THE TRUTH IS OUT THERE™

The official guide to *The X-Files*™

THE TRUTH IS OUT THERE™

The official guide to *The X-Files*™

Created by Chris Carter

Written by Brian Lowry
with research assistance by Sarah Stegall

HarperPrism
An Imprint of HarperPaperbacks

We wish to acknowledge the following still photographers for their photographic contributions to this book:
  Michael Grecco
  Chris Helcermanas-Benge
  Jack Rowand
  Ken Staniforth
  Marcel Williams

Original episodic line art: Thanks to Vivien Nishi, Greg Loewen, and Scott Steyns.

Thanks to Vivien Nishi, Rob Maier, and Peter Huff for the behind-the-scenes snapshots.

HarperPaperbacks *A Division of* HarperCollins*Publishers*
                 10 East 53rd Street, New York, N.Y. 10022

HarperPaperbacks may be purchased for educational, business, or sales promotional use. For information please write: Special Markets Department, HarperCollins*Publishers*, 10 East 53rd Street, New York, N.Y. 10022.

Cover photograph © 1995 by Twentieth Century Fox Film Corporation.
Cover photograph by Michael Grecco.
Interior design by Derek Walls.

First printing: December 1995

Printed in the United States of America

HarperPrism is an imprint of HarperPaperbacks. HarperPaperbacks, HarperPrism, and colophon are trademarks of HarperCollins*Publishers*.

Library of Congress Cataloging-in-Publication Data is on file with the publisher.

98 99 ❖   16 17 18 19

acknowledgements/dedications

This book could not have been written without Chris Carter, who generously gave of his time and his enormous energy, and the entire cast and crew of *The X-Files,* who—despite the show's credo regarding trust—were both extremely open with and accepting of a stranger among them armed with a notepad. Special thanks to Mary Astadourian for dedication beyond the call of duty; Sarah Stegall for her detailed research; Howard Gordon for patiently playing tour guide; and Frank Spotnitz, who, when it came time to find a writer, for some reason thought of an old college chum.

On a more personal note, thanks to Sally for her support; Doris, for reluctantly having a late-in-life child; and my brother Brett, with whom I used to watch *Kolchak: The Night Stalker* and, for that matter, a lot of other creepy and disgusting things.

table of contents

introduction

The truth is out there.

For more than two years, millions of television viewers have begun their weekend on that unsettling note, faithfully (and perhaps fearfully) tuning in the Fox Broadcasting series *The X-Files*.

A unique entry in primetime television on various levels, the series follows the exploits of two FBI agents, Fox Mulder (David Duchovny) and Dana Scully (Gillian Anderson), as they investigate cases that deal with paranormal phenomena. *The X-Files* has the distinction of being not only one of the few explorations of the macabre to find a regular home on network TV in recent years but also a true self-starter—that is, a show that found its audience without the benefit of having an established hit like *Seinfeld* or *Home Improvement* airing before it.

In fact, while any television series has to overcome enormous odds to achieve success, the deck seemed to be stacked against *The X-Files* from the get-go. For starters, other than the *Star Trek* franchise and its various spin-offs, there had been little track record for science fiction in the decade that preceded the series, and aside from the occasional oddity like

Twin Peaks, shows that dared to be just plain weird from time to time were even more scarce.

In a business where formula is commonplace, *The X-Files* also defied easy classification, actually being dubbed a "crime drama" by one advertising agency before its premiere. While the series does delve into UFOs and other bizarre goings-on, it is also balanced by often humorous banter between its leads and complex, intricate underpinnings involving government conspiracies and cover-ups relating to the very information the agents are trying to expose. Those episodes and incidents have come to be known as the show's "mythology" and have helped define the series as much as its trademark creepiness, resulting in popular catchphrases like "Trust no one" and "I want to believe."

Although the interplay between Mulder and Scully is sharply written, there has also been a conscious effort not to fall prey to the romantic attraction trap that has tripped up many a series. Rather, the characters' relationship has grown extremely close but remained professional, characterized by Mulder's wholehearted belief in the paranormal—driven by his sister's abduction by aliens when he was a youth—and the faith of Scully, a medical doctor, in more rational and scientific means of explaining the unknown. In fact, the character's mandate from her superiors in the pilot episode was to report on and where possible debunk Mulder's work, providing a basis for tension that gradually faded—but didn't diminish entirely, instead taking on a different cast—as the bond between them grew.

Though the pilot and the first episode dealt with UFOs, the series quickly established itself as one that was going to deal with a wide array of topics. The second episode, "Squeeze," introduced the character of Eugene Tooms, a genetic mutant who rises from hibernation to eat the livers of five victims every 30 years; "The Jersey Devil" focused on a Bigfoot-type creature outside Atlantic City; "Fire" and "Ice," two other memorable first-season entries, featured a man capable of controlling fire and a paranoid, claustrophic tale set in the ice-bound Arctic, respectively. In short, as Duchovny later put it, *The X-Files*, which at first seemed to be one of the most confining premises on television, turned out to be perhaps the most expansive.

The series also dared to be different in that it seldom provided a clear-cut resolution to cases, often leaving dangling loose ends that only added to its sense of creepiness. That proved to be a source of tension in dealings with its network, Fox, which wasn't sure how viewers would react to such unsolved and unsettling mysteries.

In addition, *The X-Files* was developed at a time when Fox had largely been focused on churning out successful comedies, with a limited track record in drama. Despite the popularity of *Beverly Hills, 90210*, most of Fox's signature series—*The Simpsons, In Living Color, Married . . . With Children*—were comedies, with the network turning to drama both as a means to speed its expansion and to fill new nights of programming. A one-hour show, naturally, would get them there that much faster than two half-hour shows, though no one was certain whether the traditional Fox audience could be counted upon to line up for such a bill of fare.

To underscore the odds involved, Fox considered 37 different program concepts during spring 1993—when *The X-Files* became a candidate to land one of the handful of slots for new series on the network's primetime lineup—and only 11 of those series hopefuls fell under the category of one-hour dramas. *The X-Files* was subsequently one of just two new shows in that genre scheduled to launch in September 1993, paired with a Western called *The Adventures of Brisco County, Jr.* Sandy Grushow, who at that time was Fox's programming chief, went out on a limb by saying he would "eat my desk" if

Bruce Campbell, who played the lead in *Brisco County*, didn't become a major TV star, although at that point no one was willing to discuss consuming any office furniture if *The X-Files* or its stars failed to have such an impact.

Then again, few could have predicted the show's eventual success given the scenario facing it. Aside from its genre's mixed track record, *The X-Files* was set to air on Friday—a night when many of the young adults and teenagers who would naturally comprise the core audience for such a program were likely to be out pursuing other, more earthbound forms of recreation.

Airing on Fox turned out to be a boon in several respects, not the least being that its lower ratings expectations as the new network on the block allowed *The X-Files*—a show characterized by its main characters' search for "the truth"—time to find something of greater importance when it comes to survival in television: a loyal audience. By the middle of its first season, critics began to take notice; word-of-mouth spread among fans, particularly computer-literate types who christened themselves X-Philes, lighting up the Internet to discuss each new episode; and the show's repeats started to be watched in greater numbers than the same hours mustered with their first telecasts. The season closed with a flourish, and when the series achieved its highest rating with its second-season premiere, *The X-Files* was off and running.

Suddenly, Fox found itself with an unlikely hit—one that not only attracted viewers but, to the surprise of many within the television industry, plaudits from the high-brow *New Yorker* and grass-roots groups like Viewers for Quality Television, as well as the prestigious Golden Globe Award for outstanding drama series. A 1995 Emmy nomination in that category—the first in Fox Broadcasting's history—only cemented the show's status as one of those rare programs capable of achieving a level of critical success that has traditionally eluded its genre while enjoying Nielsen popularity. Fan support, in fact, has reached the point where Duchovny, asked at a panel discussion what the show's long-term goal was, could rightfully joke, "Syndication."

Now that's an aim that seems well within reach. Executives at Fox, in fact, believe *The X-Files* has the potential to become a long-term franchise on the order of *Star Trek*—one that will be playing in syndication for the next 30 years.

What follows will trace how *The X-Files* was conceived and created as well as the process that allows a group of talented and dedicated producers, writers, directors, actors, and technical wizards to generate two dozen hours or more each year of contact with aliens, poltergeists, genetically engineered deviants, and even old-fashioned monsters—all with meticulous care and (in what has proven to be a constant struggle) within the constraints of a television budget. Unlike a typical episode of *The X-Files*, one conclusion—beyond an admiration for the talent involved—will be unavoidable.

The truth is in here, too.

conception and evolution

There is little in Chris Carter's upbringing to suggest the legion of extraterrestrials, demons, and spirits—not to mention the occasional paranoid conspiracy theory or two capable of making even Oliver Stone blush—that was apparently percolating inside his head.

A Southern California native who fits several popular stereotypes regarding the region—from his all-American appearance, blond hair, and penchant for casual attire to a passion for surfing that led him to write about the sport after graduating from college—Carter is the son of a construction worker and was raised in Bellflower, California, a nondescript Los Angeles suburb. Soft-spoken but intense, Carter is a true perfectionist, the sort who can rifle off the smallest imaginable detail about every episode of *The X-Files*—despite the show's arcane titles—at a moment's notice. His easygoing manner and youthful good looks can be disarming (he's been known to refer to himself as "a thirty-eight-year-old surfer"), but he also exudes a presence that tells you he's in control, without being prone to throwing his weight around.

Carter and his younger brother Craig enjoyed a fairly normal childhood. Chris grew up with a love for baseball and pitched in Little League. He took up surfing at the age of 12, and his passion for it led him to write for and eventually spend five years editing *Surfing* magazine after graduating from California State University at Long Beach with a major in journalism in 1979. He also worked as a freelance writer and traveled extensively abroad.

As with most Hollywood success stories that don't involve flat-out nepotism, the labyrinthine journey that resulted in *The X-Files* is almost as twisted as an X-File itself, with about as many different perspectives on exactly how it happened. Carter began dating his wife, Dori Pierson, four years after leaving college. A screenwriter whose credits include the feature *Big Business*, Pierson prodded Carter to write movies, and his work caught the attention of Jeffrey Katzenberg, then Disney Studios chairman, who signed Carter to a writing deal. There he was put to work writing such Disney TV movies as *B.R.A.T. Patrol* and *Meet the Munceys*.

A pickup softball game in Brentwood, California, provided another inning in Carter's career, since that was where the writer met Brandon Tartikoff, then the president of NBC Entertainment. "Chris was the left-handed, power-hitting rightfielder on the team," says Tartikoff, who, chatting with Carter during and after the games, discovered that he was a writer. After Tartikoff had a chance to read some of Carter's work he brought him over to NBC, where Carter developed a number of pilot

shows, including a female detective yarn called *Cameo by Night* starring *Sisters*'s Sela Ward; and *Brand New Life*, a sort of updated *The Brady Bunch* that aired as part of a rotating Disney series. "Chris wrote a damn good script," Tartikoff says, adding that, to a degree, he was a victim of NBC's success, since the network was riding high at the time and didn't have a need for a family series.

Carter later produced another short-lived NBC series called *Rags to Riches*—a rare musical-comedy that starred

Joseph Bologna—and developed a science-fiction action show called *Copter Cop* that Tartikoff was keen to produce before he was involved in a serious car accident that left him hospitalized for months. Not long after he recovered, Tartikoff left NBC to become chairman of Paramount Pictures and says he tried to bring Carter there, but it wasn't to be. In recent years the relationship has been mainly of a social nature, and as Tartikoff puts it, "He's too busy to play softball now."

Still, Tartikoff wasn't Carter's only admirer. His writing also impressed Peter Roth, the president of Stephen J. Cannell Productions. He read a pilot script Carter had written entitled *Cool Culture*—a show inspired by the youth culture Carter witnessed living at the beach and working for *Surfing* magazine. The script never went anywhere, but "I loved his feel for dialogue," Roth remembers, shortly thereafter trying to bring Carter in as a writer-producer on a CBS drama series called *Palace Guard.*

That show was soon canceled, but Roth kept Carter in mind when he moved from Cannell to Twentieth Century Fox as president of TV production. In 1992, he took a chance by signing a few relatively unknown producers, among them Carter. They were to develop programs through Twentieth Century Fox Television, a sister arm of Fox Broadcasting within entertainment mogul Rupert Murdoch's studio empire.

Despite his association with comedies and family-oriented Disney fare, Carter had been kicking around for years a darker concept stemming from his childhood love of programs like *The Twilight Zone, Alfred Hitchcock Presents,* and, in particular, *The Night Stalker*—a 1971 made-for-TV movie that spawned a sequel (*The Night Strangler*) and later the one-hour series *Kolchak: The Night Stalker,* which ran during the 1974–75 season on ABC.

Shortly after he came to the studio, Carter met Roth for lunch at the Twentieth Century Fox commissary—a

Q: Chris Carter has acted in one episode of the show. Which was it?

A: He appeared as one of an FBI panel interviewing Scully in the episode "Anasazi."

breezy but stylish eatery in the heart of the studio's vast lot—to mull over what sort of programs the producer would try to create. Carter indicated he'd always wanted to do his take on *The Night Stalker*, producing something "truly frightening" for television.

Roth expressed some enthusiasm for that notion, indicating that vampires, which were at the heart of the original movie, might indeed be hot given that a big-screen incarnation of *Interview with the Vampire* was in the works at that time. Carter wasn't interested in vampires per se, saying his vision had more to do with UFOs and, more broadly, the paranormal.

As Roth remembers the lunch, "We talked about what was not on the air," and the fact that giving the audience a good scare was a genre that had been absent from television for some time. Various ideas were batted around, but both Roth and Carter felt they were on the right track in trying to do a contemporary variation on *The Night Stalker*. "It was just something that had been lying there sort of dormant since I was a kid," Carter says, noting that his interest in those shows predated any ambition to be a dramatist or screenwriter, demonstrated by the hours he spent watching movies like *Mysterious Island* over and over again on local television as a kid.

In retrospect, Carter clearly sensed a void—and thus a window of opportunity—in the crowded primetime marketplace, which, with millions of dollars riding on each project, tends to be built on replicating success and not venturing down murky creative corridors. "You look at the TV schedule," he told Roth as they munched on their entrees, "and there's nothing scary on television."

Though it provided his inspiration, Carter didn't remember many specifics about *The Night Stalker*, other than how the show made him feel as a teenager. "I just knew that I couldn't get enough," he says. When he revisited the show he realized that it had a confining premise: Carl Kolchak, an unlucky newspaper reporter, kept stumbling upon vampires, werewolves, and zombies. Starring as Kolchak was Darren McGavin, who Carter considered to play Mulder's father in homage to the series, but schedules couldn't be worked out.

After his meeting with Roth, Carter began to refine his premise, trying to figure out "how not to fall into the big pit that *The Night Stalker* had fallen into" by running out of steam after one season. He knew that he needed a concept that would provide a more hospitable series framework, something sustainable week after week without stretching the parameters of credibility. The Oscar-winning movie *The Silence of the Lambs* had just been released, which helped spur the idea of using the FBI as a natural means of entry into this world of the paranormal.

With some further modification and research, Carter had his foundation—namely, that there must be somebody at the FBI investigating unexplained cases. The show, then, would focus on two FBI agents—one a believer, the other a skeptic—investigating cases involving paranormal phenomena. One of the main characters would be driven by personal experience, having witnessed the abduction of his younger sister, Samantha, when he was 12 years old.

The cherry on top for Carter came when a friend who happened to be a research psychiatrist at Yale showed him a Roper Organization survey saying, essentially, that three percent of the U.S. population believes they've been abducted by aliens. Whether those results were valid or not, Carter felt he'd found a potential wellspring of interest in a topic getting short shrift elsewhere. "I thought, 'This is too good to be true,'" he recalls.

Small personal details found their way into *The X-Files* as Carter began shaping the material. The believer, Fox Mulder, was given the maiden name of Carter's mother and first name of a kid he'd known growing up. His partner, the more doubtful Agent Dana Scully, took her moniker from Los Angeles Dodgers broadcaster Vin Scully—who to any young Southern California baseball fan owning a radio was, as Carter puts it only half jokingly, "the voice of God."

Whatever similarities Carter's concept may have shared with *The Night Stalker* in terms of the fright factor, as it evolved there were also notable differences. Reporter Carl Kolchak kept bumping into monsters by happenstance, calling for a huge suspension of disbelief. In *The X-Files*, agents Mulder and Scully would look for the paranormal after someone else encountered it, with the Bureau as a logical divining rod. "I realized what the pitfalls were in watching that show," Carter says, wanting his series to involve the agents investigating different cases each week "rather than a zombie on a motorcycle"—a reference to one of the more far-fetched *Night Stalker* plots.

Delving into his own skeptical nature, Carter also planted the seeds for what was to become an integral part of the show—namely, the assumption that there are forces at work within the government seeking to keep this information from coming to light. Specifically, Scully is essentially directed at first to do what she can to undermine Mulder's findings, and possible evidence of UFOs is hidden away in a Pentagon storage room in the pilot's concluding sequence.

Though he was still a teenager at the time of the Watergate hearings, those events clearly left their mark on Carter, who admits that coverage of the scandal and President Richard Nixon's subsequent resignation was "the most formative event of my youth." Small wonder that he named a key character Deep Throat after the Watergate reporters' shadowy source, and that he came up with lines like "Trust no one" ("My personal philosophy," he says with a laugh), "I want to believe," "Deny everything," and "The truth is out there"—the last in that series a double entendre, he suggests, nicely summing up the atmosphere he wanted the show to convey. Given his acumen for sloganeering, Carter muses, "I guess I've got a bit of the advertising man in me."

The next step involved selling the concept to a network. Executives at Fox Broadcasting, Twentieth's sister company, were Carter's first and, as it turned out, only stop. Roth and the producer met with Bob Greenblatt, Fox's vice president of dramatic series development, who in early 1995 was promoted to oversee the creation of all primetime series at the network.

"I was initially very nervous about the paranormal phenomena stuff," Greenblatt admits, fearing that such material could look "really corny and cheesy" if it wasn't executed properly. Greenblatt didn't want to end up with a rehash of *The Night Stalker*—prone to the same plot limitations—or something tongue-in-cheek like *An American Werewolf in London*. "I was afraid we couldn't pull it off," he says.

According to Greenblatt, those initial meetings in the late summer and fall of 1992 were somewhat awkward because *The X-Files* concept was so difficult to pitch verbally. Roth also remembers Carter being somewhat uncomfortable during the pitching phase, as network and studio executives second-guessed the elements within each show. "Chris and I mixed it up pretty good during that process," Roth adds. In addition, Greenblatt worried that his boss, Fox Entertainment Group president Peter Chernin, wouldn't go for a show whose premise involved chasing around in search of extraterrestrials.

"I pitched it once and they said, 'No thank you,'" Carter recalls. "I pitched it again and they finally said, 'Okay, we'll buy it, leave us alone.'"

Despite his doubts, Greenblatt remembers being struck by Carter's obvious talent and passion for the project. The seminal moment occurred for him when the producer turned in a single-spaced, 18-page outline for the pilot blocking out the scenes and even containing lines of dialogue. "It really is what the pilot episode became," says Carter, who still has that treatment.

"I was scared shitless," Greenblatt chuckles regarding his first reading of Carter's outline, having taken the summary home with him. "I knew from that story that there was something really unique here."

Carter didn't quit there, becoming, as he puts it, "my own public-relations agency." He created visual aids—charts that looked like little TV screens—as a means of selling Fox executives on the show.

Certain frustrations nevertheless continued to dog Carter, among them questions as to just how "real" the show was going to be. Reality programming like *Cops*, *Unsolved Mysteries*, and *Rescue 911* was popular, and there was some doubt at that juncture as to whether dramatic programs could compete with that sense of authenticity. "Everyone thought this has got to be as real as possible," Carter says. "No one could understand why someone would want to watch a show if it weren't true." As a concession, the pilot even carries a written statement saying that the story was "inspired by actual documented events" —the only installment to do so.

More jostling over ele-

Q: What's different that appears at the end of the opening credits in the "Anasazi" episode?

A: The words "EL 'AANIGOO 'AHOOT'E," which translates to "The Truth Is Out There" in Navajo.

ments in the show followed. In November 1992, Greenblatt got a new boss when Chernin was promoted to a job running Fox's movie division and his chief lieutenant, Sandy Grushow, was named to replace him. Fox had ordered a script at that point and Greenblatt was firmly committed to the project, but it would be largely up to Grushow whether the network would ante up to produce a pilot.

Grushow, who left Fox in September 1994 and was later chosen to head programming for a telephone company–backed venture, Tele-TV, remembers Greenblatt coming to his house over Thanksgiving weekend in 1992 to run down the scripts he'd bought as candidates for the coming season—at that point a full 10 months away. One of them was *The X-Files*, and he took note when Greenblatt told him that the creator, Chris Carter, was "a Brandon Tartikoff protégé"—good credentials, he thought, for a relatively unknown producer.

"I remember thinking to myself that it was a distinctive type of show, that there wasn't anything else on the air quite like it," says Grushow, who pored over stacks of scripts that weekend. "Distinctive" was also the watchword at Fox, which was using the programming equivalent of guerrilla warfare tactics—trying to counter the more established networks with programs not readily found on their airwaves. Grushow decided to give the go-ahead for the pilot, thinking the show might be a good substitute for the reality series *Sightings*, which also dealt with UFOs and drew a fairly sizable audience but, by the nature of its format, didn't inspire much enthusiasm among advertisers.

According to Greenblatt, the fact that the production company is also part of Fox probably helped the network make the decision to take a gamble with the show, even if there was still considerable doubt regarding its viability. "It's easier to take a flier with your sister company," he admits.

With the pilot ordered, the parties had to settle on casting the leads. As is usually the case, various actors read for each part before the field was whittled down to a few contenders. The decision on Mulder came down to David Duchovny (at the time perhaps best known for a stint as an FBI agent, albeit a transvestite one, on ABC's cult hit *Twin Peaks*), and one other actor. The alternative was "cooler, and a little more tortured" than Duchovny's take on the character, says Carter. Though Fox officials maintain Duchovny pretty much walked away with the role thanks to his wry sense of humor, which came across in the audition and meeting, Carter says he had to steer them a bit toward his preferred choice.

As for Duchovny, the actor had little enthusiasm about doing a television series at the time—his feature career having taken a promising turn with *Kalifornia*, which cast him opposite Brad Pitt. *The X-Files* turned out to be the only pilot script his manager decided to send him that year. "I read it, and I thought it was a really good story and that UFOs would get boring after three or four episodes," Duchovny recalls. "I thought I could go to Vancouver for a month and get paid, and then go on and do my next movie."

A more vigorous wrestling match ensued over Scully. Greenblatt says he knew the character "had to be real" on the heels of Jodie Foster's Oscar-winning performance in *The Silence of the Lambs*, though those associated with *The X-Files* still insist there was some muttering from within Fox about finding more of a bombshell—someone who could hold her own in a fashion show with the cast of *Melrose Place*. If some Fox officials were looking for the equivalent of *Baywatch*'s Pamela Anderson, however, Carter and Twentieth Television's casting chief, Randy Stone, immediately locked in on Gillian Anderson—a 24-year-old actress virtually unknown in television other than a guest shot on Fox's short lived series *Class of '96*.

"When she came into the room, I just knew she was Scully," Carter says. "I just felt it. . . . She had an intensity about her; intensity always translates across the screen."

Anderson had her own misgivings about doing television but circumstances had softened her reluctance— having found film work scarce and her bank account dwindling. The actress hoped a few weeks working on a television show might increase her profile, at least, when she next came calling for film roles.

What Anderson didn't fully realize was the battle taking place behind the scenes over casting her. Carter maintains that he "had to put my career on the line to put Gillian in the show," still taking some delight "in proving the naysayers wrong."

"Eve"

Scully:
"That's over
four liters
of blood."

Mulder:
"Could say
the guy was
running on
empty."

Doug
Hutchison,
who played
mutant killer
Eugene Tooms
in "Squeeze"
and later
"Tooms," sent
Chris Carter
a frozen
calf's liver
to thank him
for the work.

There were 15 to 20 people in the room when Anderson and several other actresses read for the part, and after the auditions Carter flagged her as his choice. Fox was still uncomfortable with that, so they did yet another session, bringing back Anderson (at the time only vaguely aware of what was going on behind the scenes and the drama involving her) with another group of actresses. "They didn't see the package," Carter says. "There was one actress who did an okay job, but she wasn't, in my mind, Dana Scully." Finally, Carter recalls saying, " 'Look, this is the person I want. This is Dana Scully.' And everybody looked at me and said, 'Okay.'"

Even so, there was still some head-shaking, and Carter clearly felt as if it were "me versus the world" in that room. Millions of dollars were at stake, and at this point the pilot was only days away from shooting. Anderson received notice that she'd been cast on a Thursday and boarded a plane to shoot the pilot two days later.

"We looked at a lot of actresses," says Greenblatt, adding that executives ended up screening that one episode of *Class of '96* over and over, since it was the only other piece of film they had on which to judge Anderson.

Still, doubts about Anderson didn't end with her casting. Even as footage started to come back from the pilot filming there was, Roth says, "tremendous negativity toward Gillian" from some quarters—questions as to whether the character was too cold, or if she was likable enough. Carter remembers hearing qualms about Anderson, in fact, even after the pilot was completed.

Another point of contention involved the nature of the relationship between the leads. Carter insisted that they stay clearly platonic despite those urging him to establish more sexual chemistry. "Chris from the very beginning always said, 'It's not going to be *Moonlighting*,'" notes Greenblatt.

"A big part of my job during the August to May scope of that pilot creation was protecting against that," Carter contends. "I was really the lone voice saying we cannot have these people romantically involved. There cannot be real TV sexual tension here or else the show won't work. As soon as you have them looking googly-eyed at each other, they're not going to want to go out and chase these aliens. The relationship will supplant or subvert what's going to make the show great, which is the pursuit of these cases."

Carter felt he'd made clear in the pilot that he didn't plan to allow Mulder and Scully to engage in the FBI version of *Cheers* when Anderson's character bursts into Mulder's room in a moment of panic wearing just a robe. The agent's cool response set a tone that the producer felt would carry over into subsequent episodes. (Even with that battle seemingly won, a synopsis issued by Fox's press department just prior to the show's premiere describes the connection between Mulder and Scully as growing "more complex with each case, slowly emerging as a heady mix of professional competitiveness, witty repartee, and a mutual attraction that is heightened by the intensity of their tasks and the close proximity in which they work.")

Logistically, Carter's Ten Thirteen Productions (named for the producer's birthday) and Twentieth TV had planned to produce the show in Los Angeles but couldn't find an appropriate outdoor setting for the pilot's alien abduction plot in the Pacific Northwest. The decision was ultimately made to "go where the good forests are," Carter says, shifting locations to Vancouver—a city that not only offers monetary savings compared to L.A., but which has the advantage of being able to visually approximate almost any city in North America.

Filming itself was no picnic. Because *The X-Files* got a late start, and more than 20 pilots were being shot in the Vancouver area in the crunch to get the series hopefuls ready to be considered for the fall primetime lineups, the producers didn't get their first choice in terms of hiring for technical positions, which added to the burden of working in what was then a totally foreign environment. In addition, Carter says, there was "some animosity and antagonism between the crew and some of the producers and the director," the latter being Robert Mandel, a friend of Carter's whom he personally recruited to helm the pilot.

Filming began in March 1993, and the first scene— shot at the Canadian Broadcasting Corporation—perhaps appropriately involved the sequence where Dana Scully first meets Fox Mulder, venturing into the bowels of the FBI building that he calls home to "the FBI's most unwanted." The actors had only been able to rehearse at what's called a table reading, not on the set, and Carter knew those first dailies (raw shots from that day's footage) would be closely scrutinized—in part because of the haggling that preceded Anderson's casting, in part because the nature of the actors' relationship would be central to whether the show itself would work.

That first meeting, Carter says, was "all-important to not just the show but to the future of the project. If everyone says it's not working, the next 14 or 15 days are going to be hell."

The actors, however, had an immediate rapport (Anderson has joked that Duchovny has a pretty good rapport with most women, which some of his fans would doubtless echo) despite difficult conditions. Duchovny, in fact, was taken with Anderson's grit and determination as they filmed one scene in the face of freezing rain.

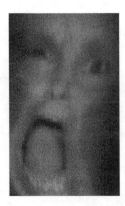

Other technical hurdles faced the production, among them getting a teenage girl's nose to bleed on cue (it was solved by running a tube alongside her face). When it was all over, William B. Davis, who plays the recurring role of the Cigarette-Smoking Man and didn't utter so much as a line in the pilot, recalls Mandel saying they'd all see each other again when the show became a series—a comment, he notes, that few took very seriously based on the survival rate of most pilots.

The two-week shoot completed, Fox received the pilot that spring just as dozens of other contenders streamed in hoping for a slot on the primetime lineup—an annual filtering process not unlike salmon heading upstream, creating enormous odds against any show making it on air, much less becoming a success. Postproduction, which includes adding music, sound effects and editing, wasn't completed until early May, only a matter of days before Fox would officially see the hour and set its fall schedule. "Each step of the way," Carter says, "until that day in May when the pilot was seen by Rupert Murdoch and the Fox brass, they really did not know what they had." In fact, when the rough cut came in, someone at Fox who'd seen it told Roth simply, "Nice try."

Greenblatt agrees that Fox still wasn't sure what it had with the show, acknowledging that as his own belief in the project mounted so did his skepticism about whether it would make the cut. During the screening for Fox executives, he recalls, "There was some nervous laughter in the room, and I thought, 'Oh, we're dead.'" The conclusion, however, was met with applause—a rare occurrence as bleary-eyed network staffers sift through dozens of series candidates.

"It screened gangbusters," says Grushow. Hands shot up immediately when he asked what everyone thought.

People spoke over each other to get their opinion in, which was unusual in such sessions. Top Fox officials—among them Murdoch and chairman Lucie Salhany, who also became a strong advocate of the show—subsequently called Roth to congratulate him on the program.

Even then, however, *The X-Files* was still the *other* drama Fox ordered that spring, with most of the network's hopes and attention focused on a Western (another genre little-seen in primetime at that point) entitled *The Adventures of Brisco County, Jr.* "*Brisco County* was still the show that most people in the company felt more passionately about," Grushow concedes. "The assumption was that *Brisco* was really going to lead the way, and *The X-Files* was going to benefit from the very significant lead-in that *Brisco* would provide for it." As a result, Fox decided to place *The X-Files* on its fall primetime lineup airing in the hour after *Brisco County*, hoping the Western would lasso viewers and deliver them to its companion. Executives hoped that the shows, airing on Friday, could provide an alternative to popular ABC comedies.

Before the season began, Fox officials were clearly more effusive in praising *Brisco County* and its star, Bruce Campbell, than *The X-Files*. In that regard, when Grushow commented that he'd "eat my desk" if Campbell didn't become a star, Duchovny's competitive spirit was piqued, feeling like *The X-Files* was being dismissed and slighted. Carter remembers Duchovny returning from an event where Grushow made those comments and joking about serving him the condiments for that meal. The attitude, Duchovny says, was that Fox was touting the other show and treating their entry as an afterthought—as if it were "and oh yeah, there's this other little show called *The X-Files*."

"No one expected that much of us," Carter says.

"I sort of wish I had said that about *The X-Files*," Grushow offers now with a chuckle. "You're always surprised when one of these things hits the way *The X-Files* has hit. . . . It's hard to ever know for sure. Anybody who ever says they do is lying, or a fool."

Yet there were soon indications even in the spring suggesting that *The X-Files* had a chance to make some noise. International broadcasters, who get to pick over U.S. shows after the network primetime schedules are set, responded with rare enthusiasm, making the series "the buzz show of 1993" on that circuit, according to Roth.

Even so, Fox still harbored various creative concerns, not the least of them being the issue of closure, or how completely and neatly the episodes would be resolved. Carter remembers having a shouting match with a Fox programming executive who wanted the endings to be more explicit, helping the audience make sense of what happened. "There's no sense to make!" Carter told him angrily. "You make the sense yourself."

"Deep Throat"

Mulder: "Tell
me I'm crazy."

Scully: "You're
crazy."

By the second season that issue, at least, had almost entirely subsided, as the network began to realize that the cryptic, spooky endings served as an integral part of the show's appeal. Carter remained adamant that he couldn't slap handcuffs on aliens, "and he was right," says Greenblatt, who adds that it's easier to give in on such matters "when you have a producer with a vision, you trust the vision, and it's working."

Carter did agree to some conciliatory modifications—part of an unavoidable evolutionary process with any series—and even he says some of those changes have been for the better. The idea of a Scully voice-over while typing up her field report notes, for example, was tacked on to the first regular episode, "Deep Throat," to mollify Fox's desire to provide resolution to the story—"bringing closure," as Carter puts it, "to a non-closed case." While he resisted the idea initially, Scully's narration "became a kind of a staple through the first season," he says, "and I think it actually added to the show."

Carter also notes that the Cigarette-Smoking Man was a mysterious figure in the pilot and was supposed to remain that way. "I never anticipated that he would be speaking as much as he is," the producer notes, "but I don't care who you are, you can't think that far ahead. The show takes on a life of its own, and you sort of have to be true to it and ride it into the sunset.

"I feel like Lewis and Clark: I know where I'm going, but I don't know what the hills and valleys and streams that I have to cross are." The same goes for Mitch Pileggi as Assistant Director Skinner, whose popularity inspired the producers to begin seeking more for the character to do.

Early reviews proved largely favorable, although some critics and reporters didn't know what to make of the macabre series and, moreover, gave it a slim chance of surviving long enough to close many cases. In its fall TV preview edition influential *Entertainment Weekly* magazine, listing synopses of new series, wrote of *The X-Files*, "We know—this show's a goner," but then during the show's second season featured the series on the cover.

After more than a year of planning and production, viewers received their first look at *The X-Files* on September 10, 1993, beginning with a story about a group of teenagers abducted in the Pacific Northwest. Mulder is first seen wearing glasses, with a poster on his wall that says I WANT TO BELIEVE. "Nobody down here but the FBI's most unwanted," he tells Scully, by way of introduction, viewing her suspiciously at first. The hour closes with Mulder calling Scully after the evidence relating to their case has disappeared, saying he'll see her the next day. As the description in Carter's original script eloquently puts it, " . . . there's no doubt from the unsettled tone in her voice that it is much more than work. It will become the defining event of her life. Nothing that comes after now—religion, motherhood, anything—will not pass through the filter of this experience."

The inherent poetry of those lines notwithstanding, the real test would ultimately be commerce—or more specifically, how many eyeballs the show could attract. The series garnered an encouraging 7.9 Nielsen rating (which translates to just over 7.4 million homes) and 15 percent of the primetime audience. That was more than satisfactory for Fox, which at the time faced a competitive handicap versus the major networks in terms of its distribution system and had little audience profile on Friday nights. "The premiere numbers got everybody's attention," Grushow says, though studio insiders say that the show's promotion time still lagged well behind *Brisco County* at that point and, indeed, for several months to follow.

Ratings gradually slipped as *Brisco*—which also bounded out of the starting gate—slowed from a gallop to barely a trot. *The X-Files* began to show signs of life

"Fire"

Scully: "I forgot what it was like to spend a day in court."

Mulder: "That's one of the luxuries of hunting down aliens and genetic mutants. You rarely get to press charges."

Q: Who is
that saying
"I made this"
at the end of
the Ten
Thirteen
logo?

A: Nathan
Couturier,
son of super-
vising sound
editor
Thierry
Couturier.

on its own in January and February, gradually climbing from April into May and scoring a best-yet 8.8 rating with its first-season finale.

Grushow points out that when Fox saw how the audience responded to *The X-Files*, the network quickly increased promotion for the show, which lagged at the outset. The executive says he told the advertising department to push the "thrills and chills aspect of the show," out of which grew the first-season promotional line, "Don't watch it alone."

Indeed, any casual glance at the Nielsen standings provides a misleading appraisal of the show's first-season performance. *The X-Files* finished the 1993–94 season ranked 113 out of 132 primetime series broadcast in terms of the number of homes tuning in; however, that ignores the fact that the show aired Friday—a night when fewer people in general, and younger viewers in particular, are apt to be home watching television—and that it routinely surpassed ratings for the show preceding it. As word-of-mouth spread, *The X-Files* was also increasingly seen by disproportionate numbers of young, educated viewers—groups that command a premium when the networks sell time to advertisers.

Though the pilot is "exactly what I wanted it to be," Carter says the course subsequent episodes have followed has proven a big surprise to him. He considers "Squeeze"—the third hour, featuring liver-eating elastic man Eugene Tooms, who emerges to commit murders every three decades—a sort-of landmark in that it strayed from the alien milieu and demonstrated "the sky's the limit" in terms of the material to be found in *The X-Files*'s bags of tricks.

Fox was equally pleased to discover *The X-Files* could play as more than just a one-note concept. "The first year we analyzed the show a lot," says Greenblatt. "We didn't want it to become 'The UFO Show.'"

Critical adulation also swelled as the first season progressed, with plaudits coming from such unlikely sources as *The New Yorker*, which glowingly described the show as having "the makings of a classic" and "as scary as *The Twilight Zone*, and much sexier." Winning the Golden Globe Award as outstanding drama and then receiving Fox Broadcasting's first-ever Emmy nomination for outstanding drama series amid a field of more conventional hours during its second season provided the last word in establishing that *The X-Files*, to borrow a phrase, was not your father's science-fiction show.

Despite limited experience overseeing a series as an executive producer (particularly on a show as complex as *The X-Files*), Carter says certain attributes—hard work, obsessiveness, his experience running a magazine, and, perhaps most of all, a motivational "fear of failure"—served him well. In the words of Fox's Greenblatt, "It's one of those rare times when a show runner was born."

Carter also made what he calls "great hiring choices," assembling a writing team with Roth's help that included co–executive producers Glen Morgan and James Wong, long-time partners who had written for such shows as *21 Jump Street* and *Wiseguy* for Cannell Productions when Roth was there (and have since moved on to create their own series, *Space: Above and Beyond*); and supervising producers Howard Gordon and Alex Gansa, whose credits included CBS's acclaimed series *Beauty and the Beast*.

Those three writing units essentially accounted for 20 of the 24 episodes the first season and managed to branch the show's alien roots out to include perils such as liver-eating contortionists, thinking computers, evil clones, psychic killers, and poltergeists. Morgan and Wong, in fact, provided some of the show's most memorable wrinkles and characters (the Lone Gunmen, Skinner, and Tooms among them) in addition to bringing considerable production know-how to the party. Carter and company thus took what might have been a limited concept and turned it into one of television's most eclectic and unique programs.

Another unplanned event in the show's evolution involved Anderson's real-life pregnancy, which came at a critical time in the show's cycle and sent panic running through executive suites in regard to what it might mean for the series's production schedule, particularly on such a two-character concept. "As an executive, if you weren't concerned about that then you didn't have a pulse," Grushow laughs. "At the time, the real question was how do we turn a potential liability into first, a non-liability, and second, a possible asset."

"I think we were all very upset," says Roth, noting that various scenarios were tossed around—down to having Scully give birth to an alien baby—before settling on the story arc, told in the memorable episodes "Duane Barry," "Ascension," and "One Breath," that explained Anderson's limited role. That plot line involved closing the X-Files unit at the end of the first season to separate Mulder and Scully, then having Scully abducted and later found in a coma. Anderson missed only one episode (the offbeat vampire tale "3") in its entirety during that period, returning to work just days after giving birth by cesarean section.

The actress herself feared she might be dropped from the show, first confiding in Duchovny about her condition, then Carter. Whatever angry rhetoric might have greeted the news from executive suites, replacing her, apparently, was never seriously considered, though her pregnancy was kept secret from the crew and press for several months. As the plan was made to go forward, nifty creative footwork was required both to work around Anderson's brief absence and in photographing her gradually metamorphosing physique. Crew members now recall with bemusement the tight shots on Anderson's face, or scenes where the actress would peek around a doorway before having her stunt double quickly run past it. As time went on, matters became more difficult, with Anderson catching breathers and even napping when she could between scenes.

Ultimately, Anderson's grit and dedication impressed everyone involved, with Roth calling her "a real trouper," in the old-time show-business sense of the word, as she filmed up to and just six days after the birth of her daughter, Piper, on September 25, 1994. Anderson acknowledges that period was difficult for her psychologically but feels she owed the show whatever she could do since such "huge exceptions" were being made on her behalf. The experience also pulled people together, since many of those who worked on the show had families, making it "the crew's pregnancy," Anderson says.

The net effect, in fact, turned out to benefit the show on virtually every level—creating, as Duchovny puts it, "a unique mythology for television." The complex alien abduction/government conspiracy story that was concocted to explain Anderson's brief hiatus actually solidified the Mulder–Scully bond, striking an extremely responsive chord with the show's hard-core fans. As Duchovny points out, there were also parallels between Scully's abduction and that of Mulder's sister, giving their relationship even more emotional resonance.

Again, Carter admits he didn't initially intend to head down that path. "I think it actually forced us to make choices that helped the show," he says. "It proved to us that people wanted shows about the characters and their lives.

"It was a way for me to do what I had resisted doing, which was to domesticate the show. I don't want to know what Mulder does with his softball team. I don't want to know what Scully does with her friends. It's just of no interest to me." Their breakup and reunion at the start of the second season, he says, provided "an interesting way to explore the characters that I hadn't anticipated doing."

Carter has come to call those episodes delving into Mulder's and Scully's histories and the show's complex interlocking conspiracies its "mythology," as opposed to the more conventional self-contained hours dealing with monsters, UFOs, etc. The pattern has become to strike a balance between the two, developing the characters through such periodic arcs while avoiding any temptation to excessively serialize the program.

Fox immediately renewed the show for a second season (*Brisco County*, alas, was put out to pasture), and more people gradually discovered *The X-Files* during the summer. Certain episodes actually drew bigger audiences for repeat airings than their first showing, and that snowball effect was evident in the second-season premiere: a 10.3 rating (which translates to more than 9.8 million households) and 19 percent of the audience, a 17 percent jump over the season finale. Still nervous about Anderson's status, Fox breathed a sigh of relief, as *The X-Files* had clearly established its credentials as a bona fide hit.

Grushow, alas, didn't get to hang around to savor that success. Most of Fox's other new shows had failed to perform well from a Nielsen standpoint, particularly the network's Sunday-night entries, which were supposed to capitalize on Fox having stolen rights to professional football from CBS. The demise of those shows actually proved to be a plus for *The X-Files*—which was placed in the Sunday lineup for a time as a stop-gap measure, introducing more viewers to the show—but didn't help

Q: In which category did *The X-Files* win its lone Emmy award?

A: Individual achievement in graphic design and title sequences during its first season.

"Shadows"

Mulder: "Hey
Scully, do
you believe
in the after-
life?"

Scully: "I'd
settle for a
life in this
one."

Grushow, who was replaced by John Matoian just a week into the new season, as *The X-Files* was taking off.

"The best that I can say about Twentieth Television and the Fox Broadcasting Company is that by and large we didn't get in the way," Grushow says now. "But at the same time, it's a show that we embraced, a show that we really focused on from a marketing perspective, which was a reflection of our belief in it."

Fox continued to struggle in the preceding hour (*M.A.N.T.I.S.* and *VR.5* were among the second-season casualties), yet despite those obstacles *The X-Files* commanded an average audience of 14.6 million viewers a week during its sophomore year, ranking 62nd out of 142 programs by that standard and becoming what networks call "an appointment series"—one viewers tune in religiously, tape, or even plan nights around. In today's television landscape, those are attributes that make *The X-Files* a show even some of Fox's competitors openly covet and admire.

To its credit, Fox's patience allowed the program to reach that plateau, and Carter says he "never got a sense that there was any fear" about the show's ratings, even at its Nielsen nadir, which gave viewers time to find the program. "I always said that we would have to create an audience on Friday nights, not steal one, and that I think that's what we have done," Carter notes.

In addition to the various entities directly involved with the show, outside forces played a part in *The X-Files*'s evolution as well. Congressional interest in the issue of television violence, spurred by Illinois Senator Paul Simon, mounted just before the show's introduction—running a different kind of chill through advertisers as well as the network departments that oversee broadcast standards.

While sparring over matters like closure, casting, and reality ran its course, Carter says the content issue remains "a boxing match that we wage each week. . . . Every episode we have to take a few frames out here and there." One of the biggest arguments arose over a scene early in the second season, in the episode titled "The Host," involving an irradiated creature, the Flukeman, killing people in the New Jersey sewers. When Fox flinched at one of the grislier moments—in which a sewer worker who had been attacked by the Flukeman literally coughs up a large worm in his shower—Carter says he told them, "If you cut this out, you're going to ruin the episode." When all was said and done, the scene stayed.

Still, Carter again finds that positive elements grew out of what began as an annoyance in the network's anxieties regarding violent content. The restrictive environment in which the show was introduced "forced us to be better storytellers," he says. "We had to do everything offscreen, imply things. I think it makes the show creepier."

Strangely enough, little mention was made at first of the show's politics, considering that the pilot and subsequent hours begin with the premise that the government is behind widespread, covert activity to prevent the public from learning about the existence of UFOs. Grushow does remember Jon Nesvig, the head of Fox's sales department, raising the issue when the show was first screened, resulting in "some sparks flying in the room."

Still, when Fox tested the show with what are called focus groups (networks never rely on their gut reactions alone) to gauge viewer response, no one even questioned the notion. "The thing that was amazing to me in that test marketing was that, to a man, everyone believed that the government was conspiring" to cover things up, Carter marvels.

Popularity has inevitably prompted closer examination of all aspects of the series, including those issues. A conservative newsletter published by the Media Research Center not long ago put *The X-Files* on its top 10 list of programs with a perceived liberal bias, citing its "proffered conspiracy theories alleging outrageous government atrocities."

Carter is amused by that charge, pointing to what some feel is an inherently conservative bent to the slogan (and Mulder's computer log-on) "TrustNo1," which is really saying in effect to be wary of government. "It's really more libertarian," he says. "Conservatives say, 'Trust us.' This is really saying, 'Don't trust anyone.' That summarizes my political views in a nutshell."

Not surprisingly, the arduous trek that took *The X-Files* from his boyhood memories to the television screen has made Carter both protective of his vision and secure in his belief that he knows what's best for it. Asked about maintaining the quality of the special effects, he says, "Part of the job—and I've learned this in the process—is never accepting 'No' for an answer. There will be a final 'No' if the answer is 'No,' but 'No' is always the first

answer you get, and you've got to make sure that the final answer you get is 'Yes.' That's really the way I proceed." Even with the constraints imposed by both a TV budget and the brutal schedule required to shoot the equivalent of a dozen feature films each year, then, the producer says, "I've done everything I wanted to do. . . . You figure out a way to do it."

If the producers had to feel their way along through the first year, Carter believes he hit his stride during the second season and now has a firm handle in how to plot out and execute the series through the third year and beyond. One of those regularly contributing ideas is Duchovny, who's become personally close with Carter (the two are occasional squash partners) and has shared story credit with him on certain episodes.

The producer has no qualms about letting his star in on that process. "He's got good ideas for the show," notes Carter. "Why not use them?" As for Duchovny, he says that once it became apparent the show would be around for a while, he had an interest as an actor in making his character as interesting as possible to play.

In terms of personal favorites, Carter mentions "Beyond the Sea," featuring Brad Dourif as a psychic serial killer ("It really sort of showed what we were capable of"); and "Ice," the Arctic-bound entry featuring a gruesome space-worm, which Duchovny has dubbed "the first really rocking episode."

The marching song for *The X-Files*, meanwhile, is onward and upward. The show is already well on its way toward becoming a cottage industry, with a big-screen movie version being discussed, merchandising opportunities exploding, and Fox's syndication wing eager to begin selling the reruns to local TV stations, well aware of the huge returns that Paramount has reaped over nearly three decades from the *Star Trek* franchise.

Carter, for his part, remains vigilant regarding overexposure while still being submerged in the series itself, spending about 12 days each month in Vancouver during production. Although some executive producers create a series and then segue in the second or third season to new projects, Carter has stated that he made a commitment to the actors to stay with the program as long as they do (Duchovny and Anderson have been signed at least through the 1997–98 TV season, which would be the show's fifth), making "X" the most prominent letter in his future.

"Everything else I do past this is a big question mark to me," he says thoughtfully. "I don't know if it'll be a hit or miss. It's a business of failure mostly. While I've got this garden growing, I want to make sure that I tend it and that it represents my best efforts."

Although Carter admits worrying occasionally where the next idea will come from (his most frequently asked question), he's equally convinced *The X-Files* will never lack for subject matter—that the show can do 20 different psychic stories and another 20 monster tales, all distinctive and original, before it's through.

That means the producer, like Mulder, faces his own unrelenting search to find what's out there—even if it's merely a new means of giving millions of TV viewers a simultaneous attack of the creeps each week. Says Carter, "I never want anything to be familiar on this show."

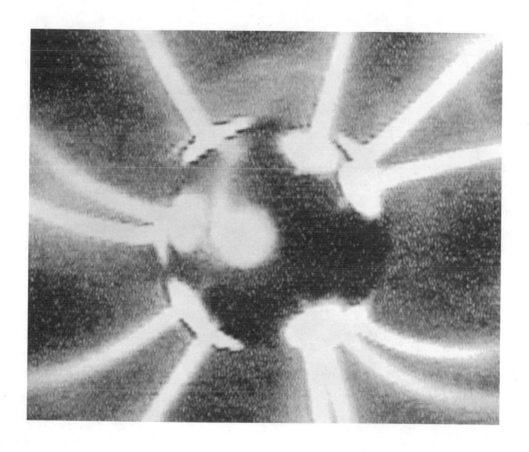

behind the scenes

If the creative essence of *The X-Files* can be distilled down to a search for truth in the face of dark forces seeking to conceal it, producing *The X-Files* involves a similar if somewhat less dramatic formula—namely, searching for quality against the tyranny imposed by the schedule and pace of primetime television.

In that particular battle, two commodities—time and money—are always most precious, and always in relatively short supply.

According to executive producer Chris Carter, parts of the battle, at least, have gotten a bit easier. After "groping in the dark" at times during the first season with "a real grab-bag of different kinds of episodes," he feels the series found its proper tone during the 1994–95 campaign—a sentiment echoed by star David Duchovny, who has become an active participant in shaping the show's future.

Launching into the third season's 24 installments, Carter has divided his task into three sets of eight and well before production was slated to begin said he knew exactly what was going to happen in those first eight episodes. "I've sort of gotten the hang of it," he says. Early in production for the third

Q: Which
episodes have
featured
altered "tag
lines"?

A: "The
Erlenmeyer
Flask" was
the first to
change the
opening tag
line of the
credits from
"The Truth Is
Out There" to
"Trust No
One." In
"Ascension,"
it was
changed to
"Deny
Everything."
In "Anasazi,"
the tag line
displayed the
Navajo trans-
lation of
"The Truth Is
Out There."

season, in fact, Duchovny and Gillian Anderson have even had a day off here and there—seemingly carrying a lighter load than they shouldered the previous year.

Carter's role is not unlike the side-show act of spinning plates, a task that requires keeping an eye on various objects simultaneously, lest one of them spin out of control. "You've got five shows going at once," he explains. "You're writing a show, prepping a show, shooting a show, editing a show, and adding the sound and music to a show." In fact, he adds, the show runner (a Hollywood term that applies to the main executive producer) really has to have his head in seven shows at the same time.

Seven shows and at least two places, since Carter, the writing staff and selected crew members spend most of their time in Los Angeles while production takes place nearly 1,300 miles away in Vancouver. The L.A. contingent includes visual effects supervisor Mat Beck and postproduction whiz Paul Rabwin, who oversees the sound, editing, Mark Snow's evocative music composition, and other measures required before raw footage can achieve broadcast quality.

Though Vancouver has become a focal point of production because of favorable financial conditions, that isn't what brought the show to the city or principally what has kept it in that location. "I'm not up there to save money at all," Carter says. "I'm there because I get to put more on screen, and I think that's what has really helped the show. The money just really goes further up there."

The X-Files actually isn't that expensive by network television standards, despite its reliance on special effects in varying degrees each week. The show falls about in the middle range for an average one-hour primetime drama, budgeted at $1.1 million per episode the first season, $1.2 million the second year and a bit more than that in season three, owing in part to salary increases (the stars have sweetened three-year deals, in recognition of the show's success) rather than a significantly expanded production allocation. Roughly 100 full-time crew members work on *The X-Files* in Vancouver, with 20 to 30 more involved at any given time depending on what's required in regard to matters like set construction.

It's a considerable hike from the studio entrance on the vast 20th Century Fox lot in squeaky clean

Century City, where valet parking attendants (that's right, valet parking attendants) meet visitors, past soundstages and backlot facades to the building where a sign reads "Ten Thirteen Productions— THE X-FILES." The Los Angeles office, housed in its own bungalow, is nicely appointed but relatively spare. Golf carts move by outside, ferrying folks around the studio, which is home to both executives and various production companies.

The office itself is bustling this particular morning, as writers move in and out—occasionally invading the space of researcher/officer manager Mary Astadourian, where various drawers full of research material are kept. In there, the scribes will find literature on the paranormal, diseases, viruses, and various monsters, with folders that carry labels like "Roswell" or "Loch Ness."

The show only began amassing its own research library in early 1995, collecting articles and copying material assembled by the writing staff while scripting episodes so it can be drawn upon at a later date. "You can lay on the bullshit really thick if you lay on a good scientific foundation," notes Carter. "The show's only as scary as it is believable. Everything has to take place within the realm of extreme possibility."

Carter's office, not surprisingly, is the largest in the building, with a couch and conference table as well as an oversized desk. The walls are decorated with articles, posters, and other paraphernalia from the series, while he taps away on a laptop computer when he has the chance to write (Carter sometimes holes up elsewhere so as not to be disturbed) or powwows with the staff in Vancouver via conference calls. On his desk sits a glass jar covered with a paper bag; when exposed, the glass jar contains what looks like an alien fetus. The jar and bag— on which is written "My God, Mulder . . . It's Trying to Communicate"—came courtesy of story editor Jeff Vlaming, who, in rather enterprising fashion, brought that particular artifact with him when the one-time *Northern Exposure* writer first came in to meet with Carter about writing for the series.

Part of the morning is devoted to the regularly

Q: What is Glen Morgan and James Wong's favorite football team?

A: The San Diego Chargers ("Die Hand Die Verletzt").

scheduled writers' meeting, with the entire staff—most of them wearing jeans or shorts, the standard dress code for producer types on a hot Southern California day—assembling to go over that week's script, blocking out the teaser and all four acts. This is the fourth meeting going over this particular script, and that episode's writer lays out the entire story on a large 4-by-5-foot bulletin board, demonstrating the "beats" in each act with anywhere from nine to eleven index cards. Each 3-by-5-inch card carries a note abbreviating what happens in the scene, with descriptions like "S SAYS MURDER, M THINKS IT'S SOMETHING ELSE" OR "GEN. HEARS CREEPY CALL; SEES FIGURE."

The other writers question each nuance, throwing out suggestions to refine the story and make sure it's clear, as they mention repeatedly, "what the X-File is" in that episode. Despite the need for exposition, Carter also stresses not letting the pace drag, wanting to spread action within the hour (or more precisely, 44 minutes or so minus commercials) allotted them. "Make sure you keep it hoppin'," he says.

Eventually, it's suggested they shift some action from the second act into the first in order to achieve the proper sense of pacing. The move requires some reconfiguration of other plot elements, but once those are blocked out the producer and other writers seem content. "That works for me," says Carter, sending the show's writer off to do another rewrite.

Carter's daily schedule, however, is just beginning. The writers' session is followed by what's known as a concept meeting—a teleconference with the staff in Vancouver to grapple with various production issues before they begin filming a new episode. Carter, Beck, Rabwin, and others huddle around the table in the producer's office. On the day in question, the crew is trying to figure out how to depict a white buffalo, chagrined to learn that because of animal protection issues they can't tranquilize a buffalo or even dye one. (Weeks later in Vancouver the matter remains unresolved, with the likelihood that the producers will either use a buffalo calf or a bovine calf—one that's lighter to begin with—employing camera tricks to whiten it further.)

Other issues involve the number of extras they can use. Carter says he'd love to see "a whole mob" of armed men in one particular scene. "Or however many we can afford in our budget," crackles across the line from

Vancouver. Casting decisions engender similar concerns, with the number of actors who have to be flown up from Los Angeles (as opposed to Vancouver locals) another matter to consider in regard to budgeting.

Because money is always an issue, and time a luxury the crew usually doesn't have, compromise and ingenuity remain key. Carter, for example, tells the location manager to find a visually interesting site "and we'll write to it," i.e., tailor the material within a certain shot that's not particularly place-specific to whatever is feasible and readily available.

Building the submarine conning tower for the "End Game."

The producers also pride themselves on finding means of scavenging resources, then developing different ways to capitalize upon them. A prime case involves the crew getting access to a Canadian Navy destroyer that was then used in three different episodes, including "Dod Kalm," when Mulder and Scully age rapidly, and "End Game," the concluding half of a two-part storyline involving an alien bounty hunter. It's fun, Carter says, "to make something out of nothing."

Episodes must be plotted down to the most minute details—in part because Carter is a perfectionist, and in part because the show is under a microscope now, with fans picking and nitpicking every conceivable aspect. Issues raised include what sort of garb Native Americans depicted should wear, with an emphasis on being as faithful as possible to tribal customs. (A Navajo group has complained because a character wore his hair down, something the elders in that tribe wouldn't normally do, in the episode entitled "Anasazi." Carter subsequently visited a Navajo reservation and attended one of their ceremonies.)

From a more practical standpoint, the Vancouver team wants to know whether they can wardrobe the actors in blue jeans because some postproduction special effects shots use a blue-screen, which essentially eliminates that color. Effects ace Beck assures them that blue jeans are fine; he'll use a green-screen if necessary to pull off the shot.

Q: What is the significance of "Steveston, Massachusetts"?

A: In "Genderbender," it is the name of the town where the Kindred live. In real life, it is a community near Vancouver beloved by the location manager for *The X-Files* for its diversity of settings.

Chris Carter,
who wrote
three of the
first five
episodes to
start the
third season,
has written
18 of the
first 54
episodes of
the series,
or exactly
one third of
the total.

The L.A. staffers are also assured that a shoot-out sequence will be top-notch, with bullet hits and ricochets plus a movie-style car explosion. Can it be done? "The answer's yes . . . with disclaimers," quips Beck good-naturedly, adding, "One big disclaimer: How much money you got?"

Beck had worked on such high-octane features as *Hot Shots* and *True Lies* before doing some work on *The X-Files* pilot (creating a vortex effect in the climactic scene), which prompted Carter to ask him to stay with the series full time. Lacking the time to work with models or miniatures on a weekly series, Beck designs all the visual effects on his Macintosh Powerbook in Los Angeles, then works with various production houses to achieve the computer-generated imagery. Beck has concocted everything from alien spacecrafts in multiple episodes to the "morphing" sequences in "Genderbender," which involved a killer who shifts back and forth from being a man to a woman, and "Colony," where an alien bounty hunter can assume anyone's likeness on a moment's notice.

Though Beck jokes about the limitations they face, that doesn't mean anyone shrinks from their assigned chores. "The effects guys always say, 'Give us more,'" Carter says.

Still, there are inevitably trade-offs and compromises that essentially come down to deciding where to fight one's battles. The producers have gone a bit overboard at the start of season three, for example, in creating what special effects chief Dave Gauthier calls "the mother of all mother ships"—a huge spacecraft facsimile that they somehow found a way to fly 170 feet in the air on a massive 165-ton crane. "Thanks for giving me some really big toys to play with," Gauthier, situated in Vancouver, recalls telling producer J. P. Finn, adding that the best part about the show is that he gets to try something different each week, with some of the less grandiose effects being the most gratifying to accomplish. An example would be the alien experimentation sequence in the Emmy-nominated episode "Duane Barry," where Gauthier was asked to create smoke wisps coming out of actor Steve Railsback's mouth. While not as flashy as the spaceship, creating the image of a thin mist spray emanating from Barry as the aliens drill into his teeth required considered technical skill for a brief and subtle moment.

The crew clearly takes enormous pride in the series, which presents them with such challenges on almost a daily basis and allows them to put their skills to the fullest possible use. Some freely admit, in fact, that they've been spoiled by their involvement with *The X-Files* and would have a hard time working elsewhere. "They'd have to drag me kicking and screaming off this show," Gauthier says.

The same goes for makeup special effects supervisor Toby Lindala, who, like some of the other staffers, really got his first crack at running such a department via the series. In reference to some of Lindala's early creations, says co-executive producer R. W. Goodwin with a chuckle, "Every few weeks I'd call and say, 'That was really disgusting.' And he'd say, 'Thank you.'"

Lindala, a young, bearded fellow who wouldn't look out of place in a heavy-metal band, fashioned some small prosthetic pieces for *The X-Files* pilot episode but received his most extensive assignment to that point creating an alien worm moving under someone's skin for the eighth episode, "Ice." At first, the gelatin-based prosthetic he'd created kept tearing, and Lindala wondered if his stint as the show's make-up effects ace might prove short-lived. "I was sweating pretty heavily," he recalls.

Still, Lindala has proven up to most any task, with the Flukeman—a costume his crew created in 10 days that had to weather water and other shooting ordeals—still his proudest accomplishment. "That was probably the most insane undertaking for a time period," says Lindala, who worked a 28- and 38-hour day during that stretch to get the suit ready in time. Even so, Lindala grew up watching monster movies and isn't complaining, relishing the opportunities the show has provided to fool around with such projects. "I love making 'em," he says.

Goodwin, a veteran producer who has worked on such series as *Life Goes On* and *Mancuso FBI*, now tries to provide more lead time to prepare such major undertakings, but in most instances Lindala and his team (four people, including Lindala, work full time in that area) have just seven days' notice to put a makeup effect together, and his services are needed in virtually every episode. His creations have included the bile-like slime

"Squeeze"

Scully: "Oh
God, Mulder,
it smells
like...I
think it's
bile."

Mulder: "How
can I get it
off my fingers
fast without
betraying my
cool
exterior?"

involved in "Squeeze" and "Tooms," alien corpses, a full-body foam make-up suit for the Alligator Man seen at the outset of "Humbug," and rigging air bladders—often a handheld device operated by one of the technicians—to provide such effects as the pulsing pustules in the episode "F. Emasculata" or the spikes that burst out of victims' throats in "Firewalker"—a process that in some instances involves using condoms filled with gelatin. Asked if he has a favorite brand, Lindala smiles. "Non-lubricated Sheiks seem to work best," he says.

The point man in Vancouver is Goodwin, responsible for recruiting several key crew members to the show, among them Rabwin and Snow, who had scored a number of television movies prior to his affiliation with *The X-Files* and who not only composes the music but performs every note, working closely with Rabwin in the juxtaposition of music with sound effects.

Careful planning remains the main hedge against both cost and time crunches, with Goodwin pointing out that in television time essentially translates directly into money. "The quicker you have to do it, the more it costs," he says, adding that while some in the industry are tempted to cut corners, "My motto is, 'Quality, whether they want it or not.'"

In some cases, that involves calculation and sacrifice. Carter—who keeps a photo of a submarine cracking through the polar ice cap on his wall—admits that he broke the piggy bank a bit to realize that image, with a 15-foot-high submarine conning tower jutting out of the ice, in "End Game." For a time after that, the show faced heightened pressure from the studio to keep costs down on subsequent episodes. Still, he points out, "We made it happen on a TV budget."

Producers must also balance their own involvement. Carter directed "Duane Barry," an acclaimed episode guest-starring Steve Railsback that aired early in the second season, for which Carter received an Emmy Award nomination in writing. The producer wants to get back behind the camera more, directing the third season's fifth episode, "The List," which he also wrote; however, that desire must be weighed against the time commitment involved in light of Carter's ongoing oversight of the entire process and multiple shows simultaneously. Similarly, Goodwin, who is responsible in part for preparing the other directors, has said he'll probably limit his directing stints to the beginning and end of the season (he handled the second-season cliffhanger, "Anasazi"), when he has a bit more time.

Kim Manners, also one of the show's pool of directors, lauds Carter for treating each installment like a mini-movie. The process gives the individual directors—who in episodic television, which is dominated by executive producers, are often viewed as transient guns for hire—the opportunity to truly ply their trade. "He insists that you go out and be a filmmaker," Manners says. "He doesn't want you to just go out and be a traffic cop." Because of that freedom, he adds, the show is "the zenith of my career."

Carter himself takes pride in *The X-Files* never settling for routine, even as he tries to manage the equivalent of juggling and tap-dancing at the same time. As for his attention to even the smallest elements in each episode, Carter—his desk awash in material from past and future episodes—simply considers that a responsibility that comes with the territory.

"If you don't know what every frame is going to look like," he says, "you're not doing your job."

making
The X-Files

The flight from Los Angeles to Vancouver, British Columbia, takes only about two-and-a-half hours, but depending on the requirements of that particular episode, for *The X-Files* crew it can be at least a world away.

A beautiful area marked by bridges, rivers, and ferryboats that also possesses the cosmopolitan allure of a big city, Vancouver offers the advantages of being a) significantly less expensive in terms of production costs than most U.S. cities, and b) able to approximate the appearance of almost any locale in North America. As a result, the Canadian city has become a hub of production, particularly for one-hour television series and made-for-TV movies.

Still, even in a city where as much television production takes place as Vancouver, *The X-Files* has made its mark. The Sutton Place Hotel, a popular night spot for production personnel visiting the city, for months offered a drink promotion featuring such concoctions as the X-File (vodka, cranberry juice, and lime), Beyond the Sea, Fire Walker, Sneaky Fox, and Starbuck. All are creations of the bartender, Debra, a self-proclaimed X-Phile—one of the show's legion of die-hard fans—who proudly points out that it's the first time all the promotional drinks have ever been tied to a single show.

The X-Files writers and directors are quite familiar with the environs, given the amount of time they spend shuttling back and forth. Unlike most television shows that shoot on location, on *The X-Files* whoever scripted that particular episode goes to Vancouver to scout out locations and do other preparatory work. "To make sure," as story editor Frank Spotnitz puts it, "everything is in sync with what the writer had in mind," from casting to production design. In the cryptic vernacular of the show, the process stems from a commitment to "purity control."

For the episode in question, that means co–executive producer Howard Gordon, the only member of the writing staff other than creator Chris Carter who has been with the show virtually since the beginning, has made the sojourn to Vancouver. "As a writer, you don't get that experience on any other show," says Gordon.

Reaching the North Shore Studios at 9 A.M., a visitor will already find Chris Carter, who flew up the night before, sitting behind his desk (a sign on it reads "Executive Leader") and on the phone, putting out fires. The offices are spacious and decorated with the expected paraphernalia, from the Lone Gunman newsletter, which hangs proudly in the art department, to pictures of a crew member posing with the Enigma (a.k.a. the Conundrum in "Humbug") over in wardrobe.

The assistant directors have appropriated a placard that says "Assistant Director Walter Skinner," the name of the series character, and used it to mark their office. Assistant director Vladimir (Val) Stefoff even jokes that he's suffering an inferiority complex, since fellow A.D. and occasional actor Tom Braidwood—who was drafted to play Frohike, one of the Lone Gunmen—"now has an 8-by-10 picture of himself on the wall," which, in fact, he does.

Already, too, there are complications with which to be reckoned, even as two recent arrivals from Los Angeles—Gordon and director Kim Manners—take the 20-minute drive from their hotel through lush wooded areas and quiet residential neighborhoods to the studio, showing up armed with oversized cups of Starbucks Coffee (which can be found on practically every street corner in Vancouver). Production ran 14 hours the previous day, till 1:26 A.M., so the start time for this day has been pushed back to noon. In addition, scaffolding left standing from the night before must be moved before the crew can set up the Lone Gunmen set. "You guys can't work around it?" producer J. P. Finn asks calmly, conceding that the constant pressures associated with the job frequently bring such matters right down to the wire. "It's not hell," he says, "but it is a hot place."

Other matters have also arisen, some remarkable in their degree of minutia. Gordon's script for the episode being prepared, for example, contains a seemingly innocuous reference to being "in the mood for some Quarter Pounders," and Fox's legal department wants them to either clear the wording with McDonald's (the hamburger's name is a trademark) or come up with something else. "That's a great line," says an only slightly exasperated Manners, whose credits include "Die Hand Die Verletzt" and "Humbug." Hours later, it's decided to change to a more generic term rather than hassle the legal issue.

The entire process involved in shooting an episode of *The X-Files*, from the first day of preparation to the last day of postproduction, usually takes six to eight weeks, with the seven days of preparation key to ensuring that the eight days of production that follow go smoothly— though even the enormous effort that goes into planning can never account for every detail that can delay filming and raise blood pressure rates all around. In the middle of the season, as time grows shorter, there's occasionally been as little as five weeks from prep to air.

At the moment, director Rob Bowman (also one of the show's producers) is finishing up production of one episode while Manners gets ready to start another two days later. A third script, still being massaged and revised by various hands, will hopefully be ready the same day.

Just two days before shooting is to begin, Manners, Gordon, Carter, and co–executive producer R. W. Goodwin cram into a small audition room, where they're scheduled to see more than 20 actors in just over an hour. Vancouver casting director Lynne Carrow has narrowed the field down to three or four choices in most instances, reading the parts of Mulder and Scully along with casting associate Wendy O'Brien to enact the scene with each candidate.

Los Angeles casting director Rick Millikan has already found a young actor who's virtually locked up the leading guest spot, but they'll still take a look at some local talent for that part as well as the others. Carrow points out that casting for *The X-Files* is no piece of cake, since it often requires finding more natural-looking actors than the high-gloss *Melrose Place* or *Beverly Hills, 90210* crowd.

The first woman reads for a smaller role, and though Manners is sold by her performance, Gordon wants one more look. She's called back in, doing the role again and making some minor adjustments. "I can go home now," she sighs. The producers settle on her for the part, though there's concern that she may not be heavy enough to play a pudgy housewife and some discussion of whether they'll need to put padding on her to make the character more corpulent.

Along the way, the producers frequently make suggestions, asking the performers (who sometimes have a minute or less to make an impression) to alter their delivery or tone and at times elaborating on the context, since the actors are given only the few pages of script that involve their character. Many of the performers seem nervous, but one young man is having trouble staying awake. "It's, like, kind of early in the morning," he says, yawning deeply. "I'm just waking up."

For some roles more than one candidate appears promising; for others, there's a dearth of acceptable choices. "You could do it," Manners says, nudging Gordon, who's quick to say, "I don't think so."

While the most pressing matter is always the episode at hand, the producers are constantly looking for performers they may want to use down the road as well. "He's got an interesting quality . . . for something," Goodwin muses after one candidate leaves, while Carter observes in another case, "This kid would be great for something else."

Manners, Gordon, and about 15 crew members, including special effects ace Dave Gauthier, production designer Graeme Murray, and others from various departments, later embark on a technical survey. They pile into an air-conditioned bus to scout out all the locations that will be involved in the upcoming shoot, usually a six-to-eight-hour pilgrimage. "And this is the easy part," laughs set decorator Shirley Inget.

Carter follows the group to the door but has too much work at the office to come along. "I'm gonna miss this one, you guys," he tells them, which is met with a collective "Aw" from the bus.

Cellular phones ring constantly, keeping the crew in near-constant contact with someone either back at the studio, in Los Angeles, or elsewhere involved in the production. Shortly, the group descends on a mini–shopping center, which will provide the setting for an action scene early in the episode. Passers-by look strangely at the gathering—art directors, most wearing shorts and T-shirts, snap pictures and measure spaces—as if they might have stumbled upon some scruffily attired tour group.

The task at hand will require turning a closed linen store into a video arcade, completely outfitting the setting, which at this point is just an empty space, in five days, while setting up a lightning strike in the parking lot. Various members of the scouting party confer in small groups, each committed to his or her own task. "We've really got a good team," Gordon notes.

Again, there are some obstacles to consider. For starters, one of the stores stays open late, meaning they may have to deal with traffic in and out of the parking lot while they're filming. In addition, the scene takes place at night, but in Vancouver during the summer, the sky stays light till well after 9 P.M. The latter proves less of an issue, but Manners can't resist teasing Gordon about the glut of night scenes with which he has to wrestle. "What writer wrote all this night stuff in the summertime?" he proclaims loudly, making sure Gordon hears him.

"Whoever it was, it's very insensitive," the writer responds.

After that, it's back on the bus for nearly an hour, reaching a remote farmhouse built near the turn of the century as, for that matter, was its 94-year-old occupant, who sits smiling patiently as the throng of visitors pass through his living room. In addition to the house (which in the episode is actually supposed to be somewhere in Oklahoma), there are also plans to shoot a key sequence on the farm, using the man's 20 cows as extras. When locations manager Todd Pittson tells him he'll be paid for the use of the cows as well, the man just shrugs. "They're here anyway," he says.

The house itself is fine, though there's some discussion as to whether they need to bring in a couch or barcalounger to furnish the scene. Staff members then take a long walk through the vast field, and inevitably someone steps somewhere he wishes he hadn't, prompting gales of laughter. The shot will also involve approximating lightning strikes, using a machine that will create

Q: When did Scully and Mulder first meet?

A: March 6, 1992.

Q: In what
episode does
Mulder first
fire his gun?

A: Mulder
fired his gun
to ward off
some white
wolves in
"Conduit."

a blinding flash. (By early the next morning, Gauthier has rigged a device using mirrors that can be buried in the ground, with little foot stands for the actor, creating an effect where the light will both flash up and spray outward. "It's truly bitchin'," he tells Manners and Gordon.)

Unfortunately, no one is sure how the cows will feel about that. "One thing I've never directed is a cow," Manners deadpans.

"But a few turkeys, eh?" quips key grip Al Campbell.

One of the more obvious advantages of filming in Vancouver now presents itself, as the crew takes a car ferry across a lovely, densely wooded river area to a quaint bed-and-breakfast for lunch—ordered en route by cellular phone, naturally, in order to speed up the process so most of the meals are waiting when the party arrives.

It's now late afternoon, but the crew presses on to survey the last two location shots. The first is a deserted road, which will be turned into a working intersection for a car-crash sequence, with the art staff erecting a 24-foot billboard that will sit 12 feet off the ground. Manners plans to use the billboard for a dual purpose, mounting a camera behind it to provide a character's point-of-view shot. The scene will also involve a car crash, so stunt coordinator Tony Morelli—a one-time kick-boxing champion who still looks like he'd be a formidable opponent—carefully scopes out the spot. The other action sequence will require leveling the top seven feet of a 20-foot-high tree after a lightning strike.

The car crash figures to shape up nicely, though Morelli may have a difficult time finding a stunt double who looks young enough to approximate the teenage driver. As for the tree, money isn't the primary issue as they debate how much they can put into the shot. "It's the time," producer Finn reminds them. "We have to shoot this in *eight* days." Eager to move along, they agree to hold a "tree meeting" later.

There's also talk about blowing up a park bench, but the idea is quickly nixed. They rent the benches, the set decoration staffers remind them, and blowing one up is expensive and thus not worth doing unless truly necessary.

The bunch straggles back to the studio around 7:30 P.M., almost eight hours after their departure. On a nearby soundstage, meanwhile, Bowman is directing stars David Duchovny and Gillian Anderson, trying to keep the level of enthusiasm up with another long night of work to do. Shooting is frequently a tedious process, with long lapses between the action as shots are set up. The two stars carry out an emotional scene in front of an elevator that isn't really an elevator, with a crew member behind the soundstage wall sliding a wooden door closed to approximate the effect. "I love it!" Bowman proclaims as the scene ends, watching the shot through a monitor and lauding his star as "One-take Duchovny."

Down the hall one finds a hospital set in the same soundstage. Across the way, in another soundstage, three men patiently stand in front of a huge blue-screen to be photographed wearing jet-black outfits and silver masks, all for the purpose of visual effects that will be added later by Mat Beck.

Crew members with a rocking horse they built for Gillian Anderson's daughter, Piper.

Outside, Anderson's baby, Piper, who was born in September 1994, plays with various staff members as well as her father, assistant art director Clyde Klotz, who's just returned from the technical survey. Piper shows off her mother's piercing eyes and frolics later with Duchovny's dog, Blue (his constant companion on the set), both seemingly fascinated with and a bit perplexed by the other. *The X-Files* is, indeed, a family affair, underscored when Goodwin brings his 10 year old son and a friend into the production office the next morning, the latter collecting autographs from everyone on that week's script.

The next day on the eve of shooting the episode being prepped, the day begins with what's known as the tone meeting, as Carter, the writer, and the director go over every aspect of the episode. A more expansive production meeting—always held on the last day of preparation for a show—follows at 11 A.M., as the entire staff associated with that episode crowds into the conference room.

Carter, Manners, Goodwin, and Gordon sit at one end, as assistant director Stefoff runs down the 52 scenes in Gordon's script (a newly revised final pink copy sits on the table, with certain sequences omitted because of time constraints) one by one, including the props and effects needed. It's a collaborative process, with every department providing its input.

The attention to detail, again, proves remarkable, driven by Carter's commitment to perfection. The cos-

X

Q: In what
episode does
Scully first
fire her gun?

A: Scully
fired a gun
to shut down
a fan motor
in "Ghost in
the Machine."

tumers are told T-shirts must be shrunken and faded to fit the guest lead actor, who won't be arriving from Los Angeles until after 9 P.M. that night. The art directors have produced an intricate series of drawings blocking out the sets and action, some of them impressively three-dimensional. "We're definitely in the '90s," Manners muses, flipping through the bundle.

The next topic of discussion involves those persistent cows, with some concern over whether the beasts can be counted on to cooperate. They will have three cow wranglers to help with the scene, but, Manners says, "If the cows wander off, we're in trouble, 'cause we have to wait till they wander back."

Another consideration involves using a dead cow the show has bought for a particular scene (the villain, capable of controlling lightning, barbecues the critter), with Carter providing assurances that the body will not go to waste and will be used in some way. Two fake dead cows have also been obtained, and with the expense Carter muses aloud about the advantages of putting "two men in a cow suit."

A later shot involves disposing of the cow, and Gordon—a city kid from New York—has actually researched the matter, calling someone in Oklahoma to find out exactly what they do with dead cows so the sequence will seem properly authentic. The process requires using a winch to drag the body onto a flatbed truck, but in light of the McDonald's headache, Carter has another suggestion. "How 'bout if we just have a truck with golden arches on the side?" he jokes, spurring laughs from everyone in the room.

After some discussion, it's also decided to have smoke traces emanating from a character who will be struck by lightning. The wardrobe department is assured the lightning flash won't hurt the costume but are told that fire retardant will be needed on one of the character's shirts. Carter also decides to use the lightning machine rigged by Gauthier to augment another sequence. "We might as well bring out all our weapons here and make it visually interesting," he says.

Manners closely examines a psychiatric hospital used in the final shot, and production designer Murray promises that the set won't too closely resemble that in the second-season episode "Soft Light," which ended with a character being held in such a room. Despite the pressure to churn out shows, *The X-Files* staff constantly resists anything that smacks of repeating themselves, wanting to keep the series fresh at every turn.

The meeting takes 90 minutes, and Finn tells department heads he'll need their budgets by three o'clock—just two-and-a-half hours away now—as personnel scatter to launch into the task at hand.

Over in Soundstage Two, meanwhile, cinematographer John Bartley, a native New Zealander who could easily pass for a college professor, is blocking out shots for the Syndicate set, where the Cigarette-Smoking Man and his shadowy cronies congregate in the third season's opening installments. It's an impressive bit of construction, with moody green walls and painted fixtures made to look exactly like expensive wooden paneling and marble counters—as one crew member puts it, "a nasty old gentlemen's club." The camera is on a dolly so it can circle the trio, with four plush chairs set up and crew members (among them assistant director and part-time actor Tom Braidwood) sitting in for the performers. The stage is permeated by a musty and slightly unappetizing odor—with a huge, metallic-looking tube piping in a smoky mist for atmosphere—but that doesn't dissuade the guest actors and extras, faced with some time to kill because their call time has been delayed two hours, from munching on a table full of cold cuts, sandwiches, and assorted snack food.

A short time later Duchovny and Anderson arrive, enjoying a few quiet moments while Piper plays nearby in a small red tub, watched carefully by her nanny. The crew breaks around 6:30 P.M. for "lunch," with a catering truck serving burgers and drinks as everyone jokes good-naturedly and gathers themselves for that night's work. Though he isn't shooting that day, actor Mitch Pileggi (who seems to create quite a stir among the female office staff) also pops by to look over dailies, or raw footage, of a fight sequence featuring him shot earlier in the week.

By now it's time to rehearse the Lone Gunmen scene, in an elaborate set that carries plenty of amusing details courtesy of the art department that are virtually impossible to discern on screen when the programs air—among them a filing cabinet with drawers labeled "Waco," "Pol Pot," "Cuba," etc., from top to bottom and a new Richard Nixon screen-saver. Blue, part border collie, watches patiently from the wings while her master works, as crew members stop occasionally to pet her.

Bowman has to deal with five actors (Anderson, Duchovny, and Gunmen Dean Haglund, Bruce Harwood, and Braidwood) in a relatively confined space, so the staging will be critical. After Bowman aligns them one way, Duchovny suggests an alternative in handling the shot, and various configurations are tried. As they begin rehearsing, everyone still seems a bit punchy, and the mood is light. Haglund keeps wanting to call a Nazi scientist "Kempler" instead of "Klemper," and Duchovny has a hard time not laughing each time Braidwood (who comes up roughly to the actor's chin) approaches him, with Frohike supposed to act relieved to see Mulder alive after the events that closed the second season. "Did you ever see the *Star Trek* where Spock thought that Kirk died?" Duchovny tells him with his trademark deadpan delivery. "That's what you want to be doing."

Production ultimately won't conclude until near 2 A.M. that morning, but for now, the actors are dismissed until the camera can be placed and the shot set up. As usual, everyone has some time to kill and—in their commitment to doing the best program possible—another long night ahead of them.

pro-files

pro-files

David Duchovny
(a.k.a. Fox Mulder)

Given his background, David Duchovny might appreciate a literary reference to describe the career path he's followed. If so, something about the best-laid plans of mice and men might come to mind.

As someone who made the jump from academia to acting, the lanky New York native has gone from being deeply rooted in the Ivy League to a profession where he periodically finds himself ankle-deep in ivy (or worse) gazing skyward at objects that will only be added later using computer-generated graphics.

By virtue of starring in *The X-Files*, Duchovny also seems destined to have a shot at major feature-film stardom, but again, not via the precise route anyone assumed he'd follow. Once his acting career began to take off with features like *The Rapture, Chaplin*, and then a starring role opposite Brad Pitt and Juliette Lewis in *Kalifornia*, Duchovny felt he was on his way and as a result had serious doubts about doing a television series. "It's like a horse race," he observes, enjoying a relaxed moment, clad in work shirt, boots, and jeans outside his trailer on *The X-Files* set in Vancouver. "You've got fifteen guys who are going to be 'the next big thing,' and three of those guys are going to finish.

X

David
Duchovny's
favorite
episodes are
"Duane Barry"
and "One
Breath."

"I was making a living," he notes. "It seemed like I would get my shot at some point."

Duchovny was willing to wait for his chance. He'd done some interesting features, and thanks to the vagaries of Hollywood, he knew a hit movie—any hit movie—would move him up to the next echelon of actors. "I always had an abiding belief that things would work out for me," he says. "I didn't know how. And then my manager, who was agreeing with me in that I didn't want to do any television, sent me the script for *The X-Files* because she thought it was a really good script. She reads all the pilots, and that was the only one she sent me."

Duchovny remembers thinking he could do the pilot—getting paid to spend a month or so in Vancouver—and then be off to his next feature. In the midst of another 12- or 14-hour day, he can only shrug at the irony, adding with a sly grin, "It didn't really work out that way."

Indeed, Duchovny, at the risk of abusing a metaphor, has probably raced past many of those horses in the race, if the number of performers who have used television as a springboard for successful feature careers is any indication. Prone to introspection as he is, however, Duchovny feels the weight of the expectations riding on him and wears the mantle of stardom uneasily, having found that sudden celebrity is not without its drawbacks on a personal level.

More than anything, agreeing to do *The X-Files* presented the actor with initial challenges he didn't anticipate, strictly from a labor standpoint. "Year one seemed like the hardest just because I had never experienced that kind of load," he recalls. "Year one was just about survival—am I *physically* going to survive? It's what I imagine those triathletes feel: When you first start competing you just want to finish, then eventually you start wanting to get a good time.

"There were many days the first year when I would just go home and think, 'I can't do it. I can't go back to work anymore.'"

Although that situation didn't ease much in terms of shooting requirements during the second season—particularly with costar Gillian Anderson's pregnancy compelling Duchovny to shoulder more responsibility for a time—the actor found the show's creative direction alone lightening the burden. "Last year I just think the work was so much better. That was kind of inspiring," he says.

Ever a tough critic, Duchovny felt there were some good episodes the first year and enjoyed doing something that was different from most primetime television shows. As for his contribution, he says he was "occasionally kind of happy with my work."

By contrast, in the second season, he believes, "we really became the best show on television," saying he's grateful that the series survived so its performers, writers and directors had the opportunity to mature together. The third season will be more of the same, he predicts, with trademark sarcasm, "before we slide back into mediocrity."

In point of fact, given the way Duchovny and executive producer Chris Carter approach matters, mediocrity is not an option. Stardom does have some advantages, in that Duchovny has been able to add his stamp to the show creatively, providing story ideas and helping contribute to *The X-Files* mythology. Neither Carter (who has become a personal friend, someone Duchovny says he'd "hang out with even if I didn't work with him") nor anyone else around the set takes the actor's input, or his frame of mind, lightly. Of Carter, Duchovny says, "He's really a wonderful producer and really receptive to my ideas—that's what I think is a wonderful producer," he adds wryly.

As for their professional relationship, Duchovny says, "We both want the show to be as good as it can be, so we don't argue. We both know we're working as hard as we can to make this a great show."

Part of Duchovny's goal has been to flesh out the character of Fox Mulder—which, he points out, was understandably vague when the show began—in order to make the part more enticing for him as a performer. "It's definitely been exciting, just something added to my experience, in terms of being able to guide the destiny of the character," he explains. "Because the character had no destiny. Like any TV show, you're forced to eventually create a history for the character that it never had."

Once *The X-Files* had survived the initial Nielsen weeding-out process and he and Carter realized the show was going to be around for a while, Duchovny offers, "it became important to me as an actor to make that history as interesting as I could."

The second-season finale, entitled "Anasazi," and revelations about Mulder's family played out in the two opening episodes of the third season, offer such mythic highlights, exploring Mulder's character and family

Q: What did David Duchovny wear to audition for the role of Fox Mulder?

A: According to Chris Carter, David wore a "tie with pink pigs all over it." Normally, however, he shuns ties, even to the extent of showing up for awards shows sans neckwear.

Q: What is
Mulder's
apartment
number?

A: 42.

history, down to his father's role in alien experimentation. Those episodes also shed light on the abduction of Mulder's sister, Samantha, which figured prominently in the character's motivation. From Duchovny's perspective, those mythic qualities can be found as well in movies ranging from *Star Wars* to *Raiders of the Lost Ark*.

Those episodes, he maintains, coupled with earlier story arcs have "created a unique mythology for television in the character, and I'm really proud of that fact—that I was conscious enough to say to Chris, 'Look, I have some ideas, I want to be involved with the creation of this myth.'"

Duchovny contends that Anderson's pregnancy and brief absence unwittingly contributed to that emotional resonance. Having Mulder search for her echoed the loss he felt in losing his sister, while Scully's abduction gave *her* an experience to draw upon—all of which, in Duchovny's eyes, provided "raw material to use in the future."

According to the actor, the depth of those episodes stands above "a kind of formula that we were drifting into in the middle of last year" with stand-alone installments dealing with whatever monsters and/or paranormal phenomena the writers could dream up. In terms of producing those hours, he contends, *The X-Files* was "maybe an interesting show, maybe better than most shows . . . but as an actor, not so interesting to play."

Now the show can go back and forth, delving into its mythology, then pulling back to do more standard and self-contained episodes. "The intensity's too much, and it can get melodramatic," Duchovny says regarding the need to break up the mythology segments, adding that the producers have achieved a "nice balance now" between the two.

Seemingly as much of a perfectionist as Carter, Duchovny acknowledges that he occasionally bristles when he's presented with a deluge of gobbledygook dialogue—those sequences where Mulder launches into remarkably detailed explanations about some event or series of events from the past. "At first it was almost impossible—it's kind of a muscular thing," he says. "You try and make it interesting from an acting point of view. . . . [But] sometimes it's just like you memorize the shit and spit it out."

At times, Duchovny admits, he worries that the longer

narrative exercises can become "the Fox Mulder bedtime story," and he'll occasionally ask the writers, "Can we tell the story a little better?" He also concedes that it's not easy crafting the equivalent of a movie each week in the time available, and that he realizes there are times when such exposition becomes necessary. As a result, Duchovny has served notice to the writers that he'll wrestle with those speeches, "but you better give me a nice scene later on to pay me back," he says.

Duchovny can be equally blunt in elaborating on his views regarding fame, given that the Internet lights up like a Christmas tree each time he takes off his shirt and people have been known to gawk or shout "Mulder" at him as he walks down the street. "Celebrity's no fun," he says flatly.

"There's really nothing nice about it. Celebrity is being known. It's no fun to be known. I imagine it's fun to be known for something good that you did, or for something noteworthy, but unfortunately the kind of celebrity television brings is monochromatic."

Clearly, it's a matter Duchovny has given considerable thought, both regarding himself and others. He describes *Kalifornia* costar Pitt, for example, as "a reserved guy," and observes that his frequent bouts with the tabloids must have been hard for him.

"I understand that it's part of the territory," he allows, "but sometimes it's hard to be amused when you're just trying to live your life and you don't feel like people snickering or pointing. In this culture that we live in, everybody wants celebrity, everybody wants to be famous. If I'm going to be famous, I'd rather be famous *for* something." With a shrug of resignation, he adds, "I don't think I have a choice at this point."

Duchovny's comfort level with fame remains low. Asked the worst part about life under the microscope, he simply says, "It doesn't leave you room to make mistakes, to do something stupid. Everything becomes kind of calculated in the worst way. You'll have an impulse and you'll go, 'Can I do that? Is anybody watching me?' It's like being Catholic," he quips.

Not that Duchovny would trade in his *The X-Files* experience. Far from it. "This is wonderful, and it affords me economic security" while hopefully creating the opportunity, he says, to do interesting feature-film work either after the series completes its run or during the hiatus periods. Though nothing is planned, there might be a

Q: What was Mulder's first case at the FBI?

A: His first assignment was the robbery ring headed by John Barnett, whom he arrested and helped convict ("Young at Heart"). Barnett "died" in prison September 16, 1989.

chance to do a film, if he can find the right material, during the break after the 1995–96 season. "There's enough time, but everything has to work out perfectly," he notes.

The travails of fame notwithstanding, things have certainly worked out, if not perfectly, pretty damn well for Duchovny. After all, how many people get to bring their dog to work with them? Duchovny's pet, Blue, a well-behaved mutt with some border collie in her, is almost constantly at his side and less apt to complain than her master. "She gets excited to go in the car every morning—much more excited than I do," Duchovny says. "This is like her pack."

He even had a chance to do a guest appearance on his favorite (or perhaps second favorite) TV series, HBO's *The Larry Sanders Show*. His one request: That he be allowed to play himself as a real jerk.

Duchovny's sense of humor is not unlike the droll one-liners Mulder tosses off, which may stem in part from the fact that he's often bemused by where he is and what he's doing. Born August 7, Duchovny was so quiet growing up in Manhattan that his brother Danny, who is four years his senior, used to enjoy telling his friends David was "retarded." Duchovny, who also has a younger sister, is reminded about his brother's comments and just laughs, saying straight-faced when asked that Danny now "works with handicapped children." (Actually, his brother is a successful commercial director.)

Duchovny admits to being shy as a youth, seldom dating during high school. His parents divorced when he was 11, and Duchovny has said in interviews those events may have contributed to both his drive to succeed academically and his personality, which at times can be construed as a bit standoffish. As for the rest of his brother's barbs, to the contrary, Duchovny was both an exceptional student and a natural athlete, playing baseball and basketball. He and Carter were even occasional squash partners until the producer was sidelined by a strained leg muscle.

After attending an all-boys prep school with the likes of John F. Kennedy Jr. and actors Zach Galligan (*Gremlins*), Billy Wirth (*Body Snatchers*), and Jason Beghe (who costarred in *The X-Files* episode "Darkness Falls"), Duchovny's academic career led to Princeton University, where he played baseball and also spent a year on the school's basketball team—a skill he showed off against Wirth, no less, in the pilot for Showtime's *Red*

Shoe Diaries. From there he moved on to Yale, earning his master's degree in English literature and also teaching. He still enjoys reading extensively, favoring the works of such authors as Norman Mailer and Thomas Pynchon, and his hobbies, along with yoga and basketball, once included reading his poetry in clubs—an avocation he has little time for with his current schedule.

Duchovny began acting as sort of a lark, taking a class along the way to help him write a screenplay. Beghe, his best friend since high school, had taken up acting himself and subsequently convinced Duchovny to audition for a commercial as a means of supplementing his income. The two had worked together periodically as bartenders, so there's some justice in that the spot Duchovny finally landed was for Lowenbrau beer.

In 1987, just short of gaining his Ph.D. at Yale in English (his dissertation topic was "Magic and Technology in Contemporary Poetry and Prose"), Duchovny began to truly pursue acting—a choice that turned out to have implications not only for Duchovny but for thousands of travelers along the Internet as well.

"It was never really a decision that I made," Duchovny says in hindsight. "I was doing both of them at once"—teaching while working on his Ph.D. and acting—"and I guess I just realized that I didn't want to be a professor."

Duchovny subsequently moved to New York but didn't find much work for a couple of years. "That was probably the hardest time of my life," he says, as he questioned both his motives in becoming an actor and whether he was truly equipped to do it.

Eventually he began appearing in off-Broadway plays and had small parts in the features *Working Girl* and *New Year's Day* before earning a role as transvestite FBI agent Dennis/Denise Bryson in the second (and as it turned out final) season of *Twin Peaks*. While conventional wisdom might have said that a romantic leading man shouldn't first meet much of the television public in a dress and high heels, Duchovny says that was never a concern. "I didn't have a career to ruin at that point, really," he notes.

"It was such a cool part in such a cool show, even though it was on the decline, everyone was just overjoyed I got the job. I was just nervous because I didn't know how to do it, didn't know how to prepare."

Duchovny also starred in the Showtime movie *Red Shoe Diaries*, which led to a recurring role as host of

Q: Who is "Danny"?

A: From early in *The X-Files*, Mulder (and later, Scully) have made phone calls to a mysterious and never-glimpsed "Danny." Danny Valodella is an omniscient and very helpful Bureau insider, who can be bribed (with one of Mulder's Washington Redskins tickets) into expediting license plate searches, adoption record searches, and the like. Chris Carter was once asked who he was; he replied, "Danny is a gnome who lives in Mulder's desk drawer."

X

Q: How did David Duchovny meet his girl-friend?

A: He was shopping for a suit (his first in many years), and asked Perrey Reeves, who had come in to shop for lingerie, which suit he should choose—the gray one or the blue one? She told him to buy both.

Zalman King's erotic anthology series. "I didn't know where it was going to go, but the pilot was good," he says. "I'm proud of it. It's where I really started to get some idea of how to do what I do."

In a similar vein, virtually all of Duchovny's features have been novel and distinctive, if not always terribly commercial in their appeal. They include costarring opposite Mimi Rogers in Michael Tolkin's offbeat and unsettling film *The Rapture*; portraying a hustler in *Julia Has Two Lovers*; and playing one of the title character's confidantes in *Chaplin*. On the lighter side, Duchovny appeared as an evil yuppie in the family comedy *Beethoven*.

According to Duchovny, *Red Shoe Diaries* proved pivotal, allowing him to exhibit a different side of what he could do. In addition, he began to feel more comfortable as an actor, describing *The Rapture* as "a difficult experience" and *Twin Peaks* as an oddity. After appearing in low-budget films that put little pressure on him, *Red Shoe Diaries* also offered him his first leading role. "To see that I could do that was very important," he suggests.

In his customary manner, Duchovny would probably be the first to say the schedule associated with producing *The X-Files* is grueling and at times frustrating, but his faith in and commitment to the series's quality pushes him along, much as he might like to grumble about the tongue-twisting dialogue and exhausting pace. As he puts it, in characteristically understated fashion, "It's hard work to make a bad show, too."

Gillian Anderson
(a.k.a. Dana Scully)

Gillian Anderson has gone her own way, and in most instances without a road map.

Anderson's experience with *The X-Files* hasn't just changed her professional career (although landing the part was, as it turned out, clearly the break of a lifetime) but her entire life, in ways that even she could hardly have foreseen at the time.

It is also a truly inspiring success story, told by someone only now beginning to absorb the flow of events that took her from the brink of going back to waiting tables to television stardom.

"At the time it always seems like forever," Anderson says. "It's only in retrospect and reading about other people's paths that I realize how lucky I was."

Anderson's odyssey began when she decided to audition for a community play while still attending high school in Grand Rapids, Michigan. Already well-traveled by that point, Anderson was born August 9 in Chicago before her family moved to Puerto Rico and then London, where she spent the next nine years. The Andersons (father Edward runs a film postproduction company, mother Rosemary is a computer analyst) returned to the United States, settling

When she
moved to
Vancouver,
Gillian
Anderson
lived in a
condominium
owned by
Steven
Williams, who
later became
the mysteri-
ous X, when
he was living
there and co-
starring on
21 Jump
Street.

Q: What
fashion
statements
did Gillian
Anderson make
in younger
days?

A: She wore a
nose ring,
and also, for
a time, dyed
her hair
blue, purple,
and black.

in Grand Rapids when Gillian, the oldest of three children, was 11.

Somewhat wild as a teenager, Anderson nonetheless harbored scientific aspirations before the acting bug bit her in high school. "Somehow, I have no idea how the transition was made from wanting to be an archeologist or a marine biologist to wanting to be an actress, but it just kind of happened," she says.

Anderson returned to Chicago to study acting at DePaul University's Goodman Theater School and was noticed by some New York–based William Morris agents at an actors' showcase. They offered to represent her in pursuing acting as a career if she moved to New York, and in short order she loaded up the car and moved to the Big Apple at the age of 22.

Working as a waitress to support herself, Anderson received the first in a series of fortuitous breaks when actress Mary-Louise Parker dropped out of the off-Broadway play *Absent Friends* two weeks into rehearsal in order to take a role in the movie *Grand Canyon*. Producers were left in a frantic rush to replace Parker, and Anderson got the part, ultimately winning a Theatre World Award for her performance.

Toiling as a waitress in two different places after what she modestly deems her "mild success" in *Absent Friends*, the actress continued to go out on auditions and after a disheartening dry spell was offered three different roles in the same day: another off-Broadway play; a low-budget feature that ended up being called *The Turning*, which starred Tess Harper and Karen Allen; and *The Philanthropist*, a Christopher Hampton play being staged at a theater in New Haven, Connecticut.

Because the play in New York would have conflicted with the other projects, Anderson opted to make a two-for-one swap and take the other two parts, doing the movie and then *The Philanthropist*. As it turned out, the latter ultimately led her to Los Angeles after she became involved with another actor in the show, following him to the West Coast and eventually moving in with him. "I'm not sure if I hadn't made those choices that I would be doing *The X-Files* right now," she muses.

Still enamored with the idea of achieving film stardom, Anderson endured considerable frustration after arriving in the movie mecca. "First of all, I swore I'd never move to Los Angeles," she admits, "and once I did, I swore I'd never do television. It was only after being out of work for almost a year that I began going in [to audition] on some stuff that I would pray that I wouldn't get because I didn't want to be involved in it."

Despite what she now calls her "very snobby view of doing television versus film," Anderson read the pilot script for *The X-Files* and found herself immediately drawn to both the character of Dana Scully and her relationship with fellow FBI agent Fox Mulder.

The X-Files, in fact, was the only pilot for which Anderson auditioned in 1993, at that point possessing little knowledge regarding what the whole process entailed. She even had to ask her manager what a pilot was and had no idea that each network commissions about four times as many pilots as they end up ordering as series. "I naively *assumed* that we were going to be picked up," she says, with the hope that landing the part and doing 13 episodes of a TV show (the number networks order for starters) would put her in a different echelon of casting. She anticipated at most committing a year to the project.

Anderson was just 24 years old at the time, and the role of Scully—a medical doctor who opts to become an FBI agent—was actually supposed to be 29 or 30. The actress's representatives fudged a bit, saying she was 27.

Contemplating whether waiting tables would again be a necessity, Anderson learned that she'd landed the part the day her final unemployment check came. Two days later, she boarded a plane for Vancouver to begin filming *The X-Files* pilot relieved to be working, but largely unprepared for where that flight would ultimately take her.

"I didn't foresee at all that it was going to become as popular as it has," she says, never thinking even after production began that the show would go longer than two or three seasons. "I often thought, 'What have I gotten myself into?' The first year was the hardest in terms of getting into the kind of grueling hours and sleep deprivation and having to perform constantly, day in and day out.

"Now, my body and my psyche are used to it, but I still can't fathom that we might go into year five or year six. I can't even think about that, because I start to panic," Anderson says with a laugh, having negotiated a contract (as has David Duchovny) through at least a fifth season.

In a fairy tale or Hollywood movie of the '30s the story might end there, but Anderson's saga was only beginning.

Gillian Anderson's favorite episodes are "Beyond the Sea" and "Irresistible."

Q: What is Dana Scully's own X-File number?

A: In "3," we saw Mulder opening an X-File regarding his partner's disappearance. He put her glasses and her badge in the file, case number X73317.

X

Q: What
literary work
inspired the
nicknames
used by
Scully and
her father?

A: *Moby-Dick*,
by Herman
Melville.
Dana Scully
called her
father
"Ahab,"
after the
tyrannical
captain who
sought the
White Whale;
he called her
"Starbuck,"
after the able
lieutenant
who served
him.

During production she began dating Clyde Klotz, an art director on the show. The two married while on vacation in Hawaii after seeing each other for roughly four months. When Anderson soon learned that she was pregnant she knew what she wanted to do, but concedes to "not completely thinking ahead about the consequences of that decision."

Concerned (and having heard rumors) that there might be pressure to recast the role, Anderson confided the news to Duchovny first, then to executive producer Chris Carter. The decision was almost immediately made to shoot around her pregnancy, though it was months before she was allowed to tell the crew or press about her condition.

Limiting Anderson's participation in the show presented no small task. Unlike an ensemble drama where a character can slip into the background and leave costars to carry the load, *The X-Files* is a two-character piece that requires its stars to sometimes work 14- and 16-hour days, with only half of Saturday and Sunday to themselves.

Still, Anderson earned the admiration of nearly everyone involved at all levels by continuing to work a grueling production schedule into her final month, up until about a week before she finally (and belatedly) gave birth. The logistics of filming, she notes, were probably more of a hardship on the directors and assistant directors who had to figure out what camera angles to use to obscure her physical changes, but Anderson admits the later months became a bit of an ordeal.

"My feet were swelling and I was exhausted, sleeping between scenes," she recalls, fondly remembering how crew members tried to help out by bringing apple boxes for her to sit on. "It became almost like the crew's pregnancy, because everyone was pulling together to make it work."

Anderson's daughter, Piper, was delivered in September 1994 by cesarean section, which wasn't anticipated and required the actress to spend the next six days in the hospital. Four days after that, she was back on *The X-Files* set, shooting scenes for the episode "One Breath." The plot had Scully—after her abduction and disappearance two episodes earlier in "Ascension"—inexplicably turning up in a Washington medical center, lying comatose in a hospital gown as her late father and a mysterious nurse seek to coax her spirit (seen floating gently in a boat just offshore) back to the land of the living.

Though the episode was designed to limit the physical strain on her, says Anderson, "It was probably one of the hardest times, because as a new mother your whole brain is focused on this child whether you want it to be or not." Instead, she found herself hooked into a bed, able to extract herself from a web of tubes only with great difficulty and thus unable to be with the baby between shots, sometimes lying there several hours at a time.

"It was excruciating psychologically," she says. "At the same time, I knew it was something that I needed to do for them. They had made huge exceptions for me in allowing me to go through with this."

Despite her childhood scientific aspirations, the actress admits that one of the more challenging aspects of her role involves the tongue-twisting medical and scientific dialogue she often has to recite. "It is hard to connect," she says. "To a certain degree, there's only so much of it that you can comprehend and understand from day to day as you're working on these lines, and then you just have to let go and trust that as an actor you can make it seem real and make it seem like you know what you're talking about."

Because of the need to keep production moving, she adds, "there's not time to be hung up on getting the lines right." In addition, Duchovny possesses what amounts to a photographic memory, so Anderson says she feels self-imposed pressure to keep pace with him.

Despite the show's motto to "Trust no one," having faith in the writers also provides a certain comfort level for the actors. As much as she admired the original pilot script, Anderson believes it's a notch below the material Carter and his ink-stained brethren have generated subsequently, with Anderson feeling the greatest affinity for those episodes—like "Beyond the Sea" and "Irresistible"—that have provided her the most expansive palate as a performer. "The scripts really lay out the degree of emotions that we're allowed to express," she says, noting that the two hours mentioned "required more of an emotional commitment, and more technical work from an acting standpoint."

In the first season, at least, Anderson also exercised regularly and "loved to do my own tumbles" and stunt-work, a practice that came to a crashing halt due to her pregnancy. In fact, Anderson remembers shooting a

Q: What was Dana Scully's father's rank?

A: William Scully is referred to in the scripts as a captain, even though in "One Breath" he appears to Dana wearing the uniform of an admiral (one star on the shoulder). Perhaps, in her mind, Scully's father was an admiral.

Q: What was
the name of
Dana Scully's
one and only
date?

A: Rob, in
"Jersey
Devil."

Q: What was
Gillian
Anderson's
first TV
role?

A: She had a
guest role on
"Class of
'96."

scene for the episode titled "Young at Heart" when serial killer John Barnett shoots Scully, who's wearing a bullet-proof vest. The actress filmed take after take where she propelled herself backward onto her back, at one point just missing the edge of a marble column behind her. On top of that, she says, "I didn't realize till later that I was pregnant at the time."

Anderson had also never handled a firearm before, which, she admits, initially felt awkward. "My hand was practically covering the whole gun," she chuckles, "but people reminded me not do that."

The show's success has raised other issues that require a different kind of dexterity. Although she says she appears "very different when not playing Scully," Anderson (who admits to being 5'3" and at times look-ing "like I'm up to his belly-button" walking beside the 6'1" Duchovny) now casts a long shadow. She acknowl-edges there are now few places she can go without being recognized; she savored the anonymity she enjoyed in parts of Europe during a trip there.

Despite the rapid course of events, those around *The X-Files* say that Anderson remains unaffected by her sud-den fame. While that notoriety hasn't become intrusive, she admits to being more protective and on edge in pub-lic. "I tend to be a very private person and want to let people in when I want them in, and not when they want to be let in," she concedes.

That said, Anderson is grateful for the way fans have responded to her character, including the fact that there's a Gillian Anderson Testosterone Brigade—a counterpart to Duchovny's female fan club, the David Duchovny Estrogen Brigade. She's also flattered that those smitten by her TV persona tend to be "computer guys," as she puts it, who write thoughtful fan mail with less panting than might be associated with other, more flamboyant television stars. "There's an intelligence to the attraction," she observes, pointing out with some pride that in England she's been called "the thinking man's crumpet."

"I actually enjoy that I *don't* get letters from guys say-ing, 'Oh you're so beautiful, I want to marry you, I can't wait till you take your clothes off,'" she continues, laugh-ing as she affects a voice that sounds like a patron of a late-night phone service. "I think I might throw up if I got something like that."

Although she appreciates the show's two-character

aspect and Scully and Mulder's deftly realized rapport, Anderson also wouldn't mind a day coming when *The X-Files* might add some more hired help, opening up the concept and allowing the central duo more spare time. With so little rest each week and roughly 10 months of production, she says, "the year becomes a blur."

Anderson says she found it difficult to unwind, in fact, when she did get time off after the frenetic pace of producing the first season. "I just did not know what to do with myself," she says. "I had this big body, waddling around. It was horrible." She may have overcompensated between the second and third seasons, loading herself up with activities.

Having made her home in Vancouver, spending time with her family is currently about all the recreation Anderson needs. She's also still interested in doing film work during the show's down time and has been encouraged to discover that the characters coming her way seem quite different from Scully. "I haven't been typecast thus far, from what I've been offered," the actress says with a certain relief, wistfully anticipating a day when—after reluctantly stumbling into television stardom—she might have time to embark on the next leg of what so far might be described as her *X-cellent* adventure.

Even Anderson admits there was a point where she had to stop, catch her breath, and absorb all the major, life-changing events that have happened to her in such a relatively short span of time. "What caught up with me," she says, reflecting on that moment, "is basically the facts of my life."

Q: What did Gillian Anderson want to be when she grew up?

A: A marine biologist.

pro-files

Mitch Pileggi
(a.k.a. Assistant
Director Walter Skinner)

If part of an actor's bag of tricks involves drawing on life experience, then Mitch Pileggi has more luggage at his disposal than most performers could even carry.

Pileggi brings unusual perspective, in fact, to his role as FBI Assistant Director Skinner, having largely grown up abroad and worked for Defense Department–related companies throughout the Middle East before returning to the United States and, at the age of 27, launching his acting career in earnest.

Still, don't ask Pileggi if *The X-Files*'s paranoid streak about covert activity and governmental conspiracies rings true. "I don't want the IRS breathing down my neck," he says with a laugh.

While his professional background may not have provided much inspiration, Pileggi did draw on part of his experience—albeit in a manner that was both unplanned and extremely personal—in creating the role of Skinner, who finds himself committed to the truth but often caught between agent Fox Mulder's hell-bent obsession with exposing secrets and the powerful and cold-blooded operatives trying to undermine his work.

"I based him on my dad a lot," says

Pileggi, whose father passed away not long after the show's premiere. "It was something that I wasn't doing consciously, but my mom and my brothers picked up on this quite a bit.

"I guess I was doing it unintentionally, and my mom called me up one time and said, 'You know, I'm watching Dad.' It really touched her."

Pileggi describes his father as "very big stuff in my life," an operations manager for a Defense Department contractor whose work led his family all over the world. At home he was a loving family man, the actor notes, while at work "he just kicked some ass. But then again, he was very tough, very stern, but very fair with his employees, too. Hopefully, that's what's coming across in Skinner."

Born April 5 in Portland, Oregon, Pileggi began traveling with his family when he was only seven and, as he puts it, "didn't stop moving till a long time later."

His father's work took him to Turkey for most of his youth, and after attending high school there and college in Germany, Pileggi began working for the same company in Saudi Arabia, shuttling back and forth to the U.S. He later did some work for another contractor in Iran.

Pileggi was in Turkey during two coup attempts and often passed through Beirut for visa purposes going into Saudi Arabia. Ultimately, he was one of the last Americans to get out of Iran as the government fell there, with barely enough fuel to reach the airport in Athens. "It was really hairy," Pileggi says. "I thought, 'You know, this sucks. I'm not sure I want to do this anymore.'"

Pileggi returned to the U.S. and, having done some acting in high school and at a junior college, "just started messing around with it." He moved to Austin, Texas, acting in a theater group before returning to California and landing roles in such television series as *Dallas, The A-Team,* and *Hooperman* as well as the movies *3 O'Clock High* and *Return of the Living Dead.*

The muscular, 6'2" actor (who says he's "a basket case" if he doesn't work out every day and, in what must be an imposing sight, loves to Rollerblade) subsequently was cast in *Shocker,* a movie directed by horrormeister Wes Craven. The producers were looking for someone "evil in a sexy kind of way" to play the role of psychotic killer Horace Pinker, and Pileggi won the part from a field of about 50 contenders. His audition, in fact, was so scary that producer Marianne Maddalena moved her chair away from him, taking a seat on the other side of the room. "She was sweating," he recalls. "It was actually very funny."

Shocker was supposed to launch an ongoing franchise, on the order of Craven's *Nightmare on Elm Street* series, but the concept fizzled after the one movie. Though Pileggi enjoyed working with Craven (and appears in the director's Eddie Murphy movie *Vampire in Brooklyn*), the role was so maniacal it didn't open a lot of doors and may have closed some by making people see him in that light.

Film and television work nevertheless followed, including parts in *Models Inc.* and the movie *Basic Instinct*. "I was in the Michael Douglas interrogation scene . . . unfortunately," Pileggi notes dryly, referring to the more celebrated sequence involving Sharon Stone by adding, "I kept trying to get him to spread his legs."

Mitch Pileggi's favorite episode is "End Game."

Pileggi auditioned for *The X-Files* unsuccessfully two or three times before he was cast as Skinner. Prior to that session he remembers thinking, "'Why are they calling me back in? They didn't hire me before.' So I went in with a bit of an attitude for this meeting [about playing] Skinner. I was kind of grumpy and not in very good humor, and fortunately, Chris thought I was acting, 'cause it suited the character."

Only later did Pileggi learn that he had lost out on the earlier parts by a hair, or lack thereof. The burly actor (who remains Los Angeles casting director Rick Millikan's proudest "find" and tends to get considerable notice from women around the set) was shaving his head at the time, which was why executive producer Chris Carter couldn't envision him in those roles. In retrospect, Pileggi says he was lucky he didn't get one of those parts because they would have been one-shots, "and then Skinner wouldn't have been available to me."

Pileggi brings considerable intensity to the role of Skinner, who, he notes, remains caught between agents Mulder and Scully on one side and the Cigarette-Smoking Man and the forces he represents on the other. "Up to this point it's just the situation he's been put in," he says, suggesting that Skinner also wants to find the truth but goes about it by more conventional means than his subordinates.

One episode that did allow more lattitude was "End Game," where Skinner steps out of character—and into "unofficial channels"—to help Scully locate and save Mulder, engaging in a memorably brutal encounter with X (played by Steven Williams). "Steven came up with some wonderful ideas," Pileggi says. "He's the one that suggested that Skinner head-butt him back, and when he said that I said, 'Yeah, that's really great.' I think that's something Skinner would have done: 'Head-butt me? Well, here, take *this*.'"

Pileggi recalls director Rob Bowman telling him to use more force shoving Williams against the elevator wall, and on the next pass he nearly put him through it. "The whole back of the elevator started coming out. We just about knocked it down," he notes.

Pileggi also received a number of letters from Vietnam veterans due to the story Skinner relates about his tour of duty during "One Breath," which the actor found particularly gratifying. The character is clearly developing his own following among fans as well, though Pileggi quickly points out that everything is relative based on the time he spends with *The X-Files* stars David Duchovny and Gillian Anderson. "I go out with to dinner with David and it's like they don't even see me, which is all right," he chuckles.

The actor expresses enormous regard for the series stars, who, he says, are extremely focused. "You listen to the technobabble that they've got sometimes and I don't know how they do it," Pileggi marvels, adding, "We have fun. We giggle, we laugh and get goofy, which you've got to do."

Pileggi now has a long-term contract with the series and says he's excited about plans for Skinner as the show progresses, adding that he loves Vancouver and has no qualms about being there as long as Skinner—to quote the character—can walk the line that Mulder keeps crossing.

After all his traveling, in fact, Mitch Pileggi sounds like someone who's found home. "This is what an actor dreams about—either having a feature career or getting a series [character] on a quality show like this," he says. "I just couldn't be happier."

pro-files

William B. Davis
(a.k.a. The Cigarette-
Smoking Man)

To answer the first question right off, no, William B. Davis is not really a smoker . . . but he plays one on TV.

Davis did smoke once but quit long before his stint on *The X-Files* and puffs herbal cigarettes while playing the menacing character known as the Cigarette-Smoking Man, or (doubtless to the chagrin of the tobacco industry) Cancer Man. It's a role series creator Chris Carter freely admits he never anticipated would speak so much or become such an integral part of the program.

The well-traveled actor and drama teacher appeared in *The X-Files* pilot as a shadowy figure who participates in covering up material found by agents Mulder and Scully, but he didn't actually speak a line until "Tooms," 20 episodes and several months later. Davis directed and taught acting for most of his professional life until he took some acting classes as a brush-up technique to help his teaching. "I started thinking, 'Maybe I've learned something here, telling people all this time what to do,'" he recalls, before beginning to pursue acting in earnest around 1980.

Born in Toronto on January 13, Davis started out as a child actor, then attended the University of Toronto and later the London Academy of

William B.
Davis's
favorite
episodes are
"End Game"
and
"Anasazi."

Music and Dramatic Art. After directing theater in England for five years he returned to Canada, where he was involved in theater and then radio for the Canadian Broadcasting Co.

Davis continued to teach and still serves as director of the William Davis Centre for Actor's Study, having moved to Vancouver to run the Vancouver Playhouse Acting School in 1985. He also kept busy acting in TV productions like *Stephen King's It, MacGyver,* and *Heart of a Child*, as well as the movies *Look Who's Talking* and *The Dead Zone*.

The Cigarette-Smoking Man has little or no history on which to base the character, and in Davis's eyes not much of a personal life about which to theorize. "I think he's just burnt," he says. "'Workaholic' would be to underestimate him. There is no other life, there is no other purpose, than what he is pursuing."

Davis laughs at the question of whether the character has a more conventional name but finds plenty of implied symbolism in how he's presented, particularly in the juxtaposition of evil with fire. Although reluctant to come out and say that he's in essence playing the Devil, "What other name could I have but Lucifer?" he asks with a sheepish smile, quickly adding that the Cigarette-Smoking Man sees himself not as evil but rather as being "on a crusade to save the world."

The Canadian native does admit that the role presents one constant challenge, since the tall, distinguished-looking actor clearly has a bit of an accent that he has to concentrate on masking in playing a lifelong Washington bureaucrat. "I have to watch my vowel sounds," Davis says.

With his acting career occupying more of his time, Davis has scaled back a bit on teaching. His students, meanwhile, have taken an interest in and developed admiration for his on-screen work, with one even suggesting that the Cigarette-Smoking Man himself is an alien who thrives on carbon monoxide. Davis shrugs it all off. "Back in the days when I was still silent," he says, with a smile that bears little resemblance to his character, "people asked me to give classes on how to *look* sinister."

pro-files

Steven Williams
(a.k.a. X)

If you're interested in getting the inside scoop on what's happening with *The X-Files*, don't ask Steven Williams: It's not that he won't tell you, but rather he *can't* tell you.

"I am still in the dark as much as the audience is about X," he says, referring to the character he began playing near the start of the show's second season, a high-level government source who has taken Deep Throat's place in helping Agent Fox Mulder, albeit with some reluctance and a decidedly ruthless streak. "They keep me so in the dark it's pathetic."

Still, the likable actor (who, in contrast to his character's grim demeanor, has a disarming and ready laugh) wouldn't have it any other way—except, perhaps, for more advance notice as to when he'll be needed to shoot and some assurance that X won't suffer the same fate as his predecessor, Deep Throat. Demonstrating X's savvy survival instincts, in fact, Williams isn't above urging people to lobby for him to hang around.

Having spent five years as Captain Fuller on the hit Fox series *21 Jump Street*, Williams certainly knows the territory, down to the Vancouver locales where *Jump Street* also filmed. He landed the role on *The X-Files* at the last minute (an actress had originally been cast in the part), based to some degree on his relationships with some fellow *Jump Street* alumni, including producer/director David Nutter and co–executive producers Glen Morgan and James Wong (*Jump Street* costar Peter DeLuise nicknamed the team "The Wong Brothers"), with whom he also worked on a short-lived Disney series called *The 100 Lives of Black Jack Savage*.

Despite his congenial nature, Williams says he has no problems getting himself into the stony frame of mind required to play X, Agent Fox Mulder's reluctant and shadowy government contact. "It's just automatic," he says. "They go 'Action,' and bam, I'm Mr. X. I'm just able to switch on and off like that and trick people."

Although the actor initially considered trying to learn what makes X tick, ultimately he decided he'd be better off maintaining a certain mystery. "The less I know about him, the more interesting he becomes. That's the way I've been playing him," says Williams. "The biggest thing about X is that he's a survivor. He's said that: 'I don't want to die.' While he is icy and cold, you can see fear in this man.

"I thought about trying to do all that stuff [to prepare], and then I thought, 'No, this is working for me.'" For that reason, Williams has done his job the old-fashioned way. As he puts it: "You read the words and look at the situation, and you put yourself there."

Acting has put Williams in a lot of different places. Born January 7 in Memphis, Tennessee, until age nine he was raised principally by his grandparents (his parents had divorced), living in a farming community where his grandfather was a baptist minister.

After a stint in the army, Williams worked as a shoe salesman in Chicago, quitting his job in 1972 to begin modeling and later working with a children's theater group. The modeling led to commercials, stage work, and eventually two nominations for the Joseph Jefferson Award.

Williams landed his first feature break in the 1975 movie *Cooley High*, followed by *The Blues Brothers* in 1980. Around that time the actor moved to Los Angeles, where steady film and television work followed, including parts in *Corrina, Corrina, Missing in Action II, Twilight Zone: The Movie,* and numerous TV shows prior to and following his role on *21 Jump Street*. In a field fraught with unemployment, Williams notes, "From

the moment I started doing this I've never had to do anything else. I've always been able to make a living acting
. . . thank God."

Though he loved the positive role model Captain
Fuller provided, Williams says he also enjoys the nasty
streak he's allowed to exhibit on *The X-Files*, from his
cold-blooded execution of another operative in the
episode "One Breath" ("I like that iciness, that cold-
ness") to X's brutal encounter in an elevator with
Assistant Director Skinner in "End Game." Close friends
have been most startled by the character, he says, telling
him, "Man, you've tapped into a dark side of yourself."

According to Williams, he actually helped stage X's
tussle with Skinner, having developed an interest in fight
choreography and the martial arts while working with
Chuck Norris on the second *Missing in Action* movie. "In
these close quarters, I said, 'How 'bout a nice head-butt
for openers?'" Williams recalls. "Skinner is the same
type of guy, so he head-butts his ass back. . . . These
aren't guys who are interested in having a long fight.
They're interested in taking you out and getting out of
there."

Williams has done most of his work with David
Duchovny, who he describes as "a pleasant guy" if not
exactly a drinking buddy. Still, the two aren't above sharing a laugh to break the tension, especially when someone flubs a line. "The stuff is so heavy sometimes that
you've got to do the other side just to lighten it up," he
says.

While he felt a bit constrained at the outset, Williams
is pleased with the way his role has unfolded and doesn't
even mind the fact that he plays one of the few recurring
characters in primetime without a regular name. Asked
what he thinks X's John Hancock might be, the actor
pauses, admitting that he hasn't given the notion much
thought. "Leroy," he says after a beat, laughing loudly.
"Leroy Williams. Which is why he calls himself 'Mr. X.'"

Steven
Williams's
favorite
episodes are
"End Game"
and "One
Breath."

pro-files

The Lone Gunmen

Created by writers Glen Morgan and
James Wong, this trio of paranoid
conspiracy theorists who publish *The
Lone Gunman* newsletter—Langly,
Byers, and Frohike—first appeared in
the first-season episode "E.B.E." and
have subsequently become recurring
characters, much to the shock of the
performers involved.

Despite their limited exposure, the
group has become extremely popular,
helping Agent Fox Mulder in his pursuit of the truth while one of its members, Frohike, spends most of his
spare time lusting after Mulder's partner, Agent Dana Scully. Stripped of
their roles and chased into the sunlight on *The X-Files* set in Vancouver,
they are:

pro-files

Tom Braidwood
(a.k.a. Frohike)

As it turns out, a snide joke and for-tuitously timed trip to the men's room reactivated Tom Braidwood's acting career, though he was and continues to be happily ensconced on the other side of the camera.

Braidwood, a first assistant direc-tor on *The X-Files*, happened to be walking by while the producers con-sidered actors to play Frohike. At that moment, director William Graham—a long-time acquaintance—noticed him and as legend has it observed, "We need somebody slimy . . . someone like Braidwood." He emerged from the bathroom to be greeted with a chorus of "Ah, Frohike," and a star was born.

Braidwood concedes that he didn't have much choice in the matter but has enjoyed his return to acting. "I always missed it," he says, and in the last year he's even been mulling over doing stage work if time permits dur-ing the summer.

Born September 27, Braidwood acted in theater before finding steady employment behind the scenes on shows like *Danger Bay* and *21 Jump Street*—the latter a credit he shares with *The X-Files* co–executive producers Glen Morgan and James Wong, who created the character and thus inadver-tently launched his second career.

Despite his duties as an A.D., Braidwood says his periodic appearances are fun for the crew (who have labeled a bicycle he rides around the studio the "Frohike Mobile") and by no means an imposition. "We've worked it out," he says. "It's usually better if I'm prepping a show. If I'm shooting, the second A.D. just takes over the set."

Lone Gunmen scenes, he adds, "are usually done pretty quick and dirty. We say, 'Did we get all our words out okay? Alright, move along.'" He also points out that his partners "get all the hard work. They have to actually tell the story. I just get to say things like 'She's hot' and 'She's tasty'" as he lusts after Agent Scully.

Based on Frohike's lecherous nature in past episodes, in fact, Braidwood says he's fond of telling people that it's "pretty tough being the only romantic interest on a major TV hit."

Tom Braidwood's favorite episode is "Dod Kalm."

pro-files

Dean Haglund
(a.k.a. Langly)

Costar Bruce Harwood returned from a gathering of *The X-Files* fans not long ago with a button for his long-haired partner in crime, Dean Haglund, that says, simply, "I'm Not Garth."

Any resemblance to the fictitious *Wayne's World* character notwithstanding, Haglund has followed his own trail of laughs into *The X-Files* lore. Well known on the Vancouver stand-up comedy and improvisation circuit, Haglund won the part of the Lone Gunmen's most flamboyant member from more than 30 aspirants who auditioned.

Born July 29, Haglund remains a member of the improvisational Theatersports team—whose stage works include such spoofs as "Star Trick: The Next Improvisation" and "Free Willy Shakespeare." He's also appeared in various movies and TV shows that shoot in the area, including *The Commish, Sliders,* and *Street Justice.*

Haglund didn't meet Harwood until he got the part of Langly, having initially read for it with a number of other actors. "Even the audition was weird, 'cause I was on the phone for half the damn audition," he jokes.

Since he usually spends Friday night on stage, Haglund was almost entirely unfamiliar with the show, though his role has lured some of the show's die-hard fans, X-Philes, out to see him live. "They watch a bunch of shows, they get really partied up and come to see me. They start screaming, and I've got to perform with my friends saying, 'Wow, who *are* those guys?'" Haglund says, while adding that there are also still folks on the comedy club circuit who've never heard of the show when the emcee introduces him by saying something like "You've seen him on *The X-Files*."

"What?" Haglund says, affecting his best "dude" impersonation. "It's *porno*?"

Dean Haglund's favorite episode is "Tooms."

pro files

Bruce Harwood
(a.k.a. Byers)

"I don't get funny lines," says Bruce Harwood of his role as Byers, the most nattily attired of the Lone Gunmen.

Not that he's complaining, since he clearly relishes his part in the series. A native of British Columbia, Harwood has appeared in such locally produced TV shows as *21 Jump Street, MacGyver,* and *Wiseguy,* as well as the recent TV movie remake of *Bye Bye Birdie.* He even played a computer technician in the ill-fated sequel *The Fly II,* but laughs when it's brought up. "It's pretty bad," he admits. "It's only funny if you know the people, because they all get slaughtered at the end."

Harwood, born April 29, sees the character of Byers—known for his severe suits—as a professorial type who moonlights as a conspiracy theorist. Like Haglund, he had zero familiarity with the show before being cast and no idea the trio would ever appear again until being called back for a second episode. "When I came on set I started hearing weird stories about how popular we were," he says.

Harwood actually attributes wardrobe to part of the Gunmen's appeal, because they look so incongruous together, with Langly a long-haired rock 'n' roll type, Byers looking like a neatly trimmed professor, and

Frohike a classic dirty old man. Writers Glen Morgan
and James Wong actually loosely based the Gunmen on a
similarly attired trio they saw at a gathering of UFO
enthusiasts. "That's why they work," Harwood suggests.
"That's how it visually defines itself."

The Gunmen play a clearly defined role, he adds, by
moving the plot along in an interesting way, sharing their
paranoid conspiracy theories with Mulder and thus providing necessary back story. Still, as a late convert to the
show, Harwood notes wryly that once he started watching the series he couldn't figure out at first "why if
Mulder has all these people helping him he's nowhere
near the truth."

That said, Harwood is eager for the trio to provide
Mulder with all the help he can handle, for as long as he
needs it, to keep himself working. "At least four or five
times a year," he adds quickly. "We're counting on that."

Bruce
Harwood's
favorite
episode is
"Humbug."

pro-files

Nicholas Lea
(a.k.a. Agent Alex Krycek)

Despite appearing in a relatively small number of episodes, Nicholas Lea—who has made his presence felt as FBI Agent Alex Krycek, a mole working for the dark forces seeking to block Mulder's work—says his affiliation with *The X-Files* has already paid dividends when casting people in Los Angeles recognize him from the show. "That instantly breaks the ice," he says, "especially for an actor who is from Vancouver and doesn't know anybody down there."

Lea didn't take up acting full time until the age of 25, after going to art school and singing in a band. After the group broke up he met an acting coach and, having always wanted to give it a try, took the plunge headfirst. "I went and quit my job the next day and started acting," he says, admitting now that he perhaps felt "a little bit bulletproof at that point."

After landing parts in Vancouver-based television shows and some low-budget features, Lea earned his first real exposure with a recurring role in ABC's *The Commish*, where he also met his girlfriend, Melinda McGraw, who played Scully's sister Melissa on *The X-Files*.

Lea did more than 30 episodes of *The Commish*, turning up on *The X-Files* in the first-season installment

X

"Genderbender" as a young man shaken by his encounter with a sex-shifting killer. The one-shot role particularly impressed director Rob Bowman, who kept him in mind for a return and immediately thought of him for Krycek—a double agent introduced as Mulder's partner in the early second-season episode "Sleepless" who, unbeknownst to Mulder, is working on behalf of the Cigarette-Smoking Man.

Born June 22, Lea was the only actor considered in Vancouver for the part, which he thought would simply be a three-episode arc. When he heard he had been cast, Lea remembers running into the gym where Melinda was working out and screaming with joy.

Like many supporting players in the series, Krycek brought with him an ill-defined past. "That's an actor's job really, to come in with a history of who that person is," Lea explains, saying he did research on the FBI and wrote an entire back story "about who this guy was and where he was from. Hopefully, then, the decisions that you make in a show are, like anybody, motivated from their past. There's a whole psychology that goes behind that."

Krycek's traitorous doings earned him the nickname "Ratboy" along the Internet, as well as a small cadre of admirers who call themselves "The Ratnicks." Lea says he's honored to have merited that kind of attention from fans.

Lea has done most of his scenes with David Duchovny, and the two have become friends, though it would be difficult to tell based on their self-choreographed fight in the second-season finale, "Anasazi." "It was really nasty," Lea says. "That's what we were after—not your regular TV fight."

With *The X-Files* having brought him new exposure, the Canadian-born Lea has also taken the somewhat reluctant step of moving to Los Angeles. "I was waiting until I really had something to offer," he says, enjoying a soda at *The X-Files* production office in Vancouver. "Because they don't cast the major roles here, I really had to go to the source."

Still, Lea adds that he'll remain ready to put on the character of Krycek—and whatever nickname the show's fans may be calling him—at a moment's notice. "I'll always drop whatever I'm doing to come up here and do this," he states, emphasizing his affection for *The X-Files* crew.

"They're the best group of producers I've ever worked with, and they've given me a huge opportunity here. It's easy to go through this business and get jobs and go, 'Yeah, see you later,' but these guys here have really opened up something for me, and that's priceless."

pro-files

Jerry Hardin
(a.k.a. Deep Throat)

In many ways the character of Deep Throat, as embodied by actor Jerry Hardin, helped establish a tone and undercurrent of gravity on *The X-Files* that was to provide the spine of the series.

Small gratitude, it would then seem, to have the nameless official—Agent Fox Mulder's high-level government contact, who sought to help him expose the truth—get shot down in the street during the first season's final episode.

Executive producer Chris Carter saw that as a key moment, proving there were no sacred cows on *The X-Files* and that everyone was in jeopardy. Hardin thought it might have had something to do with his desire to gain a more regular appearance schedule on the show, but was nonetheless pleased to enjoy a sort-of homecoming—returning to appear in a dream sequence early in the third season. The crew, he says, "welcomed me back marvelously."

As for the reasons behind his return, Hardin adds, "I like to think it's because the fans wanted me back. It's remarkable how many of the people want to meet Deep Throat. When you come right down to it, in the seven episodes I did there's probably no more than three or four minutes at a time, so I take it as a great compliment."

The veteran character actor was also pleased to revisit the role. "I've always liked the character and felt comfortable with the nature of it," he says, in his mellifluous voice. "The writing from the very beginning was very elliptical, and his sense of humor about himself and about what it was he was doing—all of those things were appealing to me. It was fun to play with."

Hardin was drawn to the writing when he signed on for the show's second episode, entitled "Deep Throat," despite certain doubts about where the character might go. "It's always vague about those recurring roles. They did say that it *perhaps* would recur, but my experience in this industry is that it's never wise to depend on that," he says with a laugh. "You take the job and run."

The veteran actor has appeared in numerous movies and TV shows but caught Carter's attention for the role playing a corrupt lawyer in *The Firm*—a part that bore some resemblance to Deep Throat. Before that Hardin costarred in the movies *Reds* and *Tempest*, while his TV credits include multiple episodes of *Star Trek: The Next Generation* and *Star Trek: Voyager* as well as *Lois & Clark: The New Adventures of Superman*.

Hardin concedes that he loves to play villains, who are "usually the much more exciting characters to create. In those situations, you're much more action-driven. In *The X-Files*, so much of what I do is language-driven, and thought-driven." Still, he says, "It pleases me that it's successful under those circumstances, in the same sense that *Star Trek* is."

In fact, Hardin sees a common bond in the success of the two franchises, both owing to strong writing that stirs viewers' imaginations. "In my opinion that again is a testimony to an interest in and a focus on language," he suggests. "If you think about it, *Star Trek* is primarily two guys or three guys standing on the captain's deck talking to each other. . . . It's language-oriented, and the language is often pretty dense."

From that perspective Deep Throat was a somewhat thankless task, given that the character had to provide complex plot strands in a limited amount of screen time, all the while remaining mysterious and purposefully ill-defined. "Those things are fun acting problems," Hardin says, referring to Deep Throat's shadowy nature. "It gives you some elbow-room as an actor to bring your own contribution to it, or a greater contribution to it. I don't consider that difficult. I consider it challenging and fun."

Acting has proven challenging and fun for Jerry Hardin since his youth. Born in Dallas on November 20, Hardin was raised in a small town outside the city. His father was a rancher, and he grew up riding horses and going to rodeos—doing, as he puts it, "all those things young cowboys do."

Still, Hardin was involved in church and school plays as a youth and participated regularly in speech and drama competitions throughout high school, eventually winning a scholarship to Southwestern University in Georgetown, Texas. That was followed by a prestigious Fulbright scholarship to study at the Royal Academy of Dramatic Art in London.

Not everyone understood, he recalls, when it came to his chosen career. "The common knowledge in that part of Texas was, 'You're a damn fool, boy. People don't make money in *that*,'" Hardin chuckles, falling into his best Texas twang.

Hardin returned after two years in Europe and began working in New York, then spent almost 12 years in regional theater. "My poor family was sort of carrying around with me," he says. His wife, also an actress, frequently did shows with him as they darted around the country.

Though he jokes about it, Hardin's parents (his father, age 91, and mother, 89, still live in Texas) were generally supportive of his decision to act, while recognizing the pitfalls. Hardin admits with a laugh that even he "did my best to discourage my own children from doing it," without much success. In fact, his daughter, Melora Hardin, is an actress whose credits include the movies *Soul Man* and *The Rocketeer*, and his son works at NBC. His wife is now a drama teacher in addition to managing young actors.

Having done most of his scenes with David Duchovny on *The X-Files*, Hardin says he was impressed by the star's "embracing of new bodies"—making newcomers or periodic visitors to the show feel comfortable and welcome. That was particularly helpful, Hardin notes, given that his own routine usually involved flying in, performing the next day, and leaving the day after that.

Even in a short time, Hardin provided some memorable highlights on *The X-Files*, including the scene in the episode "E.B.E." where Deep Throat admits to being one of three people to have executed an alien and his own execution in "The Erlenmeyer Flask." Hardin's dying words to Agent Dana Scully have stuck with the show's viewers.

Hardin says with some pride that when he's met with fans, "People by the hundreds ask me to sign 'Trust no one,' and I have to assume that my delivery of that line made it something that they felt strongly about, and that they connected strongly with that character."

THE EPISODES

X

season ①

season one

locations

Legend

#	Location	#	Location
1.	Bellefleur, OR (Pilot)	13.	Raleigh, NC (Beyond the Sea)
2.	Ellens AFB, ID (Deep Throat)	14.	Steveston, MA (Genderbender)
3.	Baltimore, MD (Squeeze)	15.	Baltimore, MD (Lazarus)
4.	Sioux City, IA (Conduit)	16.	Tashmoo Prison, PA (Young at Heart)
5.	Atlantic City, NJ (Jersey Devil)	17.	Mattawa, WA (E.B.E.)
6.	Philadelphia, PA (Shadows)	18.	Kenwood, TN (Miracle Man)
7.	Crystal City, VA (Ghost in the Machine)	19.	Browning, MT (Shapes)
8.	Icy Cape, AK (Ice)	20.	Olympic Nat'l Forest, WA (Darkness Falls)
9.	Houston, TX (Space)	21.	Baltimore, MD (Tooms)
10.	Townsend, WI (Fallen Angel)	22.	Buffalo, NY (Born Again)
11.	Marin County, CA (Eve)	23.	Colson, WA (Roland)
12.	Cape Cod, MA (Fire)	24.	Georgetown, MD (Erlenmeyer Flask)

Note: Locations were selected by site of main conflict; many episodes cover more than one location.

Map courtesy of Sarah Stegall

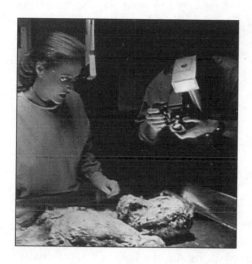

The X-Files: Pilot

First aired: September 10, 1993

Written by
Chris Carter

Directed by
Robert Mandel

Guest stars:
Charles Cioffi (Chief Blevins)
Cliff DeYoung (Dr. Jay Nemman)
Sarah Koskoff (Theresa)
Leon Russom (Det. Miles)
Stephen E. Miller (Truitt)
Zachary Ansley (Billy Miles)
Jim Jansen (Dr. Heitz Werber)
Malcolm Stewart (Dr. Glass)
Alexandra Berlin (Orderly)
William B. Davis (Cigarette-Smoking Man)
Katya Gardener (Peggy O'Dell)
J. B. Bivens (Truck Driver)
Ric Reid (Astronomer)
Lesley Ewen (Receptionist)
Ken Camroux (3rd Man)
Doug Abrams (Patrolman)

Log line: FBI agent Dana Scully is paired with maverick agent Fox Mulder, who has made it his life's work to explore unexplained phenomena. The two are dispatched to investigate the mysterious deaths of a number of high school classmates.

Principal setting: Northwest Oregon

Synopsis: Starting with text that says the story is "inspired by actual documented accounts," this first hour provides a road map for the series to follow, introducing the characters and government intrigue. The show opens with an alien abduction as a girl is found dead in the Oregon woods with two peculiar marks on her back.

In Washington, D.C., meanwhile, Dana Scully, a doctor who has spent two years in the FBI, meets with her superiors (one of whom is the Cigarette-Smoking Man, who remains silent throughout). Scully is asked if she's heard of Fox Mulder, an Oxford-educated psychologist known to be the Bureau's best crime investigator but who's earned the nickname "Spooky" because of his obsession with the paranormal. Mulder has taken on what she is told are unassigned projects outside the Bureau mainstream, known as "X-Files," and she's asked to become his partner, reporting on whether there's anything to substantiate his work.

Mulder is wary of Scully at first, saying he's "under the impression that you were sent to spy on me." He has already checked out her

background, mentioning her senior thesis, "Einstein's Twin Paradox: A New Interpretation." When she asks somewhat testily if he bothered to read it, he assures her that he did. "It's just that in most of my work," he adds wryly, "the laws of physics rarely seem to apply." The next day, they're off to investigate a series of youth murders in Oregon, South Dakota, and Texas that Mulder believes involve alien abduction and experimentation.

In Oregon, four classmates have been found dead near the woods, each with the two tell-tale marks. They exhume one of the victims only to find a non-human, almost simian shrunken form in the casket with an odd metallic device lodged in its nasal cavity. Of the remaining youths, one, the sheriff's son, is a near vegetable, and another is wheelchair-bound.

Mulder voices his abduction theory, while Scully argues that "there has got to be an explanation" of a more earthly variety. Later, the two are blinded by a sudden light, nine minutes have inexplicably elapsed, and another youth turns up dead.

Back at the hotel, Scully notices some marks on her back and, fearing they're the same as those found on the dead girl, rushes into Mulder's room. They're mosquito bites, he assures her, proceeding to explain the cause behind his obsession—how his sister was abducted at the age of eight and that the incident "tore my family apart." His success as an investigator and "connections in Congress," he says, have "allowed me a certain freedom to pursue my interests" despite efforts to thwart his work. Soon after, their hotel burns down, destroying all their evidence regarding the exhumed body and lending credence to Mulder's paranoia.

Mulder and Scully ascertain that the sheriff's son, Billy, is, in fact, the force behind the string of deaths—the aliens having implanted something in his head that left him near-comatose, to be roused when needed. The agents encounter Billy and his father in the woods, and in a blaze of light the boy is suddenly normal again—the two marks having disappeared.

Scully tells her superiors she believes Mulder's theory but can't substantiate it, other than the one remaining piece of evidence—the cylinder found in the corpse's nose, which Scully had kept in her jacket pocket. Asked about her new partner's views, Scully simply says, "Agent Mulder believes we are not alone."

Mulder calls to tell Scully that any record of the case has been erased, while the Cigarette-Smoking Man is shown depositing the alien device Scully gave the Bureau in a bin, next to similar evidence, in a huge Pentagon storage room. At least a part of the truth, it seems, is in there.

Back story: In its biggest concession to reality programming, the pilot is preceded by text saying "The following is inspired by actual documented events." Executive producer Chris Carter considers the scene where Scully takes refuge in Mulder's room wearing a robe a key moment to "really establish what I was trying to establish" in terms of the platonic nature of their relationship. "I love that scene," he says. Carter's original script also has Scully in bed at the end with a boyfriend, named "Ethan Minette," who was excised before the final cut. The clock in that scene is specifically shown to be at 11:21 P.M.—a number that will recur throughout the series, since it is the birthday of Carter's wife, Dori.

It also bears mentioning that Dr. Heitz Werber, the hypnotherapist who interviews Billy at the end, is the same one who originally took Mulder through hypnotherapy regression to access memories of his sister Samantha's abduction.

In the original script at one point Mulder and Scully literally howl at the moon.

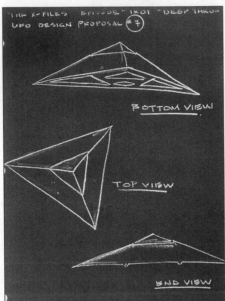

Deep Throat

First aired: September 17, 1993

Written by
Chris Carter

Directed by
Daniel Sackheim

Guest stars:
Jerry Hardin (Deep Throat)
Charles Cioffi (Chief Blevins)
Michael Bryan French (Paul Mossinger)
Andrew Johnston (Colonel Budahas)
Seth Green (Emil)
Lalainia Lindejerg (Zoe)
Vince Metcalfe (Kissell)
Gabrielle Rose (Anita Budahas)
Monica Parker (Ladonna)
Doc Harris (Mr. McLennen)
Sheila Moore (Verla McLennen)
John Cuthbert (Commanding Officer)
Brian Furlong (Lead Officer)
Michael Puttonen (Motel Manager)

Log line: Acting on a tip from an inside source (Deep Throat), Mulder and Scully travel to Idaho to investigate unusual disappearances of army test pilots.

Principal setting: Southwest Idaho

Synopsis: Mulder pulls some strings to investigate the disappearance of a test pilot at Ellens Air Force Base—the sixth pilot to turn up missing from that facility since 1963. The case, he tells Scully, has a certain "paranormal bouquet."

Before they can leave an unknown man—Deep Throat—confronts Mulder in the bathroom, saying he has "an interest in your work" and warning him to "leave this case alone."

Mulder and Scully meet with the pilot's wife, who says he'd behaved unpredictably: sprinkling fish-food flakes on his food at a dinner party, yelling at the children for no reason, and suddenly shaking as if he were having a seizure. Later they see two darting lights in the night sky, then go to the Flying Saucer Cafe—looking for "UFO nuts"—where Mulder sees a picture of a UFO that looks uncannily like a shot supposedly taken in Roswell, New Mexico in 1947. "This is gonna look real good on my field report," Scully says.

Mulder explains that Ellens is rumored to be one of six sites where parts of the wreckage of that UFO crash were taken. He believes the government is testing planes built using UFO technology, the strain of which may be causing the pilots' behavior.

Inexplicably, the missing pilot shows up, but his wife insists he's different. "That is not my husband," she says. "They've done something to him."

Mulder thinks the pilot's brain may have been "rewired" to make him forget certain things, lest he become a security risk. Soon after, Mulder and Scully are stopped by a group of armed men and told to leave immediately or suffer the consequences. Scully urges her partner to get out "while you still have a job," but he takes off alone and is caught in a secret area after seeing one of the UFOs.

Mulder is strapped to a gurney and injected with drugs. Determined to get him back, Scully takes one of the security men hostage and goes to the base, where Mulder is brought to her, groggy and glassy-eyed. "How did I get here?" he asks.

Mulder meets Deep Throat again while jogging. Deep Throat says that he can help Mulder, but that their lives may be in danger, and that "care and discretion are now imperative." His interest, he tells Mulder, is "The truth," and when the agent asks, "They're here, aren't they?," Deep Throat responds flatly, "Mr. Mulder, *they* have been here for a very, very long time."

Back story: Carter added voice-over narration by Scully after the fact as a compromise to Fox Broadcasting, which wanted more closure out of the episode. Although Carter continued to fight against pat resolutions, the narration became an ongoing device.

First appearance of "Deep Throat."

This episode is also the first one on which assistant art director Clyde Klotz worked. Mr. Klotz went on to marry Gillian Anderson on New Year's Day, 1994.

Squeeze

First aired: September 24, 1993

Written by
Glen Morgan and James Wong

Directed by
Harry Longstreet

Guest stars:
Doug Hutchison (Eugene Victor Tooms)
Donal Logue (Tom Colton)
Henry Beckman (Det. Frank Briggs)
Kevin McNulty (Fuller)
Terence Kelly (George Usher)
Colleen Winton (Lie Detector
    Technician)
James Bell (Johnson)
Gary Hetherington (Kennedy)
Rob Morton (Kramer)
Paul Joyce (Mr. Werner)

Log line: Mulder and Scully try to stop a mutant killer, Eugene Tooms, who can gain access through even the smallest spaces and awakens from hibernation every 30 years to commit murder.

Principal setting: Baltimore, Maryland

Synopsis: A businessman is murdered in his office by a killer who slithers in through an air vent. Tom Colton, a fellow Academy friend of Scully's, tells her about the case: three victims found dead with no visible means of entry, and their livers apparently ripped out by a bare hand.

Mulder joins in the investigation despite Colton's disdain for him and finds a bizarre, elongated fingerprint at the crime scene near the vent, saying the killer "ought to stick out with ten-inch fingers." The unusual fingerprint matches those found at previous murders, with five having occurred every 30 years dating back to 1903.

Mulder realizes the killer has two more murders to commit, and staking out a previous crime scene the agents catch a suspect, Eugene Tooms, slithering down a vent. An animal control officer, Tooms claims he was in the vent looking for a dead animal, in response to complaints of a bad smell coming from the air duct. Tooms passes a polygraph test and is set free before Mulder discovers that his fingerprints, when stretched by computer analysis, match those found at the previous murder sites.

Tooms soon kills again, gliding down a chimney to commit the crime. With one murder left in his cycle, Mulder says, "If we don't get him now, we won't have another chance till 2023." Mulder and Scully find the detective who investigated the 1963 murders, who says he knew that the same man was involved in '33. He shows them a picture of Tooms taken three decades earlier, and he hasn't aged.

Going to the condemned building where Tooms lived in the '60s, Mulder and Scully find a strange nest made of newspapers and bile. Mulder surmises that Tooms is a mutant who must satiate his need for human liver every 30 years and who then hibernates. Tooms, who has taken a small memento from each victim, watches from above and finds a necklace dropped by Scully.

Scully returns home, followed by Tooms. When Mulder goes back to Tooms's lair and sees the necklace, he suddenly realizes that Tooms intends to make Scully his next victim and rushes to her apartment. Mulder arrives in the nick of time, and Tooms is captured after a struggle.

In his cell, Tooms starts making another nest, and when a guard brings him food through a small opening, he looks at the aperture, and smiles.

Back story: Because the first two episode involved UFOs, Fox wanted to see a different sort of story in this hour, and in that sense "Squeeze" helped establish that *The X-Files* could be about more than just aliens each week. Although there are some parallels to *The Night Strangler*—the second *Night Stalker* movie, which involved a man who rose to commit multiple murders every twenty-one years—writers Glen Morgan and James

Doug Hutchison, playing a liver-eating mutant, is a vegetarian in real life.

Q: What was Eugene Tooms's address for 60 years?

A: 66 Exeter Street.

Wong drew their inspiration from Jack the Ripper and a large ventilator shaft outside their office. As Morgan recalls, the episode started with a simple premise when he asked Wong, "What if we were working here late at night and some guy came *through* that thing?"

Morgan concedes that when Doug Hutchinson came into the audition, Morgan thought he was too young to play Tooms, thinking, "No, this guy is wrong. He looks twelve years old." The actor won them over, however, with his impromptu reaction to director Harry Longstreet's somewhat baffling instruction to "go from a neutral position to an attack position," jarring everyone by getting into the character and snapping nastily at the director. Longstreet took some convincing, but the producers had their man.

Chris Carter says his own contribution was limited to having just returned from France and eaten a lot of *foie gras*, which made him wonder what it would be like if someone developed a taste for human liver. Morgan says they settled on the liver because it was "funnier than any other organ."

The cover of the shooting schedule for "Squeeze."

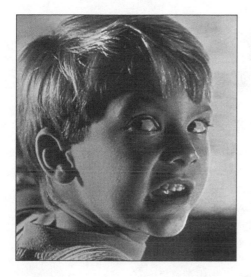

Conduit

First aired: October 1, 1993

Written by
Alex Gansa and Howard Gordon

Directed by
Daniel Sackheim

Guest stars:
Carrie Snodgress (Darlene Morris)
Joel Palmer (Kevin Morris)
Charles Cioffi (Section Chief
  Scott Blevins)
Taunya Dee (Ruby Morris)
Michael Cavanaugh (Sheriff)
Shelley Owens (Tessa)
Don Thompson (Holtzman)
Don Gibb (Kip)
Akiko Morison (Leza Atsumi)
Anthony Harrison (4th Man)
Glen Roald (M. E. Worker)
Mauricio Mercado (Coroner)

Log line: A teenage girl is abducted by aliens, compelling Mulder to confront feelings about his own sister's disappearance.

Principal setting: Sioux City, Iowa

Synopsis: A teenage girl, sleeping near her little brother, disappears at a campsite near Lake Okobogee, which Mulder describes as a "UFO hot spot." Mulder seeks out the case, and Scully is "officially" told of his sister's abduction 21 years earlier.

The missing girl, Ruby, is the daughter of a woman who reported a UFO sighting in 1967. The little brother, meanwhile, has been acting strangely, writing down a binary number sequence that Mulder sends to Washington. Shortly thereafter agents grab the mother and boy, saying the code was a highly classified defense satellite transmission.

Mulder and Scully examine the campsite and find the body of Ruby's boyfriend. Scully believes the man and the missing girl were killed by a friend and tells Mulder to "stop running after your sister." Back at the house, they notice that the boy has arranged page after page of numbers on the floor, which from above eerily reveals a mural-sized picture of Ruby. Mulder talks about his sister, telling Scully that he's been "living with it every day of my life."

Returning to the woods, the agents see a blaze of lights that turn out to be motorcycles. They find Ruby, uncon-

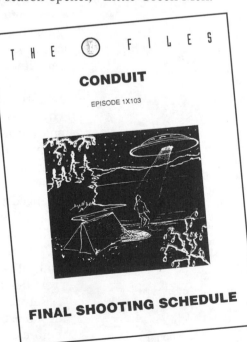

scious but alive. In the hospital, she shows symptoms of someone subjected to prolonged weightlessness, but her mother says she doesn't want her daughter to be ridiculed for discussing what's happened.

Mulder sits alone in church, weeping for his sister, while Scully listens to Mulder's hypnotic regression therapy tapes, where he recalls a voice telling him that his sister would be okay. Asked if he believes the voice, Mulder can only say, "I want to believe."

Back story: Assistant art director Greg Loewen designed the huge mural of Ruby, but colleague Vivien Nishi had to go over the printout and painstakingly write in all those 1's and 0's to make it look as if it were drawn by an eight-year-old hand. The project took several days for a shot that lasted only a few seconds.

The episode also reveals Mulder's hometown to be Chilmarc, Massachusetts, though the spelling was "Chilmark" when it turned up nearly a year later in the second-season opener, "Little Green Men."

Fox Mulder opened X-File X-40253 on his sister almost six months *before* he underwent hypno-regression to recover his lost memories.

The address in Samantha Mulder's file, 2790 Vine Street, is the former address of *The X-Files* production office in Vancouver.

T H E ⊕ F I L E S

CONDUIT

EPISODE 1X103

FINAL SHOOTING SCHEDULE

The Jersey Devil

First aired: October 8, 1993

Written by
Chris Carter

Directed by
Joe Napolitano

Guest stars:
Michael MacRae (Ranger Peter Boulle)
Gregory Sierra (Dr. Diamond)
Wayne Tippit (Detective Thompson)
Claire Stansfield (Jersey Devil)
Jill Teed (Glenna)
Tamsin Kelsey (Ellen)
Andrew Airlie (Rob)
Bill Dow (Dad)
Hrothgar Mathews (Jack)
Jayme Knox (Mom)
Scott Swanson (1st Officer)
Sean O'Byrne (2nd Officer)
David Lewis (Young Officer)
D. Neil Monk (SWAT Team Officer)

Log line: Scully and Mulder investigate murders thought to be the work of a legendary man-beast living in the New Jersey woods.

Principal setting: New Jersey

Synopsis: Opening in 1947, a man is pulled away from his car and found with his leg eaten off. Police search the woods, cornering and killing a large, unseen creature.

Cut to the present, and a homeless man is found with parts of him eaten and bite marks that appear to be human. Mulder talks about the Jersey Devil, which Scully dismisses as a folk tale, leaving Mulder alone to investigate while she goes to her godson's birthday party.

Mulder talks to some of the homeless, who tell him they've seen the creature around and that the police know about it as well. Staking out the spot, Mulder catches a glance of the beast, but he's arrested. That convinces him that the police are covering up what's happening, fearing that the truth will hurt tourism.

Mulder wants Scully to help him pursue the case, but she has a date and won't cancel. "Unlike you, Mulder, I would like to have a life," she says. Later, a park ranger tells Mulder he found the body of a male creature in the woods and turned it over to the authorities. Mulder theorizes that the creature's mate, since his death, has moved into the city to find food.

Mulder pursues the beast woman

Faking it:
The X-Files
is filmed in
Vancouver, so
Mulder was
not really in
the Atlantic
City casinos.
Instead,
Duchovny was
filmed in
front of a
blue-screen
and stock
casino
footage was
matted in
later—consid-
erably cheaper
than a location
shoot in New
Jersey would
have cost.

We discover
that Scully's
best friend
is named
Ellen; her
godson is
named Trent.

but is trapped by her, only to have her frightened off by Scully. The creature flees into the woods, where the police kill her. An examination finds a human bone in her digestive system.

Scully passes on a second date in order to work the case with Mulder. She's made her choice. When Mulder asks, "Don't you have a life?," she snaps back, "Keep it up, Mulder, and I'll hurt you like that Beast Woman did."

Meanwhile, a father and son trek through the woods, as we see a child of the two creatures hiding in the brush.

Back story: As opposed to some hairy bigfoot, Carter wanted to present the Jersey Devil as an evolutionary throwback. "The idea was not to make this a monster per se, but almost a missing link," he suggests.

Claire Stansfield, who stands about 6'1", played the beast woman and had to spend most of the episode running around naked. "That was pretty exciting," Carter says with a laugh, adding that the actress also had to have her hair tied over her breasts and wear a codpiece in some scenes to prevent those sequences from giving the audience a more thorough glimpse of the natural world than prime-time television will allow.

The subplot shows Scully trying to balance having some semblance of a personal life against the dedication (bordering on obsession) that Mulder has toward his work. She meets with a married friend, Ellen, who has a child and asks her if Mulder is someone with whom Scully might get romantically involved. Though she does go on a date, Scully opts to pursue cases with Mulder instead of that path.

The purpose of those scenes, Carter says, was "to show the life she's passing on. I just wanted to open up

Scully a little bit for the audience." On a more humorous note, Mulder at one point holds up a magazine center-fold, saying that the woman pictured claims to have been taken aboard a spaceship and held in an antigravity chamber. "Antigravity's right," Scully mutters.

Shadows

First aired: October 22, 1993

Written by
Glen Morgan and James Wong

Directed by
Michael Katleman

Guest stars:
Lisa Waltz (Lauren Kyte)
Barry Primus (Robert Dorland)
Lorena Gale (Ellen Bledsoe)
Veena Sood (Ms. Saunders)
Deryl Hayes (Webster)
Kelli Fox (Pathologist)
Tom Pickett (Cop)
Tom Heaton (Groundskeeper)
Janie Woods-Morris (Ms. Lange)
Nora McLellan (Jane Morris)
Anna Ferguson (Ms. Winn)

Log line: Mulder and Scully investigate unusual murders committed by an unseen force protecting a young woman.

Principal setting: Philadelphia, Pennsylvania

Synopsis: Lauren Kyte laments the suicide death of her boss, Howard Graves. She's later attacked by two men, who are killed by an unseen force.

Government agents call in Mulder and Scully to examine the bodies. The corpses exhibit signs of residual electromagnetic charge and appear to have had their throats crushed as if it were done from inside. Mulder posits that psychokinesis may have been involved.

Security camera tape leads the agents to Lauren, who is reluctant to talk to them. Leaving her home their car starts inexplicably, firing across the street as if of its own volition. Mulder suggests a poltergeist may be involved. "They're he-ere," rejoins Scully.

In following Lauren, they learn that Graves had a daughter who died young and would have been about Lauren's age had she survived. An enhanced photo shows an image of Graves, otherwise invisible, behind her. Lauren is subsequently awakened by Graves's voice, as blood streams down her bathtub drain, letting her know his death was a result of murder, not suicide.

Lauren confronts Graves's partner,

Dorland, telling him she knows that her boss was murdered. Soon after two assailants burst into her house but are slain just as were the first pair.

Other agents, who are with the CIA, tell Mulder and Scully that they believe Graves's company has been selling parts to a Mideast extremist group, two of whom were involved in the initial assault on Lauren. Dorland had Graves killed because he feared he was going to expose the operation. When they seek to question Lauren, Mulder dryly warns them by saying, "My advice to you is don't get rough with her."

Bureau agents raid the facility but find no evidence, until Lauren faces Dorland in his office. Suddenly, he's pinned to the wall, the door locks, pictures fly in all directions, and a knife fires into the wall to reveal a computer disk with proof of Dorland's crimes.

Lauren moves on to a new job in a new city, and when a coworker is gruff with her the woman's coffee cup begins to rattle. It's just a passing truck . . . maybe.

In the original script, Mulder tells Scully what he would like on his tombstone: "No regrets."

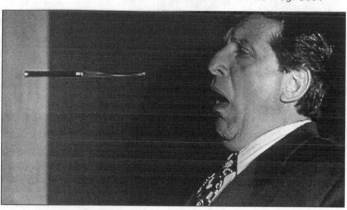

Back story: According to Glen Morgan, Fox had been pushing for the producers to do more episodes where, in essence, "Mulder and Scully investigate the paranormal and help people." As a result the incentive behind "Shadows," he says, was to provide an installment where the agents would do just that and "get them off our back" so the producers could pursue some of the more offbeat stories they had in mind. Morgan and Wong also harbored a fondness for ghost stories, and Fox executives had suggested the idea of doing some sort of episode involving poltergeists.

The show's penchant for small in-jokes is also in evidence during this hour, as the name of assistant director Tom Braidwood (well before his days of fame as the Lone Gunmen's Frohike) is used in the scene where the parking lot attendant paints over the name on the space that previously belonged to the dead man.

Ghost in the Machine

First aired: October 29, 1993

Written by
Alex Gansa and Howard Gordon

Directed by
Jerrold Freeman

Guest stars:
Wayne Duvall (Jerry Lamana)
Gillian Barber (Nancy Spiller)
Rob Labelle (Brad Wilczek)
Jerry Hardin (Deep Throat)
Blu Mankuma (Claude Peterson)
Marc Baur (Man in Suit)
Bill Finck (Sandwich Man)
Theodore Thomas (Clyde)
Tom Butler (Benjamin Drake)

Log line: A computer with artificial intelligence begins killing in order to preserve its existence.

Principal setting: Crystal City, Virginia

Synopsis: The chief executive at a high-tech firm, Eurisko, is electrocuted after saying that he plans to terminate the COS project, or Central Operating System.

Mulder's former partner, Jerry Lamana, comes to him seeking help with the case, taking Mulder's profile of the killer and presenting it as his own. Told that the murderer must have overridden the building's computer system, Scully and Mulder go see Brad Wilczek, who created the system but left the firm over a dispute with the slain CEO, Benjamin Drake.

Voice analysis shows that Wilczek was the last person to speak to Drake, and Lamana goes to arrest him but is killed when the elevator plummets to the bottom as Wilczek watches helplessly on a monitor. Wilczek confesses, though Mulder doubts he's involved and is denied access to him by authorities.

Deep Throat says the Defense Department is interested in Wilczek because he created artificial intelligence—"a learning machine" that, he surmises, killed Drake as an act of self-preservation.

Mulder asks Wilczek how to stop COS and goes to implant a virus in the system. Scully shows up as well, after a phone call reveals that someone at Eurisko accessed her computer. As they enter the building, a security camera lens follows them, and the lights go out. Boosted into an airvent, Scully is sucked toward the blades of a huge fan, while Mulder penetrates the system. A building security worker turns out to be a Defense Department spy and stops Mulder, but Scully, having freed herself, gets the drop on him and allows Mulder to introduce the virus. "Brad, why?" COS asks as it's being neutralized.

Deep Throat says Wilczek is gone, and the government is holding him to learn what he knows. Meanwhile, as workers pore over the dormant COS, a light flickers on.

Scully's FBI
ID number is
2317-616.

Back story: Producer Howard Gordon, who wrote the episode with partner Alex Gansa, says "Ghost in the Machine" still qualifies as "one of my biggest disappointments," feeling that the computer intelligence wasn't as well-defined as it needs to be compared to predecessors like those in *2001: A Space Odyssey* and *Demon Seed*.

"Fox felt it was a bit too pedestrian to be an X-File," says Gordon, who tends to be rather harsh when it comes to grading his own episodes, "and it was one of those instances where I'd have to agree with them."

The show does feature a striking visual sequence involving Scully and a vacuum-sucking fan that was, in fact, a last-minute addition when the originally scripted action involving an elevator shaft was deemed too expensive. The spinning fan blades "looked good," Gordon says, "and it was a helluva lot cheaper."

Guest star Wayne Duvall is the nephew of actor

Robert Duvall. For numerically minded fans, Scully's phone number is given as (202) 555-6431—555 being the standard prefix used in movies and television shows, since it isn't used by the phone company and thus prevents people from receiving crank calls.

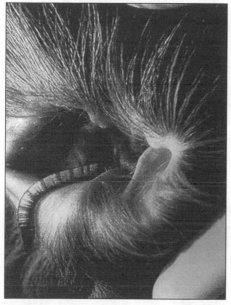

Ice

First aired: November 5, 1993

Written by
Glen Morgan and James Wong

Directed by
David Nutter

Guest stars:
Xander Berkeley (Dr. Hodge)
Felicity Huffman (Dr. Da Silva)
Steve Hytner (Dr. Denny Murphy)
Jeff Kober (Bear)
Ken Kirzinger (Richter)
Sonny Surowiec (Campbell)

Log line: Mulder and Scully and a small party are trapped in the Arctic after the unexplained deaths of a research team on assignment there.

Principal setting: Icy Cape, Alaska

Synopsis: A team sent to drill into the Arctic ice core stops sending transmissions after one of the members, in his last contact, says, "We are not who we are. It goes no further than this," into the camera. He's then attacked by another man, and they face off with guns aimed at each other before turning the weapons on themselves and firing.

Mulder and Scully pick up three doctors and scientists—Da Silva, Murphy, and Hodge—and a pilot, Bear, flying in before the next Arctic storm. They arrive to find the dead scientists and a dog that attacks Mulder, biting Bear when he tries to help. Tranquilizing the dog, they see a small form moving under its skin, while Bear notices he has developed the same dark nodules that were on the dog.

Scully finds ammonia in the victims' blood as well as a small, single-celled creature that she believes could be the larval stage of a larger animal. Mulder says if they've been exposed to an unknown organism they must employ quarantine procedure, but Bear objects, decking Mulder before he's tackled by Scully. As they restrain him, they see and cut out a strange-looking worm moving under Bear's skin at the base of his neck, causing his death.

Mulder tries to radio for help but is

David Duchovny's own border collie, Blue, is the daughter of the dog featured in this episode.

Listen closely and you'll hear Richter's line, "It all ends right here, right now" repeated by Dana Scully near the end of the episode, in a wholly different context.

told they'll be trapped for days by the storm. The worm, they realize, penetrates the hypothalamus gland in the brain, causing aggressive behavior in its host. Mulder questions whether they should kill it, saying the worm probably came to Earth from another planet—one that sustains ammonia-based life—250,000 years ago before being covered by ice. Scully says it must be stopped now.

The five survivors eye each other warily, wondering who may be infected. Mulder wakes up to find Murphy stuffed in a locker with his throat slit, and becomes the prime suspect. Squaring off at gunpoint, Scully joins the others in locking Mulder in a room. "In here, I'll be safer than you," he warns her.

Examining a blood sample, Scully finds that when larva from two different worms invade the same host they kill each other, and she proves her theory by inserting a full-grown worm into the dog, curing him.

Though Hodge and Da Silva want to use the same process on Mulder, Scully is convinced he's not infected and lets him out, but the others separate them and jump Mulder—preparing to insert the remaining worm in his ear when Hodge notices a form moving within Da Silva. Mulder brings her down, and they implant the creature in her.

After their rescue, Mulder wants to go back to the base to study the creature but is told that the military torched the place after they were evacuated. It's still there, he tells Scully, 200,000 years down in the ice. "Leave it there," she says.

Back story: There are certain similarities in this episode to *The Thing* and to the John W. Campbell, Jr., novella, *Who Goes There?* on which *The Thing* was based, inasmuch as "Ice" traps characters in a confined space with a killer who may be any one of them. Still, the idea for the hour actually started after Glen Morgan read an article in *Science News* about "these guys in Greenland who dug something 250,000 years old out of the ice." In order to give the FBI a reason to become part of the investigation, the venue was shifted to Alaska.

The episode proved a pivotal one in the career of makeup effects wizard Toby Lindala, who received his first major assignment on the show and subsequently became its resident ace in that department. Lindala remembers sweating it out when the prosthetic device he was using to create the effect of the worm moving beneath the skin started to tear. "His hands were trembling, he was so nervous," Morgan recalls.

The space worm remains near the top of *The X-Files* gross-out meter, in part because the producers got away with more than they originally anticipated. Morgan admits the plan was to let one scene involving the creature run a little long—about four seconds—"thinking Fox's standards and practices department would cut it down, and they didn't touch it."

Space

First aired: November 12, 1993

Written by
Chris Carter

Directed by
William Graham

Guest stars:
Ed Lauter (Lt. Col. Marcus
    Aurelius Belt)
Susanna Thompson (Michelle Generoo)
Tom McBeath (Scientist)
Terry David Mulligan (Mission
    Controller)
Tyronne L'Hirondelle (Databank
    Scientist)
Norma Wick (Reporter)
Alf Humphreys (2nd Controller)
David Cameron (Young Scientist)
French Tickner (Preacher)
Paul DesRoches (Paramedic)

Log line: A mysterious force is sabotaging the United States' space shuttle program and Scully and Mulder must stop it before the next launch.

Principal setting: Houston, Texas

Synopsis: In 1977, pictures from Mars showed what looked like a sculpted face in the landscape, the jumping-off point for this episode.
    Lt. Col. Belt, now supervisor of the shuttle program, was on that mission and has flashbacks of a spacewalk, seeing that same face looking down at him.
    Mulder and Scully, meanwhile, are approached by Michelle Generoo, NASA's Mission Control communications commander, who says a recent liftoff was aborted seconds before launch and that she fears a piece of equipment has been sabotaged. She wants the agents to help solve the case before her fiancé flies the next mission.
    Belt tells them there's nothing to worry about, and the shuttle launches without incident. Soon, however, communication with the spacecraft is lost, and Generoo's car crashes as the strange face zooms in at her through the fog.
    Although the shuttle is damaged, Belt tells the astronauts to deliver their payload, fearing that millions of dollars will be lost—and the space program crippled—if they don't follow through. Mulder is disillusioned, but Belt tells him things are different—that "You make the front page today only if you screw up."

Alone, Belt has another flashback, screaming as the astral presence escapes his body, heading skyward. The shuttle feels a "dull thump" and experiences an oxygen leak—what happened on Belt's mission years earlier. "There's some kind of ghost outside the ship!" the astronauts tell Houston.

The agents examine the records, which show Belt knew about the equipment flaw and possibly the O-ring failure on the *Challenger*. Belt collapses, saying the astral force "lived in me," controlling him. At his urging, they alter the shuttle's trajectory, preventing the craft from burning up on reentry. Belt himself, wrestling with the presence, leaps to his death.

Mulder, a fan of Belt's from long ago, lauds his sacrifice. "Something had possessed him. Something he had seen out there in space"—something, apparently, that didn't want company.

Back story: Chris Carter isn't entirely satisfied with this show, which was structured around the famous "face on Mars" photograph. The producer remembers lying on the bed in his hotel room in Vancouver thinking, "Wouldn't it be weird if that face came down on me?"— the exact image duplicated in relation to Col. Belt.

Certain logistical constraints contributed to Carter's frustration with this installment, among them the fact that it was impossible to show the beset astronauts in the space shuttle, making it necessary to deal with all that action offscreen. "You just can't do it on an eight-day television budget," he concedes.

"Space" was designed in part to be an inexpensive hour—after the series had exceeded its budget on some earlier episodes—using NASA footage that could be acquired at a relatively low cost. As it turned out, constructing the large control room set ended up making this the most expensive episode of the first season.

Carter admits he was a bit overwhelmed when the episode was being filmed, shooting in September as the show premiered, with reviews and other input pouring in from all sides. "Everything was happening at once," he says. "At the time we were just trying to put this balloon aloft."

Fallen Angel

First aired: November 19, 1993

Written by
Alex Gansa and Howard Gordon

Directed by
Larry Shaw

Guest stars:
Frederick Coffin (Chief Joseph McGrath)
Jerry Hardin (Deep Throat)
Marshall Bell (Commander Henderson)
Scott Bellis (Max Fenig)
Alvin Sanders (Deputy Wright)
Sheila Paterson (Gina Watkins)
Tony Pantages (Lt. Fraser)
Jane MacDougall (Laura Dalton)
Bret Stait (Corp. Taylor)
Freda Perry (Mrs. Wright)
Michael Rogers (Lt. Griffin)
William McDonald (Dr. Oppenheim)
Kimberly Unger (Karen Koretz)

Log line: Scully and Mulder investigate a possible UFO crash site, which Mulder believes the government is covering up.

Principal setting: Townsend, Wisconsin

Synopsis: An alien spacecraft crashes in the woods, but a military commander tells the radar observer to report the sighting as a meteor. Soon, the government evacuates the area, saying there was a toxic chemical spill.

Deep Throat tells Mulder that a quick retrieval team has been dispatched, meaning that he has 24 hours to locate evidence before the area is "sanitized." Mulder infiltrates the field operation, dubbed Operation Falcon, but is caught photographing the wreckage, as troops seek the escaped UFO pilot. "I suggest you forget what you saw—or what you *think* you saw," the commander tells him. Held prisoner, Mulder meets Max Fenig, a member of NICAP—the National Investigative Committee of Aerial Phenomena. Fenig tells Mulder he's familiar with his work, and that this is "like the Roswell cover-up all over again."

Scully comes to bail out Mulder, saying he's in deep trouble in Washington and that the X-Files unit may be shut down. In the interim, the military locates the alien pilot, but soldiers who encounter the translucent presence are burned horribly.

Mulder returns to find Fenig having a seizure and notices a strange inci-

X

Deep Throat's
warning to
Mulder is a
quote from Don
Corleone, in
The Godfather.
"Keep your
friends close,
but keep your
enemies
closer."

sion behind his ear—a scar Mulder has seen previously on alleged alien abductees. His presence, Mulder now believes, is no accident. Army radar, meanwhile, tracks a new "meteor"—this one much larger than the first, which, as the radar operator notes, "seems to be hovering over a small town in eastern Wisconsin."

Following Max, Mulder sees more charbroiled soldiers and Fenig bleeding from the ears. Pursuing him into a warehouse, Mulder is flung across the room by the alien presence, seeing Max suspended in the air before he disappears—abducted once again—in a burst of light.

Back in Washington, a committee grills Mulder. "How can I disprove lies that are stamped with an official seal?" he asks defiantly, telling them that "No one, no government agency, has jurisdiction over the truth." Deep Throat tells the committee chairman there is more risk in cutting Mulder loose—and letting him tell the world what he knows, "or *thinks* he knows"— than in allowing him to continue his work. "

Back story: In a sense the character of Max Fenig and his NICAP organization represent a sort of precursor to the Lone Gunmen, and the episode also foreshadows the eventual shutdown of the X-Files at the end of the season, even though the writers "hadn't the slightest clue" that would eventually occur, according to producer Howard Gordon.

Gordon says the point was "to remind the audience what Scully was there for in the first place"– namely, to act as a skeptic counterbalancing Mulder's devoted belief in the paranormal and, from the Bureau's perspective, where possible to discredit his work.

Casting directore Lynne Carrow considers Canadian actor Scott Bellis, who played Fenig, to be perhaps her proudest "find" in terms of casting the show. Gordon says there's frequently a bias toward casting actors from Los Angeles in lead roles, so when a Vancouver local lands such a part "you know they came in and just knocked our socks off," as Bellis did. Gone but not forgotten, the producers still talk about finding another role for the actor or even bringing him back as Max. After all, Gordon notes, "Abductees get returned."

Technically, thin piano wires were used to suspend Bellis in the air during the abduction sequence, without using any postproduction effects.

Eve

First aired: December 10, 1993

Written by
Kenneth Biller and Chris Brancato

Directed by
Fred Gerber

Guest stars:
Harriet Harris (Sally Kendrick)
Erika Krievins (Cindy Reardon)
Sabrina Krievins (Teena Simmons)
Jerry Hardin (Deep Throat)
George Touliatos (Dr. Katz)
Janet Hodgkinson (Waitress)
Tasha Simms (Ellen Reardon)
Tina Gilbertson (Donna Watkins)
David Kirby (Ted Watkins)
Christine Upright-Letain (Ms. Wells)
Gordon Tipple (Detective)
Garry Davey (Hunter)
Joe Maffei (Guard #1)
Maria Herrera (Guard #2)
Robert Lewis (Officer)

Log line: Two bizarre, identical murders occur simultaneously on different coasts, each involving a strange young girl.

Principal settings: Greenwich, Connecticut; San Francisco, California

Synopsis: Two men with eight-year-old daughters are killed in California and Connecticut, with each having a massive amount of blood drained from his body.

The first girl, Teena, speaks in a strangely adult manner, telling the agents that "men from the clouds" came for her father and "wanted to exsanguinate him." When she's subsequently kidnapped from a social services facility, Mulder and Scully journey to Northern California and are stunned to discover that the other girl, Cindy, is identical to the first. Both families were involved with a Dr. Sally Kendrick, who was fired from a clinic for experimenting with eugenics—the science of improving human genetic characteristics, usually through breeding.

Deep Throat tells Mulder of the Litchfield Project—a top-secret '50s eugenics program that created identical little boys named Adam and girls named Eve. At his direction, Mulder and Scully go to a home for the criminally insane where they find Eve 6, a dead ringer for Sally Kendrick. The Adams and Eves had extra chromosomes, she says, giving them heightened strength and intelligence but also causing them to become murderous. "I can top 265," she says ominously of her IQ. "We're very bright, we Eves."

Two of the Eve clones (one of whom is Kendrick) are still at large and pictures of the Eves as youths reveal them to be genetic replicas of Cindy and Teena. Mulder and Scully stake out Cindy's house, but another Eve escapes with her. Brought together, the two girls admit they "just knew" of each other's existence and each killed her father—their murderous streak having begun at an earlier age than their predecessors. Eve, who was actually trying to help them, is poisoned.

Authorities find the girls, and as Mulder and Scully take them back Mulder realizes they're actually the murderers, just before they can poison him and Scully. The girls try to escape but are caught and jailed with Eve 6. In the last scene they have a visitor: Sally Kendrick, Eve 8. "How did you know I'd come for you?" she asks.

"We just knew."

Teena and Cindy are named after the wives of producers Glen Morgan and Jim Wong, writers and producers for the show.

Back story: There's an eerie, *Boys From Brazil*–type quality in the performances by twins Erika and Sabrina Krievins. The producers initially looked for twins in Los Angeles, but child-labor laws are such that flying the children to Vancouver in light of the limited number of hours they're allowed to work during a day would have made the show "almost impossible to do," Chris Carter says. As a result, the show had to employ local talent in Vancouver and was fortunate to find the Krievins twins. "That's happened several times," the producer adds, referring to situations where the series was forced to come up with performers on short notice or for logistical reasons who then delivered excellent performances. "We've just lucked out."

The episode also features another memorable throwaway exchange between Mulder and Scully, when he says one of the girls was "abducted" and Scully corrects him by saying "kidnapped."

"Po-tay-toe, po-tah-toe," he quips.

Fire

First aired: December 17, 1993

Written by
Chris Carter

Directed by
Larry Shaw

Guest stars:
Mark Sheppard (Cecil L'ively/Bob)
Amanda Pays (Phoebe Green)
Dan Lett (Sir Malcolm Marsden)
Duncan Fraser (Beatty)
Lynda Boyd (Bar Patron)
Laurie Paton (Lady Malcolm)
Phil Hayes (Driver #1)
Christopher Gray (Jimmie)
Alan Robertson (Gray-Haired Man)
Keegan Macintosh (Michael)

Log line: Mulder and Scully encounter an assassin who can start fires with the touch of his hand.

Principal settings: Boston, Cape Cod, Massachusetts

Synopsis: Mulder is visited by an old flame (pardon the expression) from his days at Oxford, Phoebe Green, who is trying to protect a British lord vacationing in Massachusetts. Someone has killed several members of Parliament, in each case setting his victim ablaze. Mulder, who admits to a fear of fire due to an incident in his youth, wonders if it may involve a pyrokinetic—someone who can control and conduct fire.

Anticipating Sir Malcolm's arrival, the assassin kills the estate's caretaker and takes his place. Going to a local bar, he ignites his arm, torching the place. He later fatally drugs the family's driver so he can chauffeur them to a dinner in Boston.

Scully, meanwhile, profiles the killer, ascertaining that he may be "prone to excessive fantasies about women," while Mulder and Phoebe begin to rekindle their romance. Scully hurries to the hotel where the dinner is being held and finds them together, only to see that an upper floor where Sir Malcolm's children are being kept is on fire. Earning the family's trust, the caretaker helps save them.

Scully has learned that an Englishman, Cecil L'ively, who worked for two of the previous victims has recently arrived in the U.S. She then receives a composite drawing of the bar arsonist, and it's the caretaker.

Mulder discovers the slain driver at the Cape Cod home, and the house begins to erupt in flame. Mulder rescues the children while Scully confronts the killer, who explodes in flame and collapses, laughing insanely, after Phoebe douses him with a fire accelerator.

Via narration, Scully says L'ively has sustained fifth- and sixth-degree burns over his entire body but is rapidly healing and should fully recover within a month, leaving authorities uncertain how to incarcerate him. When a nurse asks if the charred suspect needs anything, he slurs, "I'm just dying for a cigarette."

Back story: Carter had been warned about the expense and problems that can arise working with fire, though the only real glitch involved a scene where Duchovny in fact suffered a burn severe enough to leave a scar on his hand.

The character of Phoebe Green—played by Amanda Pays, whose credits include *The Flash* and *Max Headroom*—was considered as a possible recurring role, owing to Carter's admiration for the actress and his love of Sherlock Homes. Carter was intrigued by the idea of incorporating a Scotland Yard detective into the show. The chemistry "didn't work as it might," he says, though Phoebe did achieve the desired effect by becoming a character, as Carter puts it, "who fans on the Internet loved to hate."

The original script included a closing exchange where Scully observes, "Well, never let it be said that you wouldn't walk through fire for a woman, Mulder," to which he replies, "And never let it be said that I wouldn't do it for you again, Scully."

The famous "black silk boxer shorts" scene was originally a "Jockey underwear" scene. . . .

The British lord, Malcolm Marsden, was named after the show's chief hair-dresser.

Beyond the Sea

First aired: January 7, 1994

Written by
Glen Morgan and James Wong

Directed by
David Nutter

Guest stars:
Brad Dourif (Luther Lee Boggs)
Don Davis (Captain William Scully)
Sheila Larken (Margaret Scully)
Fred Henderson (Agent Thomas)
Lisa Vultaggio (Liz Hawley)
Chad Willett (Jim Summers)
Lawrence King (Lucas Jackson Henry)
Don MacKay (Warden Joseph Cash)
Katherynn Chisholm (Nurse)
Randy Lee (Paramedic)
Len Rose (ER Doctor)

Log line: Scully and Mulder seek the aid of a death-row inmate, Luther Lee Boggs, who claims to have psychic abilities, to help them stop a killer who's on the loose.

Principal setting: Raleigh, North Carolina

Synopsis: Scully wakes to see her father sitting in her living room. In a flash, the image is gone, and her mother calls to say her father has died of a massive coronary.

Meanwhile, two college students are kidnapped, and death-row killer Luther Lee Boggs—condemned to the electric chair in part by Mulder's profile—says he has psychic abilities that he'll use to help find them in exchange for a stay of execution. Mulder is doubtful, believing that Boggs has orchestrated the kidnapping to save his own life. "Don't get me wrong, Luther, I want to believe," Mulder says scornfully.

Scully, however, is ready to open up to what Mulder would call "extreme possibilities" when Boggs hums "Beyond the Sea" —the song played at her father's funeral—and calls her Starbuck, her dad's pet name for her. Acting on information from Boggs, Scully finds evidence of the victims in the spot he described. "How come you don't believe me?" he asks Mulder, after they try to trick him with a fake newspaper saying the students have been found. "Agent Scully does."

Boggs also warns Mulder of a white

cross, and when the FBI raids the hostage site, Mulder is shot, his blood splattering on a white cross. The girl is rescued, but the boy and suspect—Lucas Henry, a known accomplice of Boggs—remain missing.

Scully confronts Boggs, who relates one of her childhood memories. He'll let her speak to her father and save the boy, he says, to be spared execution, but "Nobody talks," he says, "till I get a deal."

Scully says she'll make the trade, and even though he knows it's a lie, Boggs tells her where the boy is. The youth is saved and Henry killed, while Scully survives in part due to Boggs's words of warning.

Boggs tells Scully he'll deliver her father's message to her prior to his execution. Instead, she goes to Mulder's bedside. Mulder awakens, asking Scully why she didn't go to see Boggs, why she won't open herself up to the possibility of believing. "I'm afraid to believe," she confides. When Mulder replies by saying that in not going, she didn't get to hear what the message was, she says, "But I do know: He was my father."

Back story: Sheila Larken, who has played Scully's mother, Margaret, in several episodes, is married to *The X-Files* co–executive producer R.W. Goodwin. Don Davis, who portrays Scully's father, is one of five *Twin Peaks* alumni who have appeared on the show, along with David Duchovny, Jan D'Arcy ("Tooms"), Michael Horse ("Shapes"), and Michael Anderson (the midget featured in "Humbug"). Duchovny referred to Horse and Anderson as "big Michael and little Michael."

The two names for the serial killers, "Luther Lee Boggs" and "Lucas Henry," bring to mind that of actual serial killer Henry Lee Lucas. "Beyond the Sea" remains a personal favorite of both executive producer Chris Carter and Gillian Anderson, in the latter case due to the depth of emotion the script afforded her character.

In the scene where Captain Scully appears in Dana Scully's apartment, silently mouthing words, actor Don Davis was actually reciting the Lord's Prayer.

Genderbender

First aired: January 21, 1994

Written by
Larry Barber and Paul Barber

Directed by
Rob Bowman

Guest stars:
Brent Hinkley (Brother Andrew)
David Thomson (Brother Oakley)
Kate Twa (female Marty)
Peter Stebbings (male Marty)
Mitchell Kosterman (Det. Horton)
Michele Goodger (Sister Abigail)
Aundrea MacDonald (Pretty Woman)
John R. Taylor (Husband)
Grai Carrington (Tall Man)
Tony Morelli (Cop)
Lesley Ewen (Agent #1)
Nicholas Lea (Michael)
Paul Batten (Brother Wilton)
Doug Abrahams (Agent #2)

Log line: Scully and Mulder seek answers to a bizarre series of murders committed by one person who kills as both a male and a female.

Principal settings: Germantown, Maryland; Steveston, Massachusetts

Synopsis: A man dies convulsively after being seduced by a woman in a bar. Though a woman clearly entered the room, a man is seen exiting.

Mulder says the death is the fifth of its kind, involving three women and two men who suffered massive coronaries in the throes of passion. Each exhibited huge amounts of pheromones, the essence of animal attraction, containing human DNA—prompting Mulder to describe the killer as "a walking aphrodisiac" and "the ultimate sex machine."

Clues lead the agents to the Kindred, a mysterious and reclusive sect. When one of them, Andrew, touches Scully's hand, she appears shaken. Mulder and Scully meet with the group but are given few answers, and after sneaking back to their compound they see one of the members placed in a strange catacomb and revived in a bizarre ritual.

Andrew tells Scully of Brother Martin, one of the Kindred who "left to become one of you." He begins to seduce her but Mulder intervenes, at a loss as to what caused Scully to behave so oddly—about to "do the wild thing," as he puts it, with a total stranger.

The killer, meanwhile, picks up

another potential victim, but is interrupted by a cop. Suddenly, "she" is a man, punching out the officer and escaping. "The club scene used to be so simple," the perplexed victim says in the hospital.

Mulder and Scully track the killer to a motel, finding another body. After a struggle, he/she is caught, but the Kindred spirit him away. Humans, Andrew says, "enjoy pleasures we can't." A search of their farmhouse later finds the premises vacated, and a large crop circle in the hayfield. "They're gone," Mulder says—and by no earthly means of transportation.

Back story: Written by the fraternal tandem of Larry Barber and Paul Barber, this episode went through various conceptual changes during the writing process as well as at least one more specific alteration because of concerns regarding the content. The teaser sequence initially had a moment where someone's crotch starts to rot away, but the sequence was quickly toned down, with co–executive producer R.W. Goodwin saying, "If I was watching that with my kid, I'd turn it off."

Nicholas Lea, who later played the recurring role of Alex Krycek, first turns up here as the killer's would-be victim, while Kate Twa (the female half of the killer's persona) later returned in a more expansive role as a detective in "Soft Light."

Director Rob Bowman also marked his debut on the series with this hour, after working on *Star Trek: The Next Generation*. Bowman, who has become one of the show's most prolific directors, found filming in the Kindred tunnels, which had to be constructed, particularly cramped. Because of the tight logistics and close quarters an extra day of filming was required.

Asked if there was any concern about parallels between the Kindred and the Amish—the group featured in the movie *Witness,* who also shun all modern conveniences and dress in similar fashion—Carter adds wryly, "They don't watch TV, so I wasn't worried about it."

Lazarus

First aired: February 4, 1994

Written by
Alex Gansa and Howard Gordon

Directed by
David Nutter

Guest stars:
Christopher Allport (Agent Jack Willis)
Jason Schombing (Warren James Dupre)
Cec Verrell (Lula Philips)
Callum Keith Rennie (Tommy)
Peter Kelamis (O'Dell)
Jay Brazeau (Prof. Varnes)
Jackson Davies (Agent Bruskin)
Lisa Bunting (Dr. No. 1)
Russell Hamilton (Officer Daniels)
Brenda Crichlow (Reporter)
Alexander Boynton (Clean Cut Man)
Mark Saunders (Dr. #2)

Log line: When an FBI agent and a bank robber are both shot during a bank heist, the robber is killed but the agent begins to take on the criminal's persona.

Principal settings: Maryland; Washington, D.C.

Synopsis: In a stakeout, Scully shoots a bank robber while a fellow agent—Jack Willis, her former instructor and boyfriend—is seriously wounded. In the emergency room they seek to revive the agent, but the body of the robber, Warren Dupre, also writhes. Willis, after flatlining for a long time, rouses while Dupre dies.

Willis awakens, but Dupre's consciousness is within his body. He goes to the morgue, severing Dupre's fingers to take his wedding ring and disappearing, even as a tattoo that was on Dupre's forearm appears on his own.

The agent had spent a year pursuing Dupre, who, along with his accomplice/wife, Lula, killed seven people in a string of robberies. In light of Willis's strange behavior, Mulder points out that the two men died and "one came back. But which one?"

Believing he was betrayed by Lula's brother, Willis/Dupre kills him, then shows up at the crime scene. Testing his theory, Mulder gets Willis to sign a birthday card for Scully, even though they had the same birthday and it's months away.

Willis says he's found Lula, and

Scully goes with him. They catch the woman, but Willis captures Scully, telling Lula details that prove he's actually Dupre. When Scully tries to jog Willis's memory, Dupre tells her, "You killed me and let me die."

Willis falls faint because he's a diabetic and needs insulin. Lula, however, won't let him take any, admitting that she betrayed him, wanting the money for herself. She calls the FBI, asking $1 million ransom for Scully.

Isolating background noise, the agents hone in on Scully's location. Feigning his death, Willis wrests a gun from Lula and kills her, then dies—as Dupre's tattoo disappears. Scully finds that Willis's watch had stopped at the exact time he went into cardiac arrest, but isn't sure what to make of that. "It means," Mulder says compassionately, "whatever you want it to mean."

Back story: As originally written, "Lazarus" called for Dupre to jump into Mulder's body instead of Scully's old boyfriend's body, but Fox and the studio argued against that idea. The producers agreed to make the shift with more than a little reluctance, though writer Howard Gordon says in retrospect it was almost certainly for the best. "We'd wanted Mulder to experience the soul switch," he says, but there was a train of thought at that point that neither of the principals should directly experience such phenomena.

Gordon points out that introducing Scully's boyfriend provided a welcome opportunity to delve into her history. Also, the hour deftly left room for the possibility of mundane explanations as well as paranormal ones; this was the original series concept, from which it has at times strayed away. From that perspective, "Everyone's point of view was actually very well-reasoned and very well-defended," Gordon says, including the exchange between Mulder and Scully at the end when he says she can take the timing of Willis's death to mean whatever she wants.

Scully gets abducted in this episode for the first of what turned out to be several times as the series progressed.

We discover that Scully's birthday is February 23.

Chinese astrology: In the script, Dupre said he was born in the Year of the Dragon, which in the Chinese calendar would have been 1964, the same year as Scully. Instead, he says he was born in the Year of the Rat, 1960, the same year as Mulder (and Duchovny).

Young at Heart

First aired: February 11, 1994

Written by
Scott Kaufer and Chris Carter

Directed by
Michael Lange

Guest stars:
Dick Anthony Williams (Reggie Purdue)
Alan Boyce (Young John Barnett)
David Petersen (Old John Barnett)
Graham Jarvis (NIH Doctor)
William B. Davis (Cigarette-Smoking Man)
Merrilyn Gann (Prosecutor)
Jerry Hardin (Deep Throat)
Robin Mossley (Dr. Joe Ridley)
Gordon Tipple (Joe Crandall)
Courtney Arciaga (Progeria Victim)
Robin Douglas (Computer Specialist)
Christine Estabrook (Agent Henderson)

Log line: Mulder finds that a criminal he put away who was supposed to have died in prison has returned, taunting him as he commits a new spree of crimes.

Principal setting: Washington, D.C.

Synopsis: Mulder is called by his former partner, Agent Reggie Purdue, to a jewelry store robbery scene. A note has been left saying, "Fox can't guard the chicken coop"—the calling card of John Barnett, whom Mulder helped convict years earlier.

Records show Barnett died in prison four years before, but analysis shows a 95 percent probability that the handwriting is a match. Barnett had vowed vengeance against Mulder at his trial, and Mulder finds a note on his car that reads "A hunted Fox eventually dies." When Barnett calls, Mulder is sure it's him and contacts Purdue, who's strangled while he's on the phone. A note saying "Funeral first for Fox's friends—then for Fox" is left at the scene of the crime.

Further investigation shows that Dr. Ridley, who had pronounced Barnett dead, had his licensed revoked for research malpractice. Ridley was experimenting with reversing the aging process, meaning that Barnett may have looked younger than he was. Ridley shows up at Scully's door, saying Barnett is his last surviving patient, whom he experimented on by sawing off his hand and growing him a new one using salamander cells. Dying from his own experiment, Ridley also tells Scully the government financed his work.

Meeting with Deep Throat, Mulder learns that the government is bargaining with Barnett to obtain Ridley's stolen research. Barnett calls to tell Mulder he'll kill his friends one by one.

Scully has found Barnett's prints on her answering machine, and from the messages he knows Scully is heading to a cello recital. Agents stake him out there, and after Barnett shoots Scully (who survives thanks to a bulletproof vest) Mulder chases him into the hall, where he takes a hostage. Mulder—who had hesitated to shoot Barnett when he first arrested him, resulting in the death of a fellow agent—fires, killing him. Government officials labor vainly to save him, hoping to find the missing research.

Mulder muses at the irony of a life-saving cure being hidden just within reach, as the camera pans in on a non-descript-looking airport locker. He also mutters that he fears the agents "haven't heard the last of John Barnett."

Back story: Carter had another fight with Fox's standards and practices department over the scene where Agent Purdue is strangled by Barnett's salamander hand. The producer admits to losing that particular skirmish, with Fox—citing concerns about the violence issue—feeling uncomfortable about letting the murder scene drag on, so Carter shortened the sequence considerably.

John Barnett was Mulder's very first case with the Violent Crimes Unit.

This is the first episode where Mulder kills anyone.

E.B.E

First aired: February 18, 1994

Written by
Glen Morgan and James Wong

Directed by
William Graham

Guest stars:
Jerry Hardin (Deep Throat)
Allan Lysell (Chief Rivers)
Peter LaCroix (Ranheim/Druse)
Bruce Harwood (Byers)
Dean Haglund (Langly)
Tom Braidwood (Frohike)

Log line: Scully and Mulder discover evidence of a government cover-up when they learn that a UFO shot down in Iraq has been secretly transported to the U.S.

Principal settings: Reagan, Tennessee; Washington state

Synopsis: An Iraqi pilot shoots down a UFO, which crashes near a U.S. installation along the Iraq/Turkey border.

In Reagan, Tennessee, a truck driver loses power, saying he saw a saucer and lights. When Mulder tries to question the man the sheriff releases him, saying he won't cooperate. Mulder is convinced the truck was transporting an E.B.E. (extraterrestrial biological entity) across the country.

Seeking help, Mulder introduces Scully to a trio known as the Lone Gunmen—an extreme government watchdog group (one of them, Langly, brags that he had breakfast with "the guy who shot John F. Kennedy"). Scully thinks they're paranoid, until she discovers surveillance equipment in her pen.

Deep Throat gives Mulder a packet directing him to an installation in Georgia and tells him he's "on a dangerous path." Scully fears Mulder is being misled, and though he says he trusts Deep Throat, the tip turns out to be bogus. "Mulder, you're the only one I trust," Scully says, warning him that his passion is blinding him and others may use it against him.

Confronted, Deep Throat admits

he sought to divert Mulder, saying there "still exist some secrets that should remain secret."

Tracking the truck, Mulder and Scully journey to Washington state, where they are stopped suddenly by a blinding light, and find the truck abandoned. "I think we were just witness to a rescue mission," Mulder says, before realizing that it was really just another hoax designed to steer them off. Seeing the truck driver, they locate and enter a government facility with phony credentials courtesy of the Lone Gunmen, and Mulder bolts down the stairs when they're stopped by security.

There he encounters Deep Throat, who tells him of an ultra-secret pact between nations after the 1947 Roswell incident that any surviving E.B.E. would be exterminated. Deep Throat says he's one of three men to have carried out that act when he was with the CIA in Vietnam—an incident that haunted him and inspired him to use Mulder as his means to atone. "Through you," he says, "the truth will be known."

Mulder looks but there's no alien in the chamber. "I'm wondering which lie to believe," Mulder says to Deep Throat, who disappears into the night fog.

Back story: Though it features a memorable sequence where Deep Throat discusses his motivation in helping Mulder—having killed an alien while working for the CIA—this episode's most lasting and durable legacy has clearly been the Lone Gunmen, the paranoid conspiracy theorists who periodically aid Mulder. The idea first arose when producer Glen Morgan and writer Marilyn Osborn ("Shapes") went to a UFO convention in Los

Dinosaur politics:

Byers: Vladimir Zhirinovsky, the leader of the Russian Social Democrats, is being put into power by the most heinous and evil force in the twentieth century.

Mulder. Barney?

Angeles in June 1993, shortly before Morgan and James Wong began to write any material for the series.

Morgan recalls a trio of guys—dressed similar to Langly, Byers, and Frohike—sitting at a table pushing what he describes as "a mixed bag of paranoia." According to Morgan, "They started telling people about the magnetic strips in twenty-dollar bills, and in no time there were a half-dozen people tearing up ten- and twenty-dollar bills."

The Lone Gunmen were initially thrown in just for a laugh in this episode, and Morgan wasn't happy with the result, feeling he and his partner had botched things a bit in terms of execution. "We had kind of written them off," he notes, until the producers started to hear about the response to the Gunmen along the Internet. That prompted a return appearance during the second season and eventually a recurring role on the series.

Miracle Man

First aired: March 18, 1994

Written by
Howard Gordon and Chris Carter

Directed by
Michael Lange

Guest stars:
R. D. Call (Sheriff Daniels)
Scott Bairstow (Samuel)
George Gerdes (The Rev. Cal Hartley)
Dennis Lipscomb (Leonard Vance)
Campbell Lane (Margaret's Father)
Chilton Crane (Margaret Hohman)
Howard Storey (Fire Chief)
Lisa Ann Beley (Beatrice Salinger)
Alex Doduk (Young Samuel)
Walter Marsh (Judge)
Iris Quinn Bernard (Lillian Daniels)
Roger Haskett (Deputy Tyson)

Log line: The agents investigate a young faith healer who seems to use his powers for both good and evil.

Principal setting: Kenwood, Tennessee

Synopsis: The story begins 10 years ago, with a boy bringing a horribly burned man back to life. A decade later, Mulder and Scully are called in to investigate the Miracle Ministry— an evangelical ministry where the boy, Samuel, has the power to heal but has also recently laid hands upon two people who died shortly thereafter.

Samuel is missing but turns up in a local bar. "My gift has been corrupted," he says, shaking up Mulder by telling him about his missing sister, whom Mulder sees visions of throughout the episode. The boy is arrested, and at his bail hearing the courtroom is filled with locusts. Freed, Samuel touches a woman in a wheelchair who goes into a seizure and dies. Scully expresses her own doubts, reminding Mulder that she was raised Catholic, "And God never lets the Devil steal the show."

An autopsy shows the woman was poisoned with cyanide, and Mulder and Scully discover the locusts were introduced into the courtroom through an air vent. The local sheriff, meanwhile, puts two men in Samuel's cell who beat him to death.

Tracing the locusts, the agents discover that Leonard Vance, the man we first saw the boy save, has been seeking to incriminate him, eventually

Q: What was
on the
Reverend
Hartley's
vanity
license
plate?

A: "BHEALD."

In an inter-
view David
Duchovny once
said that he
would consider
Mulder Jewish
until told
otherwise.

taking his own life after seeing a vision of Samuel. Later Samuel's body is missing, with a nurse saying she saw him walk out. "I think people are looking hard for miracles, so hard that they make themselves see what they want to see," Mulder says, catching sight of an image of his sister for the last time.

Back story: "Miracle Man" marked the first script written by then supervising producer Howard Gordon without his longtime partner, Alex Gansa, with whom he'd worked on *Beauty and the Beast* as well as *Spenser: For Hire*. While television is sometimes criticized for the manner in which it treats religion, the episode is extremely respectful toward religious faith, underscored by Scully's comments regarding her Catholic upbringing.

Mulder does get in one gag at the revival meeting, however, when Scully suggests they venture backstage. "Hang on," he says. "This is the part where they bring out Elvis."

Shapes

First aired: April 1, 1994

Written by
Marilyn Osborn

Directed by
David Nutter

Guest stars:
Ty Miller (Lyle Parker)
Michael Horse (Charley Tskany)
Donnelly Rhodes (Jim Parker)
Dwight McFcc (David Gates)
Paul McLean (Dr. Josephs)
Renae Morriseau (Gwen Goodensnake)
Jimmy Herman (Ish)

Log line: Mulder and Scully travel to an Indian reservation to examine deaths caused by a beastlike creature.

Principal setting: Browning, Montana

Synopsis: A father and son shoot a fierce-looking beast that, on closer inspection, turns out to be a Native American man. During the frenzied encounter the son, Lyle Parker, is wounded by the creature before it's killed.

Mulder and Scully are told that the ranchers' cattle have been slaughtered, and that the Parkers have been involved in a boundary dispute with the local reservation. A look at the dead man's corpse, meanwhile, reveals wolflike fangs.

Mulder explains that this same region was involved in "the first X-File, initiated by J. Edgar Hoover himself," stemming from a series of murders in 1946 by a vicious animal. Although a suspect was killed, the murders resumed in 1954, '59, '64, '78 and now '94, and Mulder says even the Lewis and Clark expedition "wrote of Indian men who could change into a wolf."

The older Parker is subsequently ripped to pieces on his porch, with Lyle found nude and unconscious nearby. Scully takes him to the hospital, while Mulder visits with a tribal elder who tells him what happened in '46 and the legend of the Manitou—an evil spirit capable of changing a man into a beast.

Mulder calls the hospital, learning that Scully has taken Lyle Parker back to his ranch and that traces of his father's blood were found in his stomach—traces that could have only gotten there via ingestion. As night falls, Mulder and the sheriff hurry to the ranch, arriving just in time to shoot a creature that, in fact, is Lyle Parker.

The tribal elder provides the cryptic coda. "FBI," he says. "See you in about . . . eight years."

Back story: Fox had suggested doing a more conventional monster show, and Glen Morgan and James Wong—who had been wanting to come up with something exploring Native American mythology—proposed the Manitou, a slightly different approach to werewolves designed to serve fans of that genre while still feeling distinctive in *The X-Files* fashion. "A horror show should be able to do these legends that have been around since the thirteen hundreds," Morgan says.

When the old man points out that Mulder's name "should be Running Fox or Sleepy Fox," the agent responds, "Just as long as it's not 'Spooky Fox'"—a reference to the disparaging nickname Mulder earned at the FBI Academy (mentioned in the pilot) stemming from his belief in the paranormal.

One potentially humorous scene that failed to make the cut has a cow blocking the agents' car, with Scully waving her arms and yelling, "Baseball glove! Leather purse!" trying to shoo the beast out of the road.

Michael Horse (Charley Tskany) played Deputy Hawk in *Twin Peaks* when David Duchovny played transvestite Dennis/Denise Bryson. His opinion of David in a dress: "It's a good color on him."

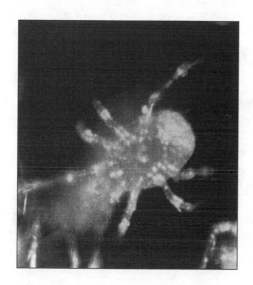

Darkness Falls

First aired: April 15, 1994

Written by
Chris Carter

Directed by
Joe Napolitano

Guest stars:
Jason Beghe (Larry Moore)
Tom O'Rourke (Steve Humphreys)
Titus Welliver (Doug Spinney)
Barry Greene (Perkins)
David Hay (Clean-Suited Man)
Ken Tremblett (Dyer)

Log line: Mulder and Scully are called in when loggers in a remote Pacific Northwest forest mysteriously disappear.

Principal setting: Olympia National Forest, Washington State

Synopsis: Frightened loggers rush to escape the woods, with two shown screaming as green glowing objects descend on them.

All 30 loggers have vanished, and Mulder says a similar incident happened in the same area 60 years ago. The forest ranger and the security chief for the logging company, Steve Humphreys, think eco-terrorists are behind what's transpired. When their car tires are flattened by spikes the quartet has to hike up to the camp, where they find a man drained of fluid inside a huge white cocoon.

One of the eco-terrorists, Doug Spinney, shows up, saying there's a force that comes out at night and devours people alive. "Darkness is our enemy," he warns them. The loggers have been cutting down old-growth trees, in the process freeing green mites that had been lying dormant. Mulder concludes they're ancient insect eggs, affected by radiation from local volcanic activity. "Maybe they woke up hungry," Spinney observes.

Humphreys leaves, only to be trapped in his car by the mites and cocooned. Meanwhile, Mulder grudgingly allows Spinney to go for help, with the promise that he'll return in the morning. Unsure whether they have enough power to keep the mites away, the ranger, Mulder, and Scully endure a scary night, with their generator failing just as the sun rises.

Spinney finally returns for them, but the car is again stopped by the terrorists' spikes. Spinney flees into the night as the bugs swarm through the air vents into the car, and hours later, Mulder, Scully, and the ranger are found cocooned. A quarantine unit treats them, saying they'll use con-trolled burns and pesticides as "eradication procedures." When Mulder asks what will happen if that doesn't work, the medical worker replies, "That is not an option, Mr. Mulder."

Though Carter says "Darkness Falls" was not specifically designed to push a message about conservation, the episode was honored nevertheless at the Environmental Media Awards.

Back story: Shooting in the forest near Vancouver, production was delayed frequently and made more difficult by heavy rains. "It was miserable," Carter recalls, noting that the actors were soaking wet much of the time and that various inserts and pick-up shots had to be added at a later time to compensate for the inclement weather.

One saving grace was the casting of Jason Beghe, who plays Ranger Larry Moore. A childhood friend of David Duchovny's, Beghe had prodded him to pursue acting and worked with him for a time as a bartender. Having him on hand (at Duchovny's suggestion) helped lighten the mood around the set, making the shoot something of a reunion and thus less of an ordeal for the cast.

Carter based the episode on his interest in den-drochronology—the reading of rings on trees—dating back to a course he'd taken in college. The green mite effects were computer-generated and added in postpro-duction, synchronized to the movements of the actors.

Tooms (a.k.a. Squeeze 2)

First aired: April 22, 1994

Written by
Glen Morgan and James Wong

Directed by
David Nutter

Guest stars:
Doug Hutchison (Eugene Victor Tooms)
Paul Ben Victor (Dr. Aaron Monte)
Mitch Pileggi (AD Walter Skinner)
William B. Davis (Cigarette-Smoking Man)
Timothy Webber (Det. Talbot)
Frank C. Turner (Dr. Collins)
Gillian Carfra (Christine Ranford)
Pat Bermel (Frank Ranford)
Jan D'Arcy (Judge Kann)
Jerry Wasserman (Dr. Plith)
Mikal Dughi (Dr. Karetzky)
Glynis Davies (Nelson)
Steve Adams (Myers)
Andre Daniels (Arlan Green)
Catherine Lough (Dr. Richmond)
Henry Beckman (Det. Frank Briggs)

Log line: Mulder becomes personally involved when Eugene Tooms, the serial killer who extracts and eats human livers, is released from prison.

Principal setting: Baltimore, Maryland

Synopsis: Tooms—the genetic mutant who kills five people every 30 years to extract their livers—is being held in a sanitarium and has come up for parole, contingent on the results of a psychiatric hearing.

His sympathetic psychiatrist stresses before the board that Tooms has been rehabilitated and is not a danger to society. Mulder also testifies but, despite Scully's signals to tone down his presentation, alarms the court by contending that Tooms is a genetic mutant, more than 100 years old, who must feed on human livers. Thinking that Mulder may be the one who belongs in a mental hospital, the panel decides to discharge Tooms despite Mulder's warning that Tooms must remain in custody for the safety of the public. "If you release Eugene Tooms, he will kill again," Mulder futilely insists. "It's in his genetic makeup."

While Mulder watches Tooms, Scully is warned by Assistant Director Skinner (with the Cigarette-Smoking Man silently at his elbow) to act "by the book." Pursuing the case, Scully returns to Frank Briggs, the detective who originally investigated Tooms, and after a search they find the remains of a missing victim—one hidden by Tooms 60 years earlier.

Tracking Tooms, Mulder dozes off but awakens just in time to thwart a murder attempt, with Tooms fleeing after wriggling through a barred window. Though he continues the surveillance, Mulder tells Scully she shouldn't be involved, fearing that the Bureau is out to shut down the X-Files and that her career may be scuttled along with his.

At Scully's urging, Mulder goes home to rest. She even calls him Fox, to which he replies, "I even made my parents call me Mulder." He leaves reluctantly—with Tooms hiding in his trunk. Entering Mulder's apartment through a vent, Tooms takes one of Mulder's shoes while he's sleeping (with the original *The Fly* playing on TV) and mars his own face, accusing Mulder of beating him. Skinner advises Mulder to take a break, and forbids him to go near Tooms.

Examination of the skeleton from 1933 shows Tooms's teeth marks on the victim. Meanwhile, the psychiatrist who fought for Tooms's release stops by to visit him and becomes his fifth victim.

Finding the body, Mulder and Scully realize Tooms will return home to begin his hibernation. The abandoned apartment building he once occupied is now a shopping mall, and Mulder descends under the escalator, confronting Tooms in his nest. Breaking free, and with Tooms in pursuit, Mulder activates the escalator, grinding Tooms to death beneath it.

Skinner reads the report, asking the Cigarette-Smoking Man if he believes it. "Of course I do," he says. Outside, Mulder looks at a caterpillar cocoon. "Change is coming," he notes wearily . . . for the X-Files.

Back story: Producers Glen Morgan and James Wong often would construct episodes around a certain moment or visual concept, as the duo did with the original "Squeeze." In this case, Morgan says he was Christmas shopping at a Los Angeles mall and saw men working on the escalator, which was open and exposed. That prompted him to consider the scare factor of an urban myth stemming from some sort of monster living underneath an escalator. And who, he thought, better to be doing that than Eugene Tooms? "Everything worked backward from there," he says.

"Tooms" remain the only encore appearance thus far by a villain, but the episode is equally noteworthy in that it features the first appearance by Mitch Pileggi as Assistant Director Skinner (who isn't seen again until the second season) and the first line of dialogue from the Cigarette-Smoking Man. The producers joke now that they didn't even know until then if William B. Davis could speak, only to be delighted by what he's brought to the role.

Guest star Hutchison was the one who suggested that he play the final scene under the escalator nude. "They covered me with Karo syrup and food coloring," he recalls, "and it was cold! I kept sticking to the walls." Despite his gruesome demise, Hutchison has used frequent appearances at *The X-Files* conventions to relentlessly lobby for a return engagement.

In this episode, the Cigarette-Smoking Man speaks for the first time.

Skinner: Do you believe him?

The Cigarette-Smoking Man: Of course I do.

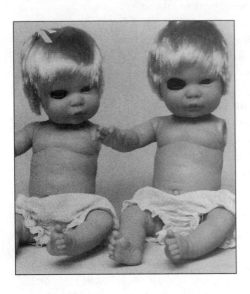

Born Again

First aired: April 29, 1994

Written by
Alex Gansa and Howard Gordon

Directed by
Jerrold Freedman

Guest stars:
Brian Markinson (Tony Fiore)
Mimi Lieber (Anita Fiore)
Maggie Wheeler (Det. Sharon Lazard)
Andre Libman (Michelle Bishop)
Dey Young (Judy Bishop)
Leslie Carlson (Dr. Spitz)
P. Lynn Johnson (Dr. Sheila Braun)
Peter Lapres (Harry Linhart)
Richard Sali (Felder)
Dwight Koss (Det. Barbala)

Log line: A series of murders is linked to a little girl who may be the reincarnated spirit of a murdered policeman.

Principal setting: Buffalo, New York

Synopsis: A lost little girl is brought into a police station and put into an interrogation room with a detective named Barbala. Moments later, he plummets to his death.

Another detective calls in Mulder. When they speak to the child's mother, she says they've gone through four nannies and that "sometimes she frightens me. . . . She sees things I can't see."

The little girl, Michelle, says she saw a man in the room, and her description fits that of another detective, Charlie Morris, who died nine years earlier. "Which means that little girl saw a ghost," Mulder suggests.

Evidence mounts that Michelle, who is eight, may have been reincarnated from Charlie Morris, who died around the time she was conceived. The girl possesses psychokinetic powers and mutilates her dolls in the manner in which Morris was killed. She also appears at the scene of an accident that results in the death of another former cop, Barbala's partner, who is killed when his scarf gets caught in a bus that drags him to his death. Reincarnation, Mulder notes, is a tenet of many major religions, adding that they're "one short step away from proving the pre-existence of the human soul."

Barbala, his partner, and Morris's partner, Fiore, were all involved in his murder. Using her powers, the girl captures Fiore and is about to kill him—destroying the house with her mind—when Mulder and Scully burst in, talking Michelle/Morris out of it. In a flash of light, it's over, as Fiore admits his complicity in Morris's death, while the girl has no memory of what's transpired. The two deaths are ruled to be accidental, and Michelle's mother refuses to allow her to be studied further. The case, despite Mulder's objections, is closed.

Back story: Dealing with reincarnation, "Born Again" is another episode that fell short of the producers' self-imposed expectations, the feeling being that the premise was perhaps too similar to the soul transfer or possession themes dealt with in some of the shows that aired around the same time. "The impetus was desperation, I believe," producer Howard Gordon quips, adding that in the final analysis the hour proved "a little too cop show-y" for his taste.

This is the first time Mulder tells the story. Instead of Scully typing computer reports we see him writing longhand in a field journal; instead of Scully's voice-over wrap-up we hear Mulder's summation.

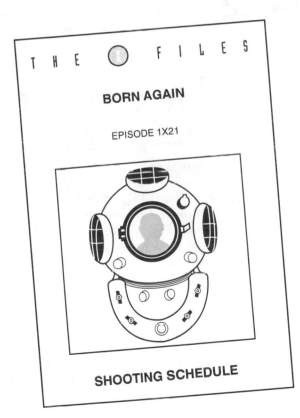

THE ◯ FILES

BORN AGAIN

EPISODE 1X21

SHOOTING SCHEDULE

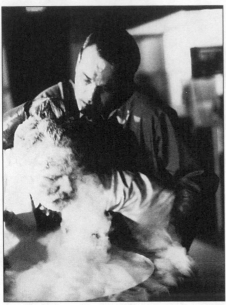

Roland

First aired: May 6, 1994

Written by
Chris Ruppenthal

Directed by
David Nutter

Guest stars:
Zeljko Ivanek (Roland Fuller)
Garry Davey (Dr. Keats)
James Sloyan (Dr. Nollette)
Matthew Walker (Dr. Surnow)
Dave Hurtubise (Barrington)
Sue Mathew (Lisa Dole)
Micole Mercurio (Mrs. Stodie)
Kerry Sandomirsky (Tracy)

Log line: Mulder and Scully investigate the murders of two rocket scientists apparently linked to a retarded janitor.

Principal setting: Colson, Washington

Synopsis: A research scientist gets sucked into an experimental jet engine, with only the retarded janitor, Roland, on hand, manipulating the keyboard to cause his death.

The scientist is the second (after Arthur Grable) of four researchers involved in the project to die. Mulder notices that there are two distinct handwriting samples on the chalkboard working out the rocket formula.

Meeting with Roland, Mulder grabs a paper on which he's been scribbling numbers. Back at the lab, Roland assaults one of the other scientists, Dr. Keats, forcing him into liquid nitrogen—his head shattering like glass when it hits the floor.

After Keats's death someone had worked on the jet formula under Grable's computer log-on, and the password matches the numbers Roland had written down. In fact, the research has been updated, they discover, during the six months since Grable's death. When they return to see Roland, he says, "I'm not supposed to talk to them." A background check shows that Roland and Grable were born the same day in the same city and are, in fact, twins.

Though he was killed, Grable's head has been preserved and cryogenically frozen, and Mulder theorizes that

Grable and Roland enjoy a psychic bond that may have been

heightened by that process and that Grable "may have reached a higher consciousness allowing him to manipulate" Roland into committing murder. When they try to question Roland, he escapes.

The last surviving doctor, Nollette, goes to the cryogenics lab and begins thawing Grable's head. In the lab, Roland tinkers with the formula—hitting the sought-after Mach 15 even as his concentration wavers as the head warms up. Nollette enters, admitting he stole Grable's work, and Roland knocks him out, locking him in the engine chamber. As it speeds up to dangerous levels the agents arrive, coaxing Roland to key in the code that shuts down the engine just in time.

Roland is to be held for examination, but Mulder has recommended his release. With the girl he loves watching from upstairs, they take him away.

Mulder tells Roland about a dream he (Mulder) had, wherein he dove down into a pool searching for his father. In the script, Mulder was searching for his *sister*.

Back story: The episode contains one truly inspired and twisted visual gag, with the scattered markings on the floor indicating where the scientist's head had shattered after being forced into the liquid nitrogen. "Any shock and horror was eliminated," Chris Carter says, "by the laugh you got when you saw those little pieces on the floor." The actual

moment is also dealt with offscreen by just the sound of the head breaking. Capping it off is Mulder's dry observation, "I don't think they'll be performing this experiment on *Beakman's World.*"

Actor Zeljko Ivanek (pronounced Zel-ko Eve-on-ek) was the first actor to read for the producers as Roland—who was seen as being pivotal in making the episode come across right dramatically—and "just blew us away," says Carter, to the point where they knew immediately he had landed the part. Born in Ljubljana, Yugoslavia, Ivanek's credits include the movies *Mass Appeal* and *Agnes of God.*

The Erlenmeyer Flask

First aired: May 13, 1994

Written by
Chris Carter

Directed by
R.W. Goodwin

Guest stars:
Simon Webb (Dr. Secare)
Jerry Hardin (Deep Throat)
Ken Kramer (Dr. Berube)
Lindsey Ginter (Crew-Cut Man)
Anne DeSalvo (Dr. Carpenter)
William B. Davis (Cigarette-
    Smoking Man)
Jaylene Hamilton (Reporter)
Jim Leard (Captain Lacerio)
Phillip MacKenzie (Medic)
Mike Mitchell (Cop)
John Payne (Guard)

Log line: Working on a tip from Deep Throat, Mulder and Scully discover that the government has been testing alien DNA on humans with disastrous results.

Principal setting: Washington, D.C.

Synopsis: A man flees from police, tossing them around like rag dolls before leaping into the bay, leaving behind a trail of green blood.

Mulder is alerted to the case by Deep Throat, tracing the escapee's car to a Dr. Berube, who abruptly cuts off any conversation. Scully says Deep Throat is toying with him, and Mulder asks him to "cut out the Obi-Wan Kenobi crap" and say what's really happening. Persevere, Deep Throat says. "You've never been closer."

Soon after, a man with a crew cut, seeking the fugitive, kills Dr. Berube. Scully takes samples of the researcher's work to Dr. Carpenter, a scientist at Georgetown, who says Berube had been cloning bacteria—each with a virus—that look like plant cells. Later, she tells Scully the DNA possesses a fifth and sixth nucleotide that exist "nowhere in nature" and are thus, by definition, extraterrestrial.

In the interim, Mulder has inadvertently been contacted by the fugitive and located a storage facility housing five men all floating in fluid-filled tanks. Mulder is chased by armed men as he leaves.

Scully apologizes to Mulder, saying that for the first time, she doesn't know

what to believe. They return to find the warehouse empty, with Deep Throat explaining that the men in the tanks were part of an experiment Berube conducted on terminal patients using alien viruses. They've probably been destroyed, he says, by "black operations" within the intelligence community—"groups within groups conducting covert activity unknown at the highest levels." Deep Throat says the fugitive, Dr. Secare, is one of those experiments and that the agents must find him "before *they* do."

Returning to Georgetown, Scully learns that Dr. Carpenter has died in a car accident along with her family. Working separately Mulder locates Secare, only to have him killed—and to be caught himself—by the Crew-Cut Man.

With Mulder missing, Deep Throat says he can get Scully access to the original alien tissue to trade for Mulder's life. Scully obtains an alien fetus, and Deep Throat insists on making the exchange, only to be shot by Crew-Cut Man as Mulder's limp body is thrown from the van. "Trust no one," Deep Throat tells Scully with his dying breath.

Two weeks later Mulder calls to tell Scully that the X-Files have been shut down and that they're both being reassigned after "word came down from the top of the executive branch." Mulder adds that he can't give up—not as long as "the truth is out there." As in the first episode, the Cigarette-Smoking Man enters a Pentagon storage room, adding the alien fetus to its contents.

X

This episode marks the departure of Jerry Hardin from the series, whose brief appearance as Deep Throat, the undercover source for Mulder, garnered much attention from fans. His dying words, "Trust no one," are substituted in the teaser for the show's usual "The truth is out there."

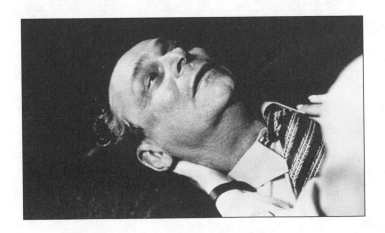

Back story: By taking the shocking step of killing off Deep Throat, Carter wanted to establish that other than perhaps the leads "everyone is expendable" on the series —a way of keeping viewers guessing as to what twists and turns may occur. Disbanding the X-Files unit also separated Mulder from Scully, providing the means to work around Anderson's pregnancy through the start of the second season.

Jerry Hardin, who played Deep Throat, recalls that his death scene was the sort of big dramatic moment "you want to take your time on and get perfect. The truth of the matter is, we were fighting the light like crazy" to get the shot completed in time before the sun came up. "It was about to be dawn," he recalls.

The episode received a nomination for an Edgar Award, an honor presented by the Mystery Writers of America.

The closing sequence of this episode exactly tracks the closing few minutes of the series pilot, right down to the time: 11:21.

T H E ⊗ F I L E S

THE ERLENMEYER FLASK

EPISODE 1X23

SHOOTING SCHEDULE

THE EPISODES

X

season ②

season two locations

Legend

1. Arecibo, Puerto Rico (Little Green Men)
2. Newark, NJ (The Host)
3. Franklin, PA (Blood)
4. New York, NY (Sleepless)
5. Marion, VA (Duane Barry)
6. Skyland Mountain, VA (Ascension)
7. Los Angeles, CA (3)
8. Georgetown, MD (One Breath)
9. Mt. Avalon, WA (Firewalker)
10. Delta Glen, WI (Red Museum)
11. Worcester, MA (Excelsis Dei)
12. Aubrey, MO (Aubrey)
13. Minneapolis, MN (Irresistible)
14. Milford Haven, NH (Die Hand Die Verletzt)
15. Folkstone, NC (Fresh Bones)
16. Germantown, MD (Colony)
17. Deadhorse, AK (End Game)
18. Fairfield, ID (Fearful Symmetry)
19. Tildeskan, Norway (Dod Kalm)
20. Gibsonton, FL (Humbug)
21. Arlington, VA (The Calusari)
22. Cumberland Prison, VA (F. Emasculata)
23. Richmond, VA (Soft Light)
24. Dudley, AR (Our Town)
25. Farmington, NM (Anasazi)

Note: Locations were selected by site of main conflict; many episodes cover more than one location.

Map courtesy of Sarah Stegall

Little Green Men

First aired: September 16, 1994

Written by
Glen Morgan and James Wong

Directed by
David Nutter

Guest stars:
Raymond J. Barry (Senator Richard Matheson)
William B. Davis (Cigarette-Smoking Man)
Mike Gomez (Jorge Concepcion)
Mitch Pileggi (AD Walter Skinner)
Vanessa Morley (Samantha age 8)
Marcus Turner (Fox age 12)
Les Carlson (Dr. Troisky)
Fulvio Cecere (Aide)
Deryl Hayes (Agent Morris)
Dwight McFee (Commander)
Lisa Anne Beley (Student)
Gary Hetherington (Lewin)
Bob Wilde (Rand)

Log line: With the X-Files shut down, Mulder secretly journeys to a possible alien contact site in Puerto Rico while Scully tries to help him escape detection.

Principal setting: Arecibo, Puerto Rico

Synopsis: The episode opens with a voice-over about the *Voyager* probe, which was sent to contact other intelligent life in the universe. Back on Earth, meanwhile, the X-Files unit has been officially closed and agents Mulder and Scully reassigned to other areas. They meet, appropriately enough, in the garage at the Watergate Hotel. "We must assume we're being watched," he says, lamenting that for all his labors he still has no physical evidence of UFOs, as he flashes back to his sister's abduction.

Summoned to meet with Senator Matheson, who has supported his work, Mulder is told to go to a site in Puerto Rico and that he has 24 hours to contact alien visitors there before a Blue Beret UFO Retrieval Team can be dispatched. "What am I looking for?" Mulder asks.

"Contact," the senator replies.

Told Mulder is missing, the Cigarette-Smoking Man assures Skinner, "She'll find him." Trying to help Mulder, Scully gains access to his computer, guessing his password (TRUSTNO1) and heading for San Juan, cleverly eluding the agents who are tailing her.

The passenger manifest that Scully scrutinizes while trying to trace Mulder's movements contains the names of many on-line X-Philes, as well as *X-Files* novel author Charles Grant.

Mulder reaches the site, where he meets a terrified man who speaks only Spanish but draws the visage of an alien on the wall. A piercing noise begins, and the man runs into the jungle, where Mulder finds him frozen to death with fear. Speaking into a tape recorder, Mulder tells Scully that he trusts "only you . . . and you've been taken from me."

A bright light floods the room, the bolted door flies open, and Mulder sees a willowy alien figure through the blinding glare. Scully arrives to find him unconscious, but he says the tapes and printouts will provide evidence of his close encounter. At that moment, however, the retrieval team shows up, forcing Mulder and Scully to quickly flee.

Back in Washington, Assistant Director Skinner chews Mulder out for abandoning his more mundane assignment. The Cigarette-Smoking Man tells Mulder, "Your time is over," but Skinner intervenes, barking at him to get out. Mulder finds the tape he escaped with is blank, meaning he still doesn't have any evidence. "I don't have the X-Files, Scully, but I still have my work," he says with determination. "And I have you, and I have myself."

Back story: In the very first episode Mulder referred to having "connections in Congress," and Senator Matheson represents the audience's first glimpse at one of those contacts. As far as the casting, "we really wanted that to be Darren McGavin," Glen Morgan admits. The producers also tried unsuccessfully to feature *The Night Stalker* star as Mulder's father, which Chris Carter deemed him to be in a symbolic way, based on the inspirational role that earlier series played in creating *The X-Files*.

Because the X-Files had been shut down, the episode "had to be kind of a new pilot," Morgan says, in the sense of altering the ground rules of the series. In addition, the flashback scene where Samantha Mulder gets abducted is different from Mulder's initial reminiscence on that event in the show's third episode, "Conduit." In the first version, Mulder and Samantha are asleep in their beds, not awake playing a board game, at the moment she's taken. According to Chris Carter, because Mulder's memories are derived from regression therapy, those images are understandably vague, explaining why he would recall the incident differently at a later time.

Senator "Richard Matheson" is named for science fiction and horror writer Richard "Somewhere in Time" Matheson. Originally, the senator was supposed to be reciting the opening monologue.

The Host

First aired: September 23, 1994

Written by
Chris Carter

Directed by
Daniel Sackheim

Guest stars:
Darin Morgan (Flukeman)
Marc Bauer (Agent Brisentine)
Mitch Pileggi (AD Walter Skinner)
Matthew Bennet (First Workman)
Freddy Andreiuci (Det. Norman)
Don Mackay (Charlie)
Hrothgar Matthews (Man on Phone)
Gabrielle Rose (Dr. Zenzola)
Ron Sauve (Foreman)
Dmitri Boudrine (Russian Engineer)
Raoul Ganee (Dmitri)
William MacDonald (Federal Marshal)

Log line: Mulder stumbles upon a genetic mutation, the Flukeman, while investigating a murder in the New Jersey sewer system.

Principal setting: Newark, New Jersey

Synopsis: A Soviet seaman is suddenly yanked into the ship's sewage system, and the body turns up later as a John Doe in a New Jersey sewer.

Mulder goes to see Skinner, who assigned him the case, and complains about being punished with meaningless assignments. Frustrated, he tells Scully he's thinking about quitting the FBI. Mulder receives an anonymous call, however, telling him "You have a friend in the FBI" and, later, that his success in this case is "imperative" if the X-Files are to be reopened.

Scully performs an autopsy on the body, finding a large fluke, or flatworm, wriggling alive inside it. Later, a sanitation worker is pulled under the water, emerging with a strange wound on his back and complaining of a bad taste in his mouth. Taking a shower, the man begins to convulse, coughing up a fluke that slides down the drain.

While Mulder investigates a sewage processing plant, a worker sees something large in the water and they flush the system, catching the Flukeman. The creature has no sex organs but primate features, and Mulder muses ironically, "It looks like I'm going to have to tell Skinner that the suspect is a giant blood-sucking worm after all." To his surprise, Skinner says the case should have been an X-File, telling Mulder, "We all take our orders from someone."

With the help of another anonymous tip, Scully identifies the first victim as a Russian. Flukeman is to be transferred to an institution, but he kills the driver and escapes into an outhouse and subsequently a sewage tanker. Mulder chases the truck to a sewage treatment plant, determined to catch the creature before it can make its way back out to sea. When the foreman falls into the water and is pulled down, Mulder leaps in after him. Seeing the Flukeman entering a drain, he drops the gate—cutting the creature in half.

Scully concludes the Flukeman was a quasi-vertebrate human caused by radiation, the Russian freighter having been disposing waste from Chernobyl. It was born, she notes, "in a primordial soup of radioactive sewage."

For his part, Mulder echoes his anonymous caller, saying, "Success in our work is imperative now, Scully. Reinstatement of the X-Files must be undeniable." When Scully asks if that came from Skinner, he says, "No. But we have a friend in the FBI."

Elsewhere, the Flukeman, or what's left of him, floats to the surface, and the eyes open. It's alive.

Back story: Darin Morgan, who played the Flukeman, is the brother of co-executive producer Glen Morgan and subsequently became a writer for the show (his credits include the memorable "Humbug" episode and the early third season episode "Clyde Bruckman's Final Repose"). The Flukeman suit was a true ordeal that at first took six hours to put on before technicians were able to speed up the process, and at one point had to be worn by Morgan for 20 hours consecutively. Because it was so difficult to remove, that meant Morgan simply had to relieve himself in the getup, almost like the scene where the astronaut has to do so in *The Right Stuff*. Carter jokes now that the assignment is a rite of passage for any aspiring writer for *The X-Files*.

Carter also had a major fight with Fox's broadcast standards over the scene where the worker pukes up the fluke —one of the more vivid sequences in the show's run— insisting that to lose that shot would ruin the episode.

"You have a friend in the FBI." The mysterious X makes his first appearance here, although we only see the back of his head as he speaks on the phone.

Gabrielle Rose returns as Dr. Zenzola; she previously appeared in the episode "Deep Throat."

Blood

First aired: September 30, 1994

Written by
Glen Morgan and James Wong

Directed by
David Nutter

Guest stars:
William Sanderson (Ed Funsch)
John Cygan (Sheriff Spencer)
George Touliatos (Larry Winter)
Kimberly Ashlyn Gere (Mrs. McRoberts)
Andre Daniels (Harry McNally)
Tom Braidwood (Frohike)
Dean Haglund (Langly)
Bruce Harwood (Byers)
John Harris (Taber)
Gerry Rousseau (Mechanic)
William MacKenzie (Bus Driver)
Diana Stevan (Mrs. Adams)
David Fredericks (Security Guard)
Kathleen Duborg (Mother)
B. J. Harrison (Clerk)

Log line: Several residents of a small suburban farming community suddenly turn violent and dangerous, prompted by digital readouts in appliances telling them to kill.

Principal setting: Franklin, Pennsylvania

Synopsis: After seeing the words "KILL 'EM ALL" on a digital elevator display, a 42-year-old real estate salesman has killed four people with his bare hands. The local sheriff, Spencer, tells Mulder it's the seventh such killing spree, accounting for 22 deaths, in an area "that only had three murders since colonial times." Mulder is stumped as to the cause but finds a residue on the culprit's finger and notes that an electronic device has been destroyed at each crime scene.

After a local woman, Mrs. McRoberts, kills an auto repairman in response to a similar display ("HE'LL RAPE YOU. HE'LL KILL YOU. KILL HIM FIRST"), Mulder and Spencer go to her house to investigate. When she tries to stab Mulder, Spencer shoots her, and an examination of the body reveals adrenaline levels 200 times normal, adrenal glands showing signs of wear, and an unknown compound. Scully suggests that combining these factors creates a substance and reaction similar to LSD. Mulder later spots a truck scooping flies into the gutter.

Mulder seeks help from the Lone Gunmen, who tell him about LSDM —an experimental insecticide that acts as a natural pheromone, invoking a fear response among insects. Checking the fields that night, Mulder is sprayed by a silent helicopter, and a town official admits they've been using the chemical. Mulder suggests someone, or some thing, is sending subliminal messages through electronic readouts, heightening existing phobias already amplified by the chemicals — subjecting the area to a controlled experiment.

A search leads them to Ed Funsch, a laid-off postal worker who has been plagued by the messages throughout. Funsch climbs a tower at the local college, firing indiscriminately with a rifle. Mulder apprehends him, after Funsch says that "they" won't let him stop.

With the suspect in custody, Mulder takes out his cellular phone. The readout says, "ALL DONE. BYE BYE," as Mulder stares mystified at the phone. Whoever, or whatever, was running the experiment is apparently finished.

Back story: "Blood" again represents one of those episodes where divergent concepts were eventually brought together and assembled into what turned out to be a rather chilling hour. Writers Glen Morgan and James Wong began with a single note, "Postal Workers," that they subsequently combined

The appliances which commanded the victims to "Kill 'em all" were worked from off camera by Ken Hawryliw and his crew. Normal appliances do not have a bright enough or large enough display to be seen by the camera. The microwave Mrs. McRoberts confronts in her scene with Mulder was actually a mockup.

with the hubbub in Southern California over malithion spraying. (Authorities had released the pesticide from helicopters to eradicate fruit flies, alarming some local residents, who weren't entirely convinced by assurances that the substance was harmless to humans while being told that it might damage the paint on their cars.)

Morgan also recalls seeing a

feature on the news magazine *20/20* about studies on DDT in the 1950s, while Chris Carter had been wanting to do something that incorporated digital readouts. "We had always tried to have regular things be scary," Morgan says, particularly objects like fax machines or cellular phones that are relatively new additions to the modern world. Morgan also admits that he doesn't have the slightest clue who or what might have been transmitting the subliminal messages and doesn't really care, leaving such things for viewers to consider.

The final transmission—"ALL DONE. BYE BYE"—has taken on a dual purpose, serving as the final shot in *The X-Files* blooper reel. The climactic scene in the bell tower was shot at the University of British Columbia.

THE ◯ FILES

BLOOD

TELEPLAY BY
GLEN MORGAN & JAMES WONG

EPISODE 2X03

KILL 'EM ALL!

SHOOTING SCHEDULE

Sleepless

First aired: October 7, 1994

Written by
Howard Gordon

Directed by
Rob Bowman

Guest stars:
Nicholas Lea (Agent Alex Krycek)
Tony Todd (Augustus Cole)
Mitch Pileggi (AD Walter Skinner)
Steven Williams (Mr. X)
Jonathan Gries (Sal Matola)
William B. Davis (Cigarette-Smoking Man)
Mitch Kosterman (Det. Horton)
Don Thompson (Henry Willig)
David Adams (Dr. Girardi)
Michael Puttonen (Dr. Pilsson)
Anna Hagan (Dr. Charyn)
Paul Bittante (Team Leader)
Claude de Martino (Dr. Grissom)

Log line: Mulder is assigned a new partner, Alex Krycek, and they investigate a secret Vietnam-era experiment on sleep deprivation that is having deadly effects on surviving participants.

Principal setting: New York, New York

Synopsis: Dr. Saul Grissom sees flames shooting into his apartment and calls 911 for help. He's found dead, but with no sign of fire in the room.

Mulder is left a tape drawing his attention to the case. With Scully assigned elsewhere, he's paired with a young agent, Alex Krycek, who (after Mulder ditches him) tells Mulder he's "followed his work" and believes in it.

Grissom ran a sleep-disorder clinic, and Scully's autopsy shows damage to his internal organs— "as if his body believed it were burning." Later another man is murdered, this time by the image of Vietnamese peasants who gun him down. The latest victim was a Marine special forces officer, stationed at the same spot where Grissom worked 24 years earlier.

The last survivor of that unit is Augustus Cole, but when they go to the V.A. Hospital to find him, he's missing. For the first time, Mulder meets with X, who tells him of a secret project to create the perfect soldier by eradicating the need for sleep. The project created a unit of killing machines, but the army lost control of them as the group began to murder at

Nicholas Lea,
who first
appeared as a
nightclub
Romeo in
"Genderbender,"
returns as
the perfidi-
ous Agent
Alex Krycek.
Internet fans
of *The X-
Files* have
dubbed him
"Ratboy" and
started a
newsletter
devoted to him.

Mitch
Kosterman
reprises his
role of
Detective
Horton from
"Genderbender."

random. Cole, who hasn't slept in 24 years, is seeking vengeance for those actions. "The truth is still out there," X says darkly, "but it's never been more dangerous."

Mulder believes Cole has developed the psychic ability to create dreams so real they can kill. Guessing that Cole will seek revenge on the other doctor involved, they go to meet him in the train station, but Cole escapes with him, "shooting" Mulder using his psychic powers.

Mulder catches up with Cole and asks him to testify about what the army has done, but Krycek, saying he saw a gun in Cole's hand, shoots and kills him. Mulder's evidence of the case disappears, and he confides to Scully about his meeting with X and the warning that closing the X-Files was "just the beginning." "Do you trust him?" Scully asks, but Mulder doesn't know how to respond.

Krycek is shown meeting with the Cigarette-Smoking Man, telling him that Mulder has "found another source" to replace Deep Throat and that Scully is "a much larger problem than you described."

Not to worry, the Cigarette-Smoking Man assures him ominously. "Every problem has a solution."

Back story: Mr. X (heard over the phone but not clearly seen in the previous episode) was actually *Ms.* X for starters, described as a woman in the original script. In fact, an actress was cast in the role, but after shooting one scene the producers decided it wasn't working and turned to *21 Jump Street* veteran Steven Williams, who had a long association with writer/producers Glen Morgan and James Wong as well as other crew members who'd worked on that series.

Nicholas Lea also makes his first appearance here as Alex Krycek, in what was to become a reasonably signifi-cant role in terms of the course of *The X-Files* "mythology."

As for the show's initial inspiration, it's been attrib-uted to a two-week bout with insomnia suffered by writer Howard Gordon, who made his solo writing debut on this episode.

Duane Barry (Part 1 of 2)

First aired: October 14, 1994

Written by
Chris Carter

Directed by
Chris Carter

Guest stars:
Steve Railsback (Duane Barry)
CCH Pounder (Agent Kazdin)
Nicholas Lea (Agent Alex Krycek)
Frank C. Turner (Dr. Hakkie)
William B. Davis (Cigarette-Smoking Man)
Stephen E. Miller (Tactical Commander)
Fred Henderson (Agent Rich)
Barbara Pollard (Gwen)
Sarah Strange (Kimberly)
Robert Lewis (Officer)
Michael Dobson (Marksman #2)
Tosca Baggoo (Clerk)
Tim Dixon (Bob)
Prince Maryland (Agent Janus)
John Sampson (Marksman #1)

Log line: Mulder negotiates a hostage situation involving a man, Duane Barry, who claims to be a victim of alien experimentation.

Principal setting: Marion, Virginia

Synopsis: In 1985, Duane Barry is shown being abducted by aliens. "Not again!" he screams, as his body slowly rises off his bed.

Cut to the present day, with Barry in a treatment facility insisting that "they're coming for me again." Seizing a guard's gun, he takes a doctor and three other people hostage, wanting the doctor to accompany him to the abduction site to prove that it's real.

Mulder is called in to negotiate. When the power suddenly goes out, Barry fires into the darkness, hitting a hostage, and Mulder is sent in along with a paramedic. As Mulder talks to him, Barry flashes back to his abduction and the experiments done on him. He agrees to let the wounded man go in exchange for Mulder.

Scully combs over Barry's medical history, finding that he's a former FBI agent who was shot in the line of duty, destroying the moral center of his brain and making him both delusional and violent. "Duane Barry is not what Mulder thinks he is," she reports to the other agents, gravely concerned.

Barry tells Mulder the government knows about the abductions, describing the site in detail. Scully, meanwhile, warns Mulder about his psychosis

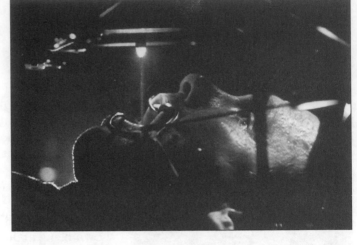

X

The case of
Phineas Gage, to
which Scully
refers, actually
happened. In
the early part
of this century,
a railway worker
placing dynamite
set off an
explosion that
drove a steel
rod more than
three feet long
through his
brain. Gage not
only survived
but suffered no
physical impair-
ment and went on
to live another
20 years.
However, his
personality
underwent a dra-
matic change,
turning him into
an irascible,
profane, and
thoroughly
unpleasant man.

through an earpiece, and eventually an FBI marksman draws a bead on Barry, wounding him.

An examination appears to validate Barry's abduction scenario, with strangely marked pieces of metal in his abdomen and sinus as well as inexplicably tiny holes drilled into his teeth. At the supermarket, Scully impulsively scans the piece of metal from Barry's stomach, and the machine goes berserk. Barry is shown jolting to consciousness, slugging a guard, and leaving the hospital.

Scully calls Mulder, telling his answering machine about the scanner. "What the hell is this thing, Mulder?" she wonders. "It's almost like somebody was using it to *catalogue* him." Suddenly, Barry appears at the window, and with a crash, Scully is heard yelling for help.

To be continued . . .

Back story: Shot during Anderson's pregnancy, the episode includes an inside joke in the supermarket scene with Scully buying pickles and ice cream. Steve Railsback, who originally came to prominence playing Charles Manson in the TV movie *Helter Skelter*, impressed everyone with his performance as Barry, but it was actually CCH Pounder who earned a guest actress Primetime Emmy Award nomination for the episode playing Agent Kasdin, Mulder's fellow hostage negotiator. Chris Carter received an Emmy nomination for writing the show, as did director of photography John S. Bartley in the category of cinematography. This is the first *X-Files* episode directed by Chris Carter.

Ascension (Part 2 of 2)

First aired: October 21, 1994

Written by
Paul Brown

Directed by
Michael Lange

Guest stars:
Steve Railsback (Duane Barry)
Nicholas Lea (Agent Alex Krycek)
William B. Davis (Cigarette-
    Smoking Man)
Sheila Larken (Margaret Scully)
Mitch Pileggi (AD Walter Skinner)
Steven Williams (Mr. X)
Meredith Bain Woodward (Dr. Ruth
    Slaughter)
Peter LaCroix (Dwight)
Steve Makaj (Patrolman)
Robyn Douglass (Video Technician)
Bobby L. Stewart (Deputy)

Log line: Mulder pursues Duane Barry in a desperate search for Scully.

Principal setting: Skyland Mountain, Virginia.

Synopsis: Mulder plays his answering machine and hears Scully being kidnapped. Her mother shows up frantic, saying she's had a dream about Dana being taken away.

Duane Barry drives down the interstate with Scully in his trunk, shooting a patrolman who pulls him over. The incident is caught on tape, and Mulder analyzes the footage, seeing Scully in the car with the help of computer enhancement. Considering what Barry had said about "ascending to the stars," he deduces that he's heading to Skyland Mountain and takes off after Scully despite Skinner's orders to stay away from the case.

Krycek calls the Cigarette-Smoking Man, alerting him to where they're going. At the mountain, Mulder takes an aerial tram hoping to beat Barry to the top, but Krycek kills the operator, stranding Mulder, who perilously wriggles out of the tram and takes off on foot.

Reaching the mountaintop, Mulder finds Barry's car empty except for a golden cross that belonged to Scully. Barry is alone, exulting, "I'm free, you sonsabitches! You can't touch Duane Barry anymore!" When Mulder presses him about Scully's whereabouts, he says only, "*They took her.*"

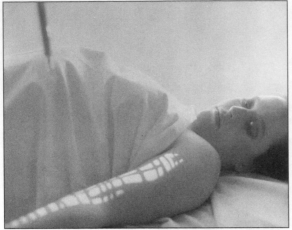

Under questioning, Barry insists that he traded Scully to "them" and didn't harm her, referring Mulder to shadowy figures in the hall. When Mulder springs on him and chokes him, he says wide-eyed, "They'll tell you where she is. The military's in on it. Just ask 'em."

Mulder leaves Barry alone, imagining Scully being experimented upon, her belly distended. He returns to find Krycek with the prisoner, and moments later Barry goes into cardiac arrest and dies.

Krycek meets with the Cigarette-Smoking Man, asking why they don't simply kill Mulder. To do so, he's told, "risks turning one man's religion into a crusade." Scully has been taken care of, he notes, adding that Krycek "needs to keep Mulder's trust."

Mulder tells Skinner that he believes Barry was poisoned, that the results are being covered up, and that the military knows Scully's whereabouts. Taking Krycek's car, Mulder goes to Senator Matheson seeking help, but X intercepts him, saying the senator can't help him "without committing political suicide."

"They have something on him?" Mulder asks. "They have something on everyone, Mr. Mulder," X says icily. "The question is when they'll use it."

Back in the car Mulder notices cigarettes in the ashtray and realizes to whom they belong. He accuses Krycek of killing Barry and the technician, but when the agent is summoned, he has disappeared. Frustrated, Skinner says he's doing "what they fear the most"—reopening the X-Files.

Mulder meets with Scully's mother, offering her the cross he found. She tells him hopefully to "give it to Dana . . . when you find her."

A prenatal premiere: Yes, that is actually Gillian Anderson's pregnant torso shown in the "examination" scene, where Mulder's imagination is showing him what might be taking place with his partner. She was only a few weeks away from the birth of her first child, Piper, a daughter. She was born September 25, 1994.

Back story: The conversation between Krycek and the Cigarette-Smoking Man represented an effort to explain why the forces seeking to thwart Mulder's work don't simply kill him—a response to various fans, among them science fiction writer Harlan Ellison, who've put that question to Chris Carter.

David Duchovny also performed his own stunts in the aerial tram sequence, hoping to provide a greater sense of authenticity in the scene.

3

First aired: November 4, 1994

Written by
Chris Ruppenthal, Glen Morgan, and
    James Wong

Directed by
David Nutter

Guest stars:
Frank Military (The Son/John)
Perrey Reeves (Kristen Kilar)
Frank Ferrucci (Det. Nettles)
Tom McBeath (Det. Munson)
Gustavo Moreno (The Father)
Justina Vail (The Unholy Spirit)
Malcolm Stewart (Commander Carver)
Ken Kramer (Dr. Browning)
Roger Allford (Garrett Lore)
Richard Yee (David Yung)
Brad Loree (Fireman)
John Tierney (Dr. Jacobs)
David Livingstone (Guard)
Guyle Frazier (Officer)

Log line: Mulder investigates a series of vampiresque murders in Hollywood and finds himself falling for a mysterious woman who is a prime suspect.

Principal setting: Los Angeles, California

Synopsis: A businessman is killed by a woman and her accomplice, who are seen biting his arm, drawing blood.

Mulder returns to his office after having obviously been away for months. He removes plastic from his desk and looks at Scully's X-file, removing the small cross that belonged to her. He subsequently shows up at the L.A. murder scene, explaining that there have been six similar killings in Memphis and Portland where the victim is drained of blood, with writing in blood on the wall. Assuming he's on to a cult, Mulder catches one of the trio responsible, John, at a blood bank. "Don't you want to live forever?" he asks Mulder. "Not if drawstring pants come back into style," Mulder replies.

Assuming the suspect's vampire beliefs are delusional, Mulder leaves him in an open cell hoping fear of sunlight will scare him enough to talk. When the sun hits him, however, John burns to death horribly.

A stamp on John's arm leads Mulder to a Hollywood club where he encounters Kristen, a mysterious woman. "You've lost someone," she

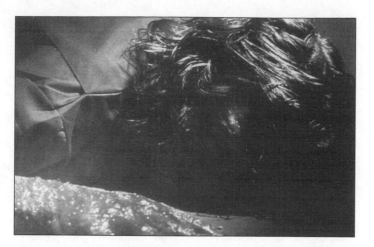

says eerily. When Mulder refuses to taste her blood, she leaves with another man. Mulder follows them but is beaten up by the man, who is soon set upon and killed himself. The coroner tells Mulder there are three sets of human bite marks on the victim.

Mulder tracks down Kristen, realizing that she's no longer part of the cult. She explains that she and John got into "blood sports" but when they met the others things became "unnatural." She's since been running from the trio, who've pursued her from city to city.

She and Mulder presumably have sex—the act is not shown—awakening to discover that John has returned from the dead and is there with his compatriots. "Everybody else just dies, but we come back," he tells her.

Mulder and Kristen escape, killing the female leader of the trio by impaling her on a wooden post. Since John has said that "Only one of us can kill us," Kristen tastes her blood to become one of them, then drenches the house in gasoline and sets it ablaze. Four bodies are found in the remains, and Mulder is left alone, clutching Scully's cross.

Back story: "3" is the only installment where Mulder has a sexual close encounter, with his paramour played by David Duchovny's real-life girlfriend, Perrey Reeves. "I thought, 'This guy's a monk. Let's let him be a human,'" Carter says. "Especially in [Scully's] absence, it seemed like a perfect opportunity to do it."

The "Club Tepes" featured in the episode is named after Prince Vlad Tepes, or Vlad the Impaler, the inspiration for

This is the only X-Files episode ever to be made without Gillian Anderson.

Tom McBeath, who appears as Detective Munson, appeared in "Space."

Bram Stoker's *Dracula*. In the final scene, the Unholy Spirit also says in Transylvanian "I will live forever."

The episode is not without its detractors, among them Duchovny, who says the hour has style but suffers from lapses in logic. "Why do I let her shave me, for God's sake?" he muses.

One Breath

First aired: November 11, 1994

Written by
Glen Morgan and James Wong

Directed by
R.W. Goodwin

Guest stars:
Sheila Larken (Margaret Scully)
Melinda McGraw (Melissa Scully)
Tom Braidwood (Frohike)
Jay Brazeau (Dr. Daly)
Mitch Pileggi (AD Walter Skinner)
Dean Haglund (Langly)
Bruce Harwood (Byers)
Nicola Cavendish (Nurse Owens)
Steven Williams (Mr. X)
Don Davis (Captain Scully)
William B. Davis (Cigarette-Smoking Man)
Lorena Gale (Nurse Wilkins)
Ryan Michael (Overcoat Man)
Tegan Moss (Young Dana Scully)

Log line: Scully is found alive but in a coma, and Mulder must fight to save her life.

Principal setting: Washington, D.C.

Synopsis: One of the most deeply layered episodes in the show's run, the episode begins with Scully still missing and her mother reminiscing about Dana's childhood. Mulder stresses that they must not give up, and Scully turns up mysteriously, alive but comatose in a D.C. hospital. "Who brought her here?" Mulder demands, to no avail.

In gauzily shot images, Scully's soul floats in a boat tethered just offshore, while a strange woman and her late father try to coax her in. Mulder, meanwhile, absconds with Scully's chart, showing it to the Lone Gunmen, who tell him that someone has experimented on Scully's DNA. Back at the hospital, a man steals Scully's blood sample and Mulder pursues him, only to encounter X. "You want to see what it takes to find the truth?" X asks, ruthlessly killing the thief, execution-style.

Elsewhere, the Cigarette-Smoking Man warns Skinner to "sit" on Mulder, or "they" will. A stranger provides Mulder the means to find the Cigarette-Smoking Man, who Mulder confronts at gunpoint. "I've watched presidents die," he says, adding when Mulder threatens to kill him, "I have more respect for you, Mulder. You're becoming a player."

Still guilt-ridden over his role in

Scully's condition, Mulder tenders his resignation, but Skinner—after relating a grim story about his own service in Vietnam—tells him, "Your resignation is unacceptable."

X turns up again, arranging an ambush so Mulder can seek vengeance against Scully's abductors. Instead, at the urging of Scully's sister Melissa, Mulder goes to sit with Scully at the hospital, returning to find his apartment ransacked.

Scully awakens, finding Mulder by her side. "I had the strength of your beliefs," she tells him. Mulder returns her cross to her, while Scully learns that the nurse who spoke so soothingly to her during her coma—helping woo her back from death—has never worked at that hospital.

Glen Morgan states that he named Nurse Owens after his own grandmother.

Back story: Gillian Anderson, still a bit wobbly and exhausted just days after giving birth by cesarean section, spent most of the episode in a hospital gown with tubes sticking out of her for hours at a time, occasionally falling asleep while filming some of her scenes. The producers had considered making Scully's sister, Melissa, a romantic interest for Mulder but later nixed the idea.

The episode also lightly pokes fun at the show's fans on the Internet, with one of the Lone Gunmen telling Mulder he should join them Friday in "hopping on the Internet to nitpick the scientific inaccuracies of *Earth 2.*"

"I'm doing my laundry," Mulder quips.

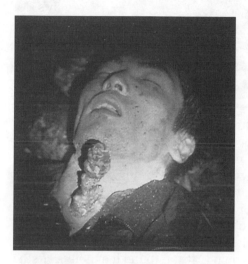

Firewalker

First aired: November 18, 1994

Written by
Howard Gordon

Directed by
David Nutter

Guest stars:
Bradley Whitford (Dr. Daniel Trepkos)
David Lewis (Vosberg)
Tuck Milligan (Dr. Adam Pierce)
Leland Orser (Jason Ludwig)
Torben Rolfsen (Technician)
Shawnee Smith (Jesse O'Neil)
Hiro Kanagawa (Peter Tanaka)
David Kaye (Eric Parker)

Log line: Mulder and Scully stumble upon a deadly life form while investigating the death of a scientist studying an active volcano.

Principal setting: Mt. Avalon, Washington

Synopsis: A team of scientists exploring Mt. Avalon has sent a distress signal from the volcano, and videotape shows one of their party lying dead. The group is exploring the site with the aid of Firewalker—a robot that can descend deep into the earth's core.

Mulder suggests Scully "give yourself some time" after her abduction ordeal and coma, but she insists that she wants to work. "I've already lost too much time," she says.

Reaching the research site along with another scientist, Pierce, who had been working with the research team, Mulder is attacked by a member of the party. The survivors—Ludwig, Tanaka, and O'Neil—fear the expedition's leader, Trepkos, a brilliant scientist who went crazy and murdered Erikson, the man seen dead in the videotape. Mulder finds Trepkos's notes, which mention "a new life-form"—a subterranean organism, silicon-based, that can survive within a volcano. Elsewhere, Trepkos ambushes Pierce while he surveys the site and chokes him to death. "No one can leave," Trepkos says.

Tanaka collapses, and as they transport him to get help he runs off. From a distance, they see a snakelike spike

The flash-
lights Mulder
and Scully
use in this
episode and
throughout the
first two
seasons are
xenon flash-
lights made
by Maxabeam.
Costing about
$4,000 apiece,
they are used
by search and
rescue parties
in the
wilderness,
and can pro-
ject a beam
of between 3
and 6 million
candlepower.

burst out of his throat—a spore, Scully says, that grew inside him until reaching reproductive maturity.

Mulder says he must find Trepkos, while Scully studies the spore. Ludwig leads Mulder into the caverns, but Trepkos slays him, then burns the body. "It's not him I'm trying to kill," Trepkos says, as the spore moves within Ludwig; rather, he's trying to destroy the spore that's infected all his colleagues. Firewalker brought back the spore, he says, and then Erikson found it and infected the others, who are all hosts.

Scully's tests show the spore must be inhaled immediately upon release or it becomes harmless, and Mulder, realizing she's in danger with O'Neil, rushes back. Overtaken by the spore, O'Neil cuffs herself to Scully, who throws her into a plexiglass chamber just before the spore bursts out against the window.

Trepkos, who was involved with O'Neil, returns to see her body. "I told her . . . it would change her life," he says sadly. Mulder tells rescuers there were only two survivors, allowing Trepkos to stay, carrying O'Neil into the caverns below.

Back story: "Firewalker" sprang from two news items producer Howard Gordon had read about Project Dante, a NASA-funded robotic explorer that had been sent into a volcano. It also fits with a certain genre the show likes to tap into at least once or twice each season in which a scientific, military, or industrial party (as in "Ice" or "Darkness Falls") encounters some difficulty in a remote location and the FBI is sent in to investigate.

Gordon saw Trepkos's obsession and the toll it exacted upon him in terms of losing someone he loved as a means of exploring the darker side of Mulder's commitment to his search. "The natural endpoint of this quest for the truth is madness," he notes, suggesting that Mulder's decision to let Trepkos go at the end represents the bond in that respect between Mulder and Trepkos—their shared *Heart of Darkness*.

Toby Lindala's spike/tendril effect "won the gross-out award at that point in time," Gordon adds, also lauding David Nutter's direction.

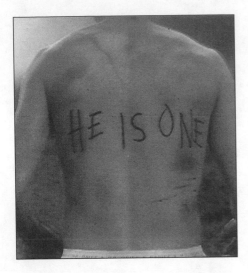

Red Museum

First aired: December 9, 1994

Written by
Chris Carter

Directed by
Win Phelps

Guest stars:
Gillian Barber (Beth Kane)
Steve Eastin (Sheriff Mazeroski)
Lindsey Ginter (Crew-Cut Man)
Mark Rolston (Richard Odin)
Paul Sand (Gerd Thomas)
Bob Frazer (Gary Kane)
Robert Clothier (Old Man)
Elisabeth Rosen (Katie)
Crystal Verge (Woman Reading Words)
Cameron Labine (Rick)
Tony Sampson (Brad)
Gerry Naim (1st Man)
Brian McGugan (1st Officer)

Log line: Mulder and Scully investigate a possible connection between a rural religious cult and the disappearance of several teenagers.

Principal setting: Delta Glen, Wisconsin

Synopsis: A teenage boy disappears, then is found 12 hours later with the words "He is one" scrawled on his back. Mulder says there have been several victims in the area, each found hysterical with fear. The local sheriff thinks possession may be involved and suspects the Church of the Red Museum, a local cult that believes in soul transference and eschews eating meat.

A teenage girl is also seized and later found with the writing on her back. Tests show she has a strange opiate in her blood, and the Red Museum's head, Odin, is a former doctor. They arrest him, and his acolytes assemble in town.

An old man takes Mulder and Scully to a farm, where they see men injecting the cattle with genetically engineered growth hormone. "People around here've changed, gotten mean," he tells them, with seven rapes in the last year by high school boys. He believes the hormone is responsible, and when Scully notes that it's been proven safe, he shoots back, "Says who? The government?"

That night, a small plane crashes, killing the pilot and his passenger, Dr. Larsen, who possesses a briefcase full of cash. Larsen had treated each of the abducted teens since childhood, giving them vitamin shots. "Looks like the good doctor may have been delivering more than babies," Mulder muses, looking over the scorched bills.

Crew-Cut Man, who killed Deep Throat, arrives on the scene, executing one of the men who'd been injecting the cattle. The sheriff's son is then abducted and found dead.

Noticing a secret space behind the first abducted boy's bathroom, Mulder realizes the landlord, Gerd Thomas, has been abducting the children. Thomas says the kids have become monsters because of Larsen's tests, and a check of the substance reveals the same alien DNA Scully acquired in an earlier episode. "Purity control," Scully says, referring to a label used in "The Erlenmeyer Flask."

Mulder surmises that an experiment has been conducted on the town, and the perpetrators are now covering their tracks. For safety he takes the remaining teens to the Red Museum, then goes to the meat-packing plant, encountering Crew-Cut Man. He eludes Mulder, but the sheriff—still mourning his son—kills him.

Crew-Cut Man has no identity, not even fingerprints on file. Scully's voice-over concludes that the town was part of an experiment on the effect of alien DNA, with the Red Museum as a control group. "The case," she says, "remains open and unsolved."

Back story: An aborted attempt was made to do an unprecedented inter-network crossover on this particular episode between *The X-Files*, which airs on Fox, and CBS's *Picket Fences*, which is set in the fictitious town of Rome, Wisconsin. Both shows are produced through Twentieth Century Fox Television, and the CBS drama aired in the hour after *The X-Files*. CBS was instrumental in nixing the idea—a decision that took on a bit of irony given that the two shows became direct competitors in September 1995. The *Picket Fences* episode did feature an FBI agent investigating a similar type of case.

Excelsius Dei

First aired: December 16, 1994

Written by
Paul Brown

Directed by
Stephen Surjik

Guest stars:
Frances Bay (Dorothy)
Teryl Rothery (Nurse Charters)
Eric Christmas (Stan Phillips)
David Fresco (Hal Arden)
Sab Shimono (Gung Bituen)
Tasha Simms (Laura Kelly)

Log line: Mulder and Scully uncover strange goings-on in a nursing home after a nurse is attacked by an unseen force.

Principal setting: Worcester, Massachusetts

Synopsis: Michelle, a nurse in the Excelsius Dei convalescent home, is pinned down and raped by an invisible attacker. She accuses one of the patients, Hal Arden, an old man who laughs off the claim. "I'm seventy-four years old. I've got plumbing older than this building," he says, having just left the bathtub and opening his towel to prove it. "And it don't work much better, either."

After the agents leave, Hal's roommate, Stan, cautions him to be more careful lest he "ruin it for us all." He takes a pill, and refuses when Hal presses him for one. Moments later, Hal—seemingly choked by an unseen hand—dies.

The doctor who runs the facility says he's making progress treating the Alzheimer's patients using an experimental drug. Mulder thinks the nurse's charge is contrived, but Scully, for once, isn't so sure.

Returning to the facility they see one of the orderlies plummet to his death—an unseen power knocking him out the window and bending his fingers off the ledge. Stan is somehow involved.

One of the patients, Dorothy, talks to the invisible figures, who we can see in shadows assembling around Scully. Mulder asks about an Asian orderly, Gung, and finds mushrooms growing in his room—as well as a missing orderly buried in the soil. Gung admits to giving the patients mushrooms for medicinal purposes but says "something has gone very wrong," that "the souls who died here continue to suffer" and have been awakened. When he goes to find his stash of capsules they're missing.

Mulder notes that mushrooms have long been used by shamans to visit the spirit world and suggests that "something has been unleashed here." At that point he and Michelle are locked in the bathroom, which begins flooding with water, even as Stan goes into a seizure. Mulder finally breaks free, and the spirits disappear.

Plans are made to deport Gung, while the patients, with the treatment no longer in use, relapse to their vegetative states. In the final shot we see Stan, staring blankly into space.

Back story: To shoot the climactic sequence where the bathroom door bursts open, special effects supervisor Dave Gauthier built a tank and flooded the hallway with more than 3,300 gallons of water. An earlier moment implying that the nurse who was attacked, Michelle, was a lesbian can be found in the script (her lover enters their apartment as the agents question her) but failed to make the final cut. "It just felt gratuitous at that point," Carter says.

Shelia Moore, who appeared in "Deep Throat," makes a return as the director of the home.

Tasha Simms, who played the mother of Cindy Reardon in "Eve," here returns as the daughter of Stan Phillips.

Aubrey

First aired: January 6, 1995

Written by
Sara Charno

Directed by
Rob Bowman

Guest stars:
Deborah Strang (B. J. Morrow)
Morgan Woodward (Old Harry Cokely)
Terry O'Quinn (Lt. Brian Tillman)
Joy Coghill (Mrs. Ruby Thibodeaux)
Robyn Driscoll (Detective Joe Darnell)
Peter Fleming (Officer #1)
Sarah Jane Redmond (Young Mom)
Emanuel Hajek (Young Cokely)

Log line: Mulder and Scully investigate the possibility of genetic transferring of personality from one generation to another in connection with a serial killer.

Principal setting: Aubrey, Missouri

Synopsis: B. J. Morrow is having an affair with her boss, Lt. Tillman, and tells him she's pregnant. Inexplicably, she finds herself later in a field, digging up the body of an FBI agent who's been missing since 1942.

Before his disappearance, the agent, Sam Chaney, had been investigating a serial killer who carved the word "sister" into the chests of female victims and painted on the wall with their blood. The killer was never caught.

Talking with Scully, B. J. admits she's pregnant and having strange nightmares. She doesn't know how she found the body. Scully discovers that the word "brother" is carved in the ribs. Tillman tells them there was a recent homicide featuring the same M.O., and another body turns up with "sister" carved on it.

Flipping through old mug shots, B. J. picks out Harry Cokely, who was convicted of raping a woman in 1945 and carving "sister" on her. Yet when Mulder and Scully visit Cokely, he's feeble—77 years old and on an oxygen machine. "I can't leave the house without this damn thing," he sneers, when questioned as to his whereabouts. "I sit here in front of the TV twenty-four hours a day."

B. J. awakens with a vision, soaked with blood, "sister" carved on her chest. She says she saw Cokely in her dream and rushes to a house, ripping up floorboards to reveal the bones of Chaney's missing partner. It's a house Cokely rented 50 years earlier.

Mulder and Scully visit the woman Cokely raped, and she admits to having a baby after the assault that she gave up for adoption. Mulder thinks Cokely's descendant is responsible—the killer's genetic memory having been passed on. "Genetic traits often skip generations," he notes. The agents discover that B. J. is Cokely's granddaughter.

Mulder fears B. J. will try to finish what Cokely started, and she does go after her grandmother. "Someone has to take the blame, little sister," she snarls, but seeing the "sister" carved on the woman fazes her, and instead she hunts down Cokely. Mulder finds him slashed up and is ambushed by B. J., who holds a razor to his throat before dropping the weapon when Cokely dies.

Scully hypothesizes that B. J.'s pregnancy may have been "a catalyst for her transformation." She's held in a psychiatric cell on suicide watch, after trying to abort her unborn child, a boy, which Tillman is trying to adopt.

Back story: "Aubrey" turned out to be a true team effort by the writing staff, as Sara Charno began with the concept of 50-year-old murders and the transfer of genetic memory, eventually combining that idea with a separate one she'd been mulling over about a female serial killer. Certain changes were still being made right before shooting, such as the scene in the fourth act where Mulder is attacked by B. J., who as revised sees the face of the slain FBI agent from decades earlier when she looks at him.

Producers Glen Morgan and James Wong—who provided numerous contributions to the script—suggested casting Morgan Woodward in the role of Cokely, having remembered the veteran actor from an episode of *21 Jump Street* he'd done while they were producing that series. Woodward's credits also include the original *Star Trek*, *Battle Beyond the Stars* and countless bad-guy roles in TV and movie Westerns. Guest star Terry O'Quinn played a killer himself, it bears noting, in *The Stepfather* series.

Despite the grim storyline there's some amusing banter between the leads, allowing Scully to give as good as she gets. When Mulder accuses her of engaging in a "pretty extreme hunch," for example, Scully quickly counters by saying, "I seem to recall you having some pretty extreme hunches."

The bones and skulls used here and in "Our Town" are not real bones. They are plastic bones which must be "aged" with paint and chemicals, and have the plastic seams filed off. Not only would real bones cost a great deal more, but they would give the cast of *The X-Files* the creeps. . . .

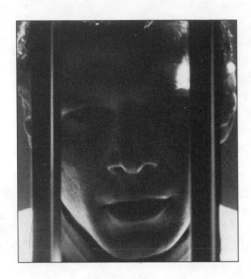

Irresistible

First aired: January 13, 1995

Written by
Chris Carter

Directed by
David Nutter

Guest stars:
Nick Chinlund (Donnie Pfaster)
Robert Thurston (Jackson Toews)
Bruce Weitz (Agent Moe Bocks)
Denalda Williams (Marilyn)
Christine Willes (Karen Kossoff)
Deanna Milligan (Satin)
Glynis Davies (Ellen)
Tim Progosh (Mr. Fiebling)
Dwight McFee (Suspect)
Maggie O'Hara (Young Woman)
Kathleen Duborg (Prostitute)
Mark Saunders (Agent Busch)
Ciara Hunter (Coed)

Log line: A psycho who collects hair and fingernails from the dead steps up his obsession to killing his soon-to-be-collectibles himself.

Principal setting: Minneapolis, Minnesota

Synopsis: A mortuary worker, Donnie Pfaster, is caught by his boss taking locks of hair off a corpse. Mulder and Scully are later called in by a Minneapolis agent, Moe Bocks, to examine a desecrated grave. Though Mulder is convinced this isn't an X-File (he took the case because he had tickets for the Redskins-Vikings football game), Scully seems shaken by the crime.

Mulder calls the perpetrator "an escalating fetishist"—one whose compulsion is growing to the point where he "may resort to homicide to procure more corpses." Donnie subsequently picks up a prostitute and murders her, taking various tokens from her body. He later fixates on a coed in his class, but when he approaches her she escapes and he's arrested.

Disturbed by the case, Scully has a nightmare in which she imagines herself as one of the victims. She awakens with a scream. Mulder alerts her that the police have a suspect in custody, but it's the wrong guy—being held, in fact, in a cell across from Donnie, who's released after getting Scully's name from a cellmate.

Back in Washington, Scully discusses her fears with a counselor. Though she says she'd trust Mulder with her life, Scully confides, "I don't want him to know how much this is bothering me. I don't want him to think he has to protect me." Meanwhile, the agents find a fingerprint that leads to Donnie's apartment, where they find hair and a finger but not the suspect.

When Scully returns to Minneapolis, Donnie is waiting to surprise her, forcing her car off the road. She's held bound and gagged while Mulder tracks the suspect to Donnie's late mother's house. Donnie prepares to bathe Scully as part of his ritual. "Would you say your hair is normal, or dry?" he oozes. When he approaches her Scully breaks away, grappling with him before Mulder and other agents crash in. She finally breaks down, crying on Mulder's shoulder.

Pictures show Donnie as a child, then grown, glowering from behind bars. The idea of such a human monster is, Mulder says in voice-over, "as frightening as any X-File."

Back story: One of the few episodes with no paranormal angle to it, "Irresistible" still proved chilling enough in its Jeffrey Dahmer-esque overtones that Fox's program standards department rejected the initial script as "unacceptable for broadcast standards." Carter was forced to change the character from a necrophiliac to a "death fetishist," diminishing any overt sexuality in Pfaster's obsession. Nick Chinlund, who's memorable in the role, has also appeared in Showtime's series *Red Shoe Diaries*, the erotic anthology series hosted by David Duchovny.

This is Dwight McFee's third appearance in *The X-Files*, having previously appeared in "Shapes" and "Little Green Men."

It's also worth noting that when Pfaster's cellmate tells him Scully's name he adds "like the baseball announcer"—a reference to Dodger broadcaster Vin Scully, who did, in fact, provide the inspiration for the character's moniker. The show remains one of Gillian Anderson's favorite episodes.

The football game that Mulder and Scully are missing is Washington v. Minnesota, two teams that each had a "Carter" in their ranks; in one scene a television announcer mentions a catch by Cris Carter.

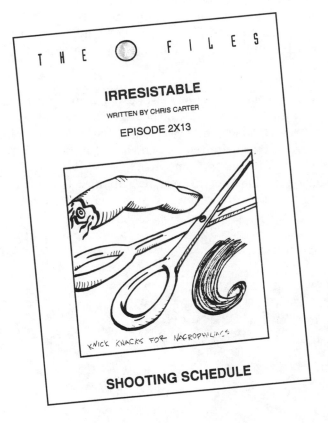

THE ◯ FILES

IRRESISTABLE

WRITTEN BY CHRIS CARTER

EPISODE 2X13

KNICK KNACKS FOR NACROPHILIACS

SHOOTING SCHEDULE

Die Hand Die Verletzt

First aired: January 27, 1995

Written by
Glen Morgan and James Wong

Directed by
Kim Manners

Guest stars:
Susan Blommaert (Mrs. Paddock)
Dan Butler (Jim Ausbury)
Heather McComb (Shannon Ausbury)
P. Lynn Johnson (Deborah Brown)
Shawn Johnston (Pete Calcagni)
Travis MacDonald (Dave Duran)
Michelle Goodger (Barbara Ausbury)
Larry Musser (Sheriff John Oakes)
Franky Czinege (Jerry Thomas)
Laura Harris (Andrea)
Doug Abrahams (Paul Vitaris)

Log line: Mulder and Scully journey to a small town to investigate a boy's murder and are caught between the town's secret occult religion and a woman with strange powers.

Principal setting: Milford Haven, New Hampshire

Synopsis: The local Parent-Teachers Committee meets, talking about the usual topics. Before adjourning, however, they light a candle and pray in unison . . . to the Lords of Darkness, chanting, "Die Hand Die Verletzt" (Subtitles: "His is the hand that wounds").

Four teenagers later venture into the woods, with the boys trying to scare their dates by reading a prayer to Satan. Suddenly, rats appear at their feet, and when they start to flee one of the boys is grabbed by the throat. His body is later found with the eyes and heart cut out.

A local cop tells Mulder and Scully there are rumors of Satan worship and dark rites in the town, which Scully dismisses as folklore—until it begins raining toads. A substitute teacher, Mrs. Paddock, shows up at the school, and while the agents question the students involved, the PTC group meets, with one of them, Calcagni, saying that "Something is here . . . a presence" that's responsible for the death. They tell the agents that occultists are behind what's happened, and when a water fountain drains counterclockwise—which should be impossible in the Northern hemisphere, we're told—Mulder concludes something is there as well. Mrs. Paddock, meanwhile, opens her drawer, revealing the dead boy's heart and eyes.

While dissecting a pig embryo Shannon, the daughter of one of the PTC leaders, sees the pig heart beating, and shrieks, reliving images of satanic rituals and molestation. When she returns after class to make up the work, Paddock concentrates on the girl, whose eyes glaze over as she raises the scalpel, slashing her own wrists. Mulder detects the smell of incense in Paddock's office, which is used in Black Mass rituals.

Calcagni says Shannon's death was a sign from the evil presence. "We must rekindle our faith," he tells the group, saying they must use the girl's death to get rid of the FBI. Her stepfather, Ausbury, admits to Mulder they've been worshipping dark forces, using children's blood in ceremonies and posthypnotic suggestion to repress memories until they reach adulthood.

He also says they've become lax about some of the rites, that they'd "slip over" the ones they didn't want to do. "Did you really think you could summon the Devil, then ask him to behave?" Mulder inquires.

Receiving a call from Scully that turns out to be bogus, Mulder handcuffs Ausbury in the basement, where he's devoured by a huge snake, as Paddock is shown licking her lips, her eyes serpentine. They return to find only crushed bones, and remember the python in Paddock's room.

Calcagni tells the others they must kill the agents or suffer the same fate as Ausbury, "if it's not already too late." They surprise Scully and Mulder and prepare to sacrifice them, but Paddock takes control of Calcagni, who shoots his companions before turning the shotgun on himself. "It is already too late," Paddock says mockingly.

The agents find a note on the chalkboard—"Goodbye. It's been nice working with you"—as the power flickers back on.

The characters "Paul Vitaris" and "Deborah Brown" are named after prominent on-line X-Philes.

P. Lynn Johnson previously appeared in "Born Again" where, curiously, her character was named "Braun," a variant of "Brown."

Back story: One of the show's creepiest episodes, "Die Hand" was the last hour written by Glen Morgan and James Wong, who left the series to devote their time to developing and producing a new show, Fox's *Space: Above and Beyond*. The pair used Paddock's cryptic line on the chalkboard, "It's been nice working with you," for another more sentimental purpose—to serve as their parting aside to the cast and crew.

Again, part of the script grew out of the Morgan and Wong flair for constructing episodes around individual scenes, with Morgan proclaiming enthusiastically at one point, "We need an episode where a snake eats a guy." Amphibians also figured prominently in the sequence where toads rain from the sky, with real toads—dropped from only a few feet so as not to harm them—eventually being substituted for fake ones that proved to be too heavy as they caromed off the umbrellas.

Airing on the eve of Super Bowl XXIX, the producers—long-suffering San Diego Chargers fans—also indulged themselves in a little personal gag in the opening credits, where they were listed as James "Chargers" Wong and Glen "Bolts, Baby" Morgan. Though the Chargers were routed two days later by the San Francisco 49ers, Morgan insists he isn't superstitious enough to believe that those credits had anything to do with jinxing his team.

"Crowley" High School evokes the memory of British ceremonialist Aleister Crowley, whose theories on "magick" shocked his contemporaries and heavily influenced the development of modern Wicca.

T H E ◯ F I L E S

DIE HAND DIE VERLETZT

TELEPLAY BY
Glen Morgan & James Wong

EPISODE 2X14

ominus
Inferus
Vobisum!"

SHOOTING SCHEDULE

Fresh Bones

First aired: February 3, 1995

Written by
Howard Gordon

Directed by
Rob Bowman

Guest stars:
Kevin Conway (Pvt. McAlpin)
Daniel Benzali (Col. Wharton)
Katya Gardner (Robin McAlpin)
Matt Hill (Pvt. Harry Dunham)
Jamil Walker Smith (Chester Bonaparte)
Bruce Young (Pierre Bauvais)
Roger Cross (Pvt. Kittel)
Steven Williams (Mr. X)
Callum Keith Rennie (Groundskeeper)
Peter Kelamis (Lt. Foyle)

Log line: Mulder and Scully journey to a Haitian refugee camp after a series of deaths, finding themselves caught in a secret war between the camp commander and a Voodoo priest.

Principal setting: Folkstone, North Carolina

Synopsis: A soldier, Private McAlpin, sees maggots instead of cereal in his breakfast bowl, then drives off in a panic, crashing into a tree with voodoo markings on it. His death marks the second death in a week of a soldier assigned to the local Immigration and Naturalization Service processing center, where Haitian refugees are being held. The military calls it suicide, but the soldier's wife suspects a voodoo curse.

The base commander, Colonel Wharton, says the soldiers are under stress because the refugees hate them. Scully goes to examine McAlpin's body but finds a dog's corpse in its place. Mulder meets with Bauvais, one of the refugees, who says Wharton won't let them return home, "which is all we ask."

Driving away, they nearly hit a figure walking in the road. It's McAlpin, who Mulder believes to have been made a zombie, causing him to wonder about the other Marine who died. When they try to exhume him, his body has been snatched.

One of the soldiers says the agents are "in the middle of something you don't understand," that Bauvais warned Wharton he'd "take his men, one by one . . . take their souls" if the refugees weren't allowed to go. Wharton has Bauvais beaten, and X tells Mulder the colonel is seeking revenge for the deaths of his men on the last U.S. mission in Haiti. "The Statue of Liberty's on vacation," X notes sardonically.

Scully finds the soldier who tried to warn them dead in Mulder's room, with McAlpin standing there holding a bloody knife. When they return to question Bauvais, they're told he killed himself. "I'll assume your business here is finished," Wharton says flatly.

Further investigation shows that McAlpin and the missing soldier both filed complaints against Wharton for his treatment of the refugees. At the cemetery, Mulder spots Wharton performing a voodoo rite over Bauvais's coffin. Mulder is stunned, but Bauvais rises to confront Wharton, who's found dead, while Bauvais is shown lying peacefully in his casket.

As they prepare to leave, Mulder and Scully are told that a young boy who had helped them, Chester, died six weeks earlier in a base riot. Wharton's coffin, meanwhile, is lowered into the ground, with him screaming inside it, very much alive.

Back story: News clippings again provided the seed for this episode, after producer Howard Gordon saw two articles about three suicides involving U.S. servicemen in Haiti, while the internment of Haitian refugees also remained very much in the news. Rob Bowman, who's directed a number of Gordon-scripted episodes, "did a great job," the writer says, in mining his script for chills.

The design painted on the tree into which McAlpin crashes his car is a "vever," a sign belonging to the 'loa' or spirits honored in voudoun. Bauvais explains the vever as a loco-miroir, or mirror of the soul.

Guest star Daniel Benzali (who went on to star in the ABC series *Murder One*, practicing law instead of voodoo) was "kind of a bold choice," Gordon adds, in that he didn't necessarily look like a military man but "just had that quality" the producers were after. Though there are no subtitles, when Colonel Wharton performs his voodoo ritual at the end he says in French, "To the spirits of the stars. To the spirit of the moon."

"Fresh Bones" was the highest-rated episode of the first two seasons.

Tetrodotoxin is a powerful paralytic found in puffer fish. As Scully points out, it is considered a delicacy in Japan. Such meticulous care is required in its preparation that, to prevent poisoning, only specially trained and licensed chefs are permitted to prepare it.

Colony (Part 1 of 2)

First aired: February 10, 1995

Written by
Chris Carter;
story by David Duchovny and Chris Carter

Directed by
Nick Marck

Guest stars:
Brian Thompson (Pilot)
Dana Gladstone (Dr. Prince/Gregor)
Megan Leitch (Samantha Mulder)
Peter Donat (Bill Mulder)
Tom Butler (CIA Agent Chapel)
David L. Gordon (FBI Agent)
Andrew Johnston (Agent Weiss)
Tim Henry (Federal Marshal)
Michael McDonald (MP)
Mitch Pileggi (AD Walter Skinner)
Capper McIntyre (Jailer)
Bonnie Hay (Field Doctor)
Rebecca Toolan (Mulder's Mother)
James Leard (Sgt. Al Dixon)
Linden Banks (The Reverend Sistrunk)
Kim Restell (Newspaper Clerk)
Richard Sargent (Captain)
Ken Roberts (Proprietor)
Michael Rogers (1st Crewman)
Oliver Becker (2nd Doctor)

Log line: Mulder and Scully track an alien bounty hunter, who is killing medical doctors who have something strange in common.

Principal setting: Northeastern U.S.

Synopsis: Mulder is rushed into an emergency room suffering from extreme hypothermia. In voice-over, he says that he's learned there is intelligent life beyond Earth, "that they're among us, and they have begun to colonize."

Flash back two weeks to the Beaufort Sea in the Arctic Circle, where a government research vessel rescues a Russian pilot who has crash landed. The pilot turns up at an abortion clinic in Scranton, killing a doctor who oozes green fluid from the wound.

Mulder is sent three obituaries, all for abortion clinic doctors who look exactly alike with no records of their birth. Concluding that there may be more of the doctors, and that the killer is following a geographic pattern, he locates another in Syracuse, sending a field agent to investigate. The agent encounters the pilot and shoots him, but he oozes the same green fluid, causing the agent to collapse as if poisoned. When Mulder and Scully arrive, the killer "morphs" into the deceased agent's likeness. Mulder returns to Washington, where he is surprised to learn that the agent in Syracuse was found dead.

Mulder meets a CIA agent,

Ambrose Chapel, who says the doctors are Soviet clones known as Gregor, and that they are being killed under a secret agreement. When they find another Gregor, however, he leaps several stories to the ground, miraculously surviving and running off before the pilot catches him.

Scully wonders why Mulder believes Chapel. "Whatever happened to 'Trust no one?'" she asks.

"I changed it to 'Trust everyone,'" Mulder quips. "Didn't I tell you?"

Mulder is summoned home on a "family emergency" to Martha's Vineyard, where he's stunned to find his sister, Samantha, who's been missing for 22 years. She tells him the Gregors are her adoptive parents and in actuality alien visitors being killed by an alien bounty hunter who can appear as anyone. "As anyone? You've got to be kidding me," Mulder says, exasperated. Samantha alone can identify the bounty hunter, and Mulder suddenly realizes Scully could be in danger as well.

Investigating on her own, Scully encounters the last four Gregors, who request protection and are placed in federal custody. Disguised as an agent, the pilot gains access to the jail, killing them all.

Mulder shows up at Scully's room, but when the phone rings, it's Mulder on the line. "Scully? Are you there?" she hears, looking toward the man facing her.

To be continued . . .

Back story: This was the first episode to be told in flashback—simply another device, in Carter's eyes, to maintain a degree of freshness in the different storytelling devices used in the series.

In the old-fashioned know-how department, after a

technician devoted hours to creating a sound effect for the alien stiletto, which the writers had told him they wanted to "sound like alien technology," coproducer Paul Rabwin settled the matter by vocally making a "Phffft" sound into the microphone. Despite all the high-tech efforts, that wound up being the sound effect they used.

This is a return appearance for Andrew Johnston, who played Colonel Budahas in "Deep Throat." Also, Tom Butler, who played Benjamin Drake in "Ghost in the Machine," here returns as Agent Chapel. And Jim Leard, who appeared as Captain Lacerio in "The Erlenmeyer Flask," returns to interrogate the Reverend Sistrunk as Sargeant Dixon.

End Game (Part 2 of 2)

First aired: February 17, 1995

Written by
Frank Spotnitz

Directed by
Rob Bowman

Guest stars:
Brian Thompson (Pilot)
Dana Gladstone (Dr. Prince/Gregor)
Megan Leitch (Samantha Mulder)
Peter Donat (Bill Mulder)
Colin Cunningham (Lt. Wilmer)
Mitch Pileggi (AD Walter Skinner)
Steven Williams (Mr. X)
Garry Davey (Captain)
Andrew Johnston (Agent Weiss)
Allan Lysell (Able Gardner)
J. B. Bivens (Sharpshooter)
Oliver Becker (2nd Doctor)
Beatrice Zeilinger (Paramedic)
Bonnie Hay (Field Doctor)

Log line: Mulder tracks an alien bounty hunter who has taken Scully prisoner while discovering that his sister may not be who she seems.

Principal settings: Maryland, the Arctic Circle

Synopsis: A navy submarine encounters a strange vessel and, after firing upon it, is rocked by a huge shock wave.

Picking up where the previous hour left off, Scully realizes the man with her is not Mulder and pulls her gun on him, but the pilot tosses her aside easily and takes her hostage. He hopes to trade her for Samantha, who tells Mulder the only way to kill their pursuer is by piercing the base of his skull.

The clones, she says, are the progeny of two visitors from the 1940s who are trying to establish an Earth colony by genetically merging with humans. She says they work in abortion clinics to access fetal tissue. Because the experiment wasn't sanctioned, a bounty hunter has been dispatched to terminate the colonists.

A trade is set up on a bridge in Bethesda, and Mulder asks Skinner to aid him. "If I ever needed your help—your trust—I need it now," he says. As Mulder prepares to swap Samantha for Scully, Skinner waits nearby with a sharpshooter, but the bounty hunter grabs Samantha and the two plummet into the water below.

Distraught, Mulder informs his father that Samantha has been lost again. She's left him instructions, however, if they are separated to meet her at a clinic, where he finds several Samantha clones—the woman who claimed to be his sister was using him for their case. They admit that Mulder has been manipulated but also say his sister is alive. At that point the bounty hunter arrives and Mulder is knocked out, awakening to find the clinic burning and all the clones gone.

X reluctantly tells Mulder the pilot's craft was found in the Arctic and that an attack fleet was dispatched to prevent him from leaving. Scully finds a note from Mulder saying he's left for parts unknown, not wanting her to know any more. "I won't let you jeopardize your life and your career," the message says.

Realizing the danger he faces, Scully seeks Skinner's help, asking if there's "any way you might locate him through unofficial channels." She subsequently contacts X, who won't speak to her but is met by Skinner. "Did you tell her what she needs to know?" he asks tersely, engaging X in a brutal struggle before X draws his gun, pointing it at Skinner's head. "I've killed men for far less," he says.

"Pull that trigger and you'll be killing two men," Skinner responds, moments later giving Scully the information—saying it was obtained through "unofficial channels."

Mulder finds the submarine in the Arctic, and a soldier who is in fact the bounty hunter. Throwing Mulder around like a child, he asks, "Is the answer to your question worth dying for?" Mulder persists, and the pilot tells him yes, his sister is alive. "Can you die now?" he says,

leaving him to perish on the ice as the conning tower of the sub sinks into the ice.

Back where the previous episode started, Scully rushes to Mulder's side, using her knowledge of the alien-bred retrovirus to save him. "Ultimately," she says in voiceover, "it was science that saved Agent Mulder's life." Mulder rouses, seeing Scully at his bedside, and tells her he "found something I thought maybe I'd lost: faith to keep looking."

Back story: To create the polar ice cap in which the submarine is lodged, 140 tons of snow and ice were trucked into a soundstage that was refrigerated for five days in order to capture the Arctic conditions and make sure viewers could see the actors' breath. The conning tower—the image that first inspired the episode—stood 15 feet high, operating on a hydraulic system that allowed it to move up and down six feet.

"End Game" is also memorable for the confrontation between X and Skinner. Mitch Pileggi recalls taking a few accidental shots to the groin in slamming Steven Williams against (and nearly through) the fake elevator wall. Williams suggested the dueling head-butts, saying there was a psychological as well as physical aspect to the encounter. The scene grew out of a need to have Scully discover where Mulder was, since only X knew. Finally, Carter simply told writer Frank Spotnitz, "Why can't we just have Skinner beat the information out of X?"

The weapon used by the pilot in this episode was built of aluminum and clear acrylic. No spring could be found powerful enough to eject the stiletto-like point fast enough, so the crew ran a rubber hose up Brian Thompson's sleeve and activated it pneumatically from off camera.

Fearful Symmetry

First aired: February 24, 1995

Written by
Steven DeJarnatt

Directed by
James Whitmore Jr.

Guest stars:
Charles Andre (Ray Floyd)
Jack Rader (Ed Meecham)
Jayne Atkinson (Willa Ambrose)
Lance Guest (Kyle Lang)
Bruce Harwood (Byers)
Tom Braidwood (Frohike)
Dean Haglund (Langly)
Garvin Cross (Red Head Kid)
Tom Glass (Trucker)
Jody St. Michael (Sophie)

Log line: Mulder and Scully investigate animal abductions from a zoo near a known UFO hot spot.

Principal setting: Fairfield, Idaho

Synopsis: An invisible force shatters windows, crumples cars, and sends a workman fatally flying. Later, an elephant suddenly appears in the road—43 miles from the zoo where it was safely locked up—and is found dying.

Mulder believes that somehow an invisible elephant did the damage. At the zoo he and Scully meet the chief of operations, Ed Meecham; Willa Ambrose, who's been brought in above Meecham; and Kyle Lang, from the Wild Again Organization, a group dedicated to liberating circus and zoo animals.

Mulder teleconferences with the Lone Gunmen, who say the zoo is near a major UFO hotspot and that no animal there has ever brought a pregnancy to term.

Scully, meanwhile, believes the W.A.O. is involved and tracks a member to the zoo, where, with a flash of light, the tiger is suddenly outside its cage and the man is mauled to death by a phantom attacker.

Mulder suggests they question Sophie, Ambrose's gorilla, who speaks using American Sign Language. The ape keeps repeating, "Light, afraid." At Mulder's urging, they perform an autopsy on the elephant, who—despite having never mated—has been pregnant. "That's impossible,"

Ambrose declares. Still, the same proves true with the tiger, who turns up across town and is killed by Meecham. Because of the incidents, the zoo is closed.

Mulder thinks the animals are being abducted by aliens and artificially inseminated, and that the embryos are harvested before they're returned. Though Sophie has never mated, when questioned she expresses fear that "Baby go flying light."

When Sophie is taken into custody for transfer back to her homeland, Ambrose goes to Kyle for help, who at first declines but later shows up at Sophie's cage and gets crushed to death. Mulder tails Meecham, who Ambrose paid to kidnap Sophie. When Mulder is locked in a room with the panic-stricken ape, she charges him. Dazed, he sees Sophie disappear in a blinding flash. Ambrose translates her final gestures as "Man Save Man."

Sophie turns up miles away and is killed by a car. Meecham and Ambrose are charged with manslaughter in Kyle's death, but Mulder is left to ponder the animal abductions, and Sophie's final message. Given the rate of extinction, he wonders, could it be an act of alien conservation? "Or," he muses, "in the simple words of a creature whose own future is uncertain, will man save man?"

This is the only time the Lone Gunmen group has appeared without Dean Haglund's "Langly" character.

Back story: There was some concern that the elephant would be reluctant to run toward the truck for the teaser sequence, but as it turned out the beast loved the truck, and the problem became keeping the pachyderm away from it.

Episode titles in the series are always obscure, and this one comes from William Blake's poem "The Tyger," and the lines, "Tyger, tyger burning bright/In the forests of the night:/What immortal hand or eye,/Could frame thy fearful symmetry?" The construction site where the tiger is shot is also named Blake Towers after the poet.

Dod Kalm

First aired: March 10, 1995

Written by
Howard Gordon and Alex Gansa

Directed by
Rob Bowman

Guest stars:
John Savage (Henry Trondheim)
Mar Anderson (Halverson)
Dmitry Chepovetsky (Lt. Harper)
David Cubitt (Captain Barclay)
Vladimir Kulich (Olafsson)
Claire Riley (Dr. Laskos)
Stephen Dimopolous (Ionesco)
John McConnach (Sailor)
Bob Metcalfe (Nurse)

Log line: Mulder and Scully fall victim to a mysterious force aboard a navy destroyer that causes rapid aging.

Principal setting: Norwegian Sea

Synopsis: Soldiers abandon a U.S. Navy destroyer, and 18 hours later the remaining crew members are found in a lifeboat, shriveled and aged. Mulder says the boat had been missing for 42 hours before the survivors were located, but when Scully sneaks in to see one of them, the man, who's supposed to be 28, "looks ninety."

Mulder says ships also disappeared in 1949 and 1963, with nine total events occurring in the same area along the 65th parallel. He believes there may be a wrinkle in time, with the government—based on the Philadelphia Experiment—trying to manipulate wormholes on Earth. "I'm betting the military never stopped the work it began fifty years ago," he suggests.

Journeying to Norway, the agents finding a ship's captain, Trondheim, who takes them to the destroyer. They crash into the vessel and board the ship, which exhibits corrosion as if 20 or 30 years have passed. "It's a ghost ship," Trondheim says, until they spot a sign that reads "Commissioned 1991." Mulder and Scully find mummified corpses, even as Trondheim's boat steams off, stranding them. Mulder believes time is speeding up on the ship.

Q: How many
languages
other than
English have
appeared in
The X-Files?

A: 13.
French
("Fresh
Bones"),
Creole
("Fresh
Bones"),
Russian ("The
Host"),
Italian
("Anasazi"),
Japanese
("Anasazi"),
Romanian
("The
Calusari"),
Transylvanian
("3"), Latin
("Die Hand
Die
Verletzt"),
Navajo
("Anasazi"),
Spanish
("Little
Green Men"),
German ("Die
Hand Die
Verletzt"),
and Norwegian
("Dod Kalm").

Trondheim's first mate is killed, and they find the ship's captain, Barclay, a 35-year-old man who soon dies of old age. Trondheim is then attacked by a pirate whaler, Olaffson, who shows no ill effects from the aging.

When Mulder, Scully, and Trondheim rest, they awaken to find themselves 30 years older. Scully theorizes that the process may be related to free radicals—reactive chemicals containing extra electrons that attack DNA and proteins, causing the body to age. She surmises that the ship may be drifting toward a meteor at the ocean's floor or in an iceberg which is acting like a giant battery that's causing them to age rapidly.

Mulder, however, soon realizes the real problem stems from contaminated water, with the only safe water in the sewage system, which has kept Olaffson alive. Scully finds they all have impossibly high concentrations of salt in their system, with Mulder—who had been seasick and thus dehydrated—worst off of all. "I think I just lapped George Burns," he jokes weakly.

Trondheim doesn't want to waste water on him, and locks himself with their remaining store in the sewage hold. He's drowned, however, when the ship shudders and ocean water floods the room.

Mulder bemoans their fate, while Scully tells him that from her near-death experience, "One thing I'm certain of, as certain as I am of this life: We have nothing to fear when it's over." He loses consciousness, as Scully writes down her final thoughts.

She awakens in a hospital, Navy SEALs having found them. A doctor was able to save them thanks to information in Scully's log. The ship, she's told, sank less than an hour after their rescue.

Back story: Although the producers and actors thought that this would be a respite after some truly demanding episodes—with just one location in which to shoot and a small cast to manage—

"Dod Kalm" turned out to be enormously difficult for everyone from a production standpoint.

The concept was built around the fact that, for a few weeks, the show had access to a Canadian navy destroyer that had been used in earlier episodes. Howard Gordon was asked to tailor a script around that setting. "'This'll be a great rest for everyone,'" he remembers Chris Carter telling him.

Unfortunately, filming on the ship was freezing cold and so cramped that it was difficult to set up certain shots, while people frequently banged their heads against the ceiling. In addition, the actors had to endure three to four hours of makeup for their aging sequences on certain days before the cameras could roll. "Everyone was exhausted as it was," muses Gordon, who wrote the episode with former partner Alex Gansa, so for the actors having to come in early for makeup on top of it was "about the worst thing I could have done to them."

As a result, there's an outtake where Gillian Anderson—in heavy makeup, flawlessly delivering her monologue about Scully's certainty that they have nothing to fear from the hereafter—concludes the sequence by saying she's sure of one thing: "Howard Gordon is a dead man."

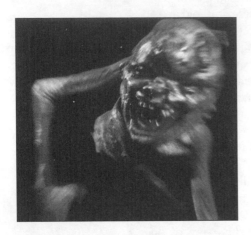

Humbug

First aired: March 31, 1995

Written by
Darin Morgan

Directed by
Kim Manners

Guest stars:
Jim Rose (Dr. Blockhead)
The Enigma (The Conundrum)
Michael Anderson (Mr. Nutt)
Wayne Grace (Sheriff Hamilton)
Vincent Schiavelli (Lanny)
Gordon Tipple (Hepcat Helm)
Alex Diakun (Curator)
John Payne (Glazebrook)
Alvin Law (Reverend)

Log line: Mulder and Scully investigate the bizarre death of a retired escape artist in a town populated by former circus and sideshow acts.

Principal setting: Gibsonton, Florida

Synopsis: Jerald Glazebrook, a reptile-skinned circus performer suffering from a condition known as ichthyosis, lounges in his pool after frolicking with his two decidedly normal kids. He is attacked by an unseen creature, filling the water with blood.

Mulder says the attack is similar to 48 other assaults over the last 28 years, and they attend Glazebrook's funeral—a raucous affair interrupted by the thrill-seeking Dr. Blockhead, who emerges from under the casket and pounds a nail into his chest. "I can't wait for the wake," Mulder quips.

The town is filled with sideshow performers, and one of them, Hepcat, tells the agents about the Fiji Mermaid, a legendary P. T. Barnum act that supposedly was just a dead monkey with a fish's tail sewn on. Mulder is intrigued, however, since the killer left tracks that appear to be simian.

Mulder and Scully check into a trailer-park motel, where they meet Mr. Nutt, the midget proprietor, and Lanny, a man with a congenital twin growing out of his side, who now spends his days drinking and toting luggage. That evening, Hepcat is attacked by the same creature.

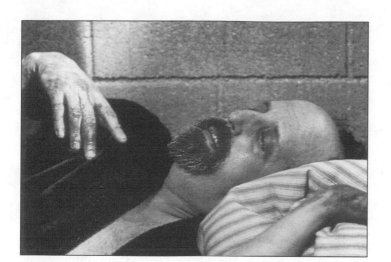

Jogging the next morning, Mulder sees a heavily tat-tooed man emerging from a stream, wolfing down a live fish. It's the Conundrum, a circus geek who eats any-thing.

Hepcat is found dead, and the killer must have entered through a window only a contortionist might have navigated. They question Blockhead, and Scully checks out the local museum. Scully then discovers that the sheriff was actually once Jim Jim the Dog-Faced Boy, but when they find him digging in his backyard, nothing sinister is involved. Mr. Nutt, meanwhile, is grabbed through his doggie door and killed, with one of Blockhead's pins found in his palm.

The suspect surprises even Scully, who'd expected something more "exotic." When they bring Blockhead in to jail, however, they find that Lanny—sleeping off one of his binges—has been attacked, and that it's actually his twin, Leonard, who's been inadvertently committing the murders, somehow disjoining himself from Lanny's body. "I don't think he knows he is harming anyone," Lanny says sadly. "He's merely seeking . . . another brother."

Mulder and Scully chase the scurrying Leonard into a fun house, but he escapes to the trailer park, attacking the Conundrum. When the agents arrive the Conundrum lies there unharmed, rubbing his stomach contentedly.

Lanny passes away, and Leonard can't be found. Spoofing David Duchovny's budding sex-symbol image, Blockhead laments the day when everyone will look "just like him," as Mulder unwittingly strikes a heroic pose. "Imagine going through your whole life looking like *that*," he says with disgust.

Gillian Anderson actu-ally ate at least one live cricket during the filming of this episode, to the aston-ishment of cast and crew.

Blockhead and the Conundrum, meanwhile, motor off into the sunset, the latter looking a bit indigested. It is, he tells Mulder, speaking for the first time in the episode, "probably something I ate."

Back story: Undoubtedly bizarre, this foray into dark comedy grew out of a suggestion by Glen Morgan to his brother Darin to do an episode about circus freaks. Darin watched a tape of the Jim Rose Circus, casting Rose and the Enigma (neither of whom had acted before) in key roles. After that, the extras casting folks "beat the bushes," as director Kim Manners put it, to find the other characters featured.

Though writers usually only stay through the prep phase, Darin Morgan remained throughout filming to make sure the hour captured his vision. Manners—who'd directed only one of *The X-Files* previously—admits to being taken aback by the notion of doing a comedic version, which Carter (ever fond of baseball analogies) has likened to throwing the show's audience a knuckleball. Whatever the pitch, "Humbug" proved a major hit with fans.

More *Twin Peaks* associations: Michael Anderson appeared in *Twin Peaks* as did David Duchovny.

The Calusari

First aired: April 14, 1995

Written by
Sara Charno

Directed by
Michael Vejar

Guest stars:
Joel Palmer (Charlie/Michael Holvey)
Lilyan Chauvin (Golda)
Helene Clarkson (Maggie Holvey)
Ric Reid (Steve Holvey)
Oliver and Jeremy Isaac Wildsmith
  (Teddy Holvey)
Christine Willes (Agent Kosseff)
Bill Dow (Dr. Charles Burk)
Kay E. Kuter (Head Calusari)
Jacqueline Dandeneau (Nurse Castor)
Bill Croft (Calusari #2)
Campbell Lane (Calusari #3)
George Josef (Calusari #4)

Log line: A young boy's unusual death leads Mulder and Scully to a superstitious old woman and her grandson, who may be possessed by evil.

Principal setting: Arlington, Virginia

Synopsis: An unseen presence unhooks a two-year-old child from a restraining device at a kiddie park and—using a helium balloon as bait—leads him across a miniature train track, where the child is killed. While the parents react with shock, his eight-year-old brother, Charlie, looks on dispassionately.

Three months later, Mulder analyzes a photo of the event, which with digital enhancement shows what looks like a figure pulling the balloon—"some kind of poltergeist activity," he concludes.

Mulder meets with the parents. The father, Steve, is a State Department official who met his wife, Maggie, in Romania. They insist the boy's death was an accident, but Scully sees Charlie's grandmother drawing a swastika on his hand, and the woman yells at her daughter, "You marry a devil! You have devil child!"

Scully finds documentation of the boys' recurrent illnesses and suggests this may be a case of Munchausen by Proxy—where a parent or caretaker induces symptoms in a child. Under questioning, Steve admits things have been strange since his mother-in-law came to live with them and says that the woman both dotes on Charlie and seems to fear him. Steve agrees to take Charlie to a social worker, upsetting both Maggie and her mother. As he prepares to leave with the boy, however, the garage door-opener catches his tie, strangling him as the boy screams.

A police investigation finds dead roosters in the old woman's room, while Mulder notices a strange ash in the garage and is told it's Vibuti—Holy Ash, something that materializes out of thin air. The grandmother shuttles the boy off with three dark-suited men, who perform a strange ritual, with the image of Charlie appearing in the mist, cursing them in Romanian. When the social worker arrives and they find Charlie dazed, Maggie orders the men to leave.

Mulder recognizes mugwort, an herb recognized since medieval times in Europe as a charm against evil. During the exorcism, the Calusari also employ dragon's blood, which is actually a plant; it is named for its color.

The grandmother locks herself in the room with Charlie, but objects fly around and she's knocked to the ground. Charlie stands over her, dropping the two roosters, suddenly very much alive, who peck her to death. Ash is again found at the scene.

Mulder questions the three men, who are Romanian holy men, known as the Calusari. They say they are trying to cleanse the house of an evil that is "still here," one that has been there through history and "doesn't care if it kills one boy or a million men."

Under questioning by the social worker Charlie shrieks that he didn't kill his grandmother, that "Michael did it." Maggie gasps, saying Charlie never knew about his stillborn twin, and that her mother wanted to perform a ritual of separation to divide their souls lest the world of the dead follow the boy. Charlie has a seizure and is hospitalized, but Michael appears, attacking the nurse with a metal rod and asking his mother to take him home.

When the agents see the two leaving Scully pursues them while Mulder goes for help, recruiting the Calusari. As they perform an exorcism at the hospital, Scully enters Maggie's house, finding her pinned to the ceiling. Just as Michael is about to stab Scully, the Calusari complete their ritual, and in a blink, he's gone, leaving nothing but ash.

"Be careful," an elder Calusari warns Mulder, speaking of the evil that was within Charlie. "It knows you." In voice-over, Mulder says the case remains unsolved.

Back story: The producers agonized about the teaser sequence, which involved the death of a very small child, as well as the general darkness of the whole hour, since Maggie loses her mother, husband, and one of her sons.

Again, part of the action was structured to incorporate an interesting moment Chris Carter had thought up outside the context of this episode—in this case, a garage-door opener hanging. The producer did have to compromise with Fox's standards department, however, shortening the sequence and obscuring the father's face so as to soften the impact of the strangulation.

There are clearly echoes of *The Exorcist* and *The Omen* to be found here, among them the scene where the boy speaks in a language not his own. For those rusty in their Romanian, when Charlie stands over his grandmother before her death he says, "You are too late to stop us."

Christine Willes reprises her role as an FBI social worker, having previously appeared in "Irresistible."

The material oozing out of the walls during the exorcism scene is called amrith, a "honey-like, viscous liquid" manifested during an exorcism. Also mentioned is Vibuti, or Holy Ash, supposedly materialized out of thin air during a paranormal event. These physical displays of spiritual phenomena are commonly cited in spiritualist literature.

F. Emasculata

First aired: April 28, 1995

Written by
Chris Carter and Howard Gordon

Directed by
Rob Bowman

Guest stars:
Charles Martin Smith (Dr. Osborne)
John Tench (Steve)
Angelo Vacco (Angelo Garza)
Morris Paynch (Dr. Simon Auerbach)
John Pyper-Ferguson (Paul)
Dean Norris (U.S. Marshal Tapia)
Mitch Pileggi (AD Walter Skinner)
William B. Davis (Cigarette-Smoking Man)
Lynda Boyd (Elizabeth)
Alvin Sanders (Bus Driver)
Kim Kondrashoff (Bobby Torrence)
Chilton Crane (Mother at Bus Station)
Bill Rowat (Dr. Torrence)
Jude Zachary (Winston)

Log line: When a plaguelike illness kills 10 men inside a prison facility, Scully is called to the quarantine area while Mulder tracks two escapees.

Principal setting: Cumberland Prison, Virginia

Synopsis: A scientist, Dr. Robert Torrence, finds the carcass of a wild boar with grotesque boils on it while collecting insects in the Costa Rican rain forest. One of the sores bursts open, splattering him with a puslike substance. We next see the doctor radio for help, himself now covered with the sores. Rangers find him as vultures pick at his body.

A convict, also named Robert Torrence, receives a package with a bloody pig's leg in it. Eighteen hours later he too is covered with boils, as white-suited specialists in quarantine garb examine him.

Realizing something strange is happening, two of the convicts, Paul and Steve, escape. Mulder and Scully are sent in to join the manhunt but are suspicious when they see the quarantine conditions.

Scully is given few answers by a scientist, Dr. Osborne, who says he's with the Center for Disease Control and that 14 men have been infected with "a flulike illness," 10 of them dying. Scully noses around on her own, discovering that the dead men's bodies are being incinerated. One of the pustules bursts onto Osborne, who recoils in horror. Scully learns the package was sent by drug manu-facturer Pinck Pharmaceuticals and finds a dead insect in one of the sores.

Mulder, meanwhile, pursues the convicts, who have taken refuge at the house of Paul's girlfriend, Elizabeth. Steve is already ill and inadvertently infects her before agents crash in, finding Steve dead and Paul already gone.

Infected himself, Osborne admits he's not with the CDC but works for Pinck, which was financing explo-ration of new rain forest species and received samples of the parasitoid *F. Emasculata*—a bug carrying the disease-causing parasite, which attacks the immune system, the larvae burrowing into a host when the pustules erupt.

Mulder tells Skinner they must warn the public, but Cigarette Smoking Man says they must "control the dis-ease by controlling the information" and preventing panic. When Mulder says he wants no part of it, he's told he already is.

Osborne also tells Scully she must try to warn people, saying, "Don't believe for a second that this is an isolated incident." When Scully leaves to test her own blood she returns to find Osborne among the bodies being inciner-ated. "No one will corroborate your story," one of the medical workers notes coldly, adding, "Just be glad things are under control."

Mulder questions Elizabeth but has no answer when she wonders why people aren't being alerted to the con-tagion. She finally admits that Paul has boarded a bus for Toronto, while Scully tells Mulder that with the other evidence destroyed only the convict can help them get the truth out.

Mulder boards the bus, but when Paul notices him he takes a boy hostage, one of his sores bulging near the youth's face. Paul lets everyone else off, but as Mulder questions him a shot rings out. Paul lies dead, and in a heartbeat the quarantine personnel rush in, whisking Mulder away.

Though Mulder wants to go public, Skinner says to leave it alone. "You never had a chance," he says. Because the scientist and prisoner had the same name, the controlled experiment with the virus can be dis-missed as a mere postal error. "We can't prove a thing, Mulder," Scully notes. "They made sure of it."

"Watch your back," Skinner warns them ominously. "This is just the beginning."

Q: What does the "F" in "F. Emasculata" stand for?

A: Faciphaga. The insect that serves as the vector for the infection is properly termed *Faciphaga emasculata*.

Angelo Vacco,
who plays
"Angelo
Garza," is a
production
assistant in
the offices of
Ten Thirteen
Productions in
Los Angeles;
Chris Carter
wrote the part
for him.

Mulder and
Scully use
their cellular
phones more
often in this
episode than
any other.
During Seasons
One and Two,
they usually
used a Nokia
101 or 121. The
programmable
alphanumeric
face came in
handy in
"Blood," when
the crew pro-
grammed
Mulder's cellu-
lar display to
read "All Done,
Bye Bye."

Back story: In the scene where the escaped convict is holding the boy at gunpoint on the bus, makeup effects supervisor Toby Lindala had to operate a handheld device—with a tube leading to the makeup applied to the actor—in order to make the sores on the felon's cheek bubble outward. "I was jammed underneath one of the bus seats with these extras basically stepping on my head," he says.

The producers debated whether to delay the airdate because of its proximity to the release of the similarly themed movie *Outbreak* but ultimately decided that the episode stood on its own.

For those interested, Mulder gives his badge number, JTT047101111, to obtain pay phone call records from a phone-company operator.

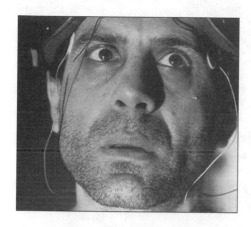

Soft Light

First aired: May 5, 1995

Written by
Vince Gilligan

Directed by
James Contner

Guest stars:
Tony Shalhoub (Dr. Banton)
Kevin McNulty (Dr. Davey)
Kate Twa (Det. Ryan)
Nathaniel Deveaux (Det. Barron)
Steven Williams (Mr. X)
Guyle Frazier (Barney)
Forbes Angus (Govt. Scientist)
Donna Yamamoto (Night Nurse)
Robert Rozen (Doctor)
Steve Bacic (2nd Officer)
Craig Brunanski (Security Guard)

Log line: An experiment in dark matter turns a scientist's shadow into a form of instant death.

Principal setting: Richmond, Virginia

Synopsis: An executive lounging in his hotel room hears a man knocking at another door. When the business-man goes to the door he makes contact with the shadow, which seemingly drags him into the floor. Panicked, the man who cast the shadow, Dr. Chester Banton, rushes down the hall.

Scully agrees to help Detective Kelly Ryan—a student of hers at the Academy—who's investigating three cases of apparent abduction. Mulder notices a strange smudge on the carpet also found at the other two crime scenes.

Checking the second victim's house they find a train ticket and note showing that the man also came in on the train. They instruct Ryan to send police to the station, and two officers encounter Banton. "Stay away from me," he warns, but the two approach and are vaporized when they touch his shadow.

Examining security camera tape from the days of the other disappearances, Mulder notices Banton, blowing up the picture to see a logo for Polarity Magnetics—where the first victim worked—on his jacket.

At Polarity they meet Dr. Davey, who says Banton has been missing for five weeks after suffering an accident experimenting with dark matter using a particle accelerator. Banton was locked in the chamber during a test, burning an image in the wall similar to the images at the other scenes.

Back at the train station Mulder observes that soft light casts no shadows. They spot Banton and corner him, with Mulder alertly shooting the lights out as Scully nears his

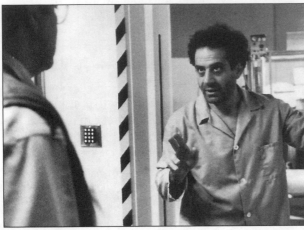

shadow. Held in a psychiatric hospital, Banton tells them his shadow is like a black hole, reducing matter to pure energy. The government is after him, he fears, wanting to perform a "brain suck" to learn what he knows and willing to kill to obtain it, which risks unleashing the shadow force. "If I die, there could be nothing left to tether this thing," he says.

Mr. X's weapon of choice here and in "One Breath" is a Sig Sauer P228. A highly compact model, it has the stopping power required for quick and dirty work in basements and in the dark.

The police, with Ryan's help, elbow the agents out, planning to move Banton to county jail. Mulder contacts X for help, but he refuses, pointing out that he was exposed to Scully and Skinner before and doesn't want to put himself in jeopardy. When Mulder says he can trust them, X replies, "Dead men can't keep promises. The next time the blood and regret could be yours."

That night, however, X shows up at the hospital with two "paramedics" saying he's there to transfer Banton. As they strap him down, emergency lights flicker on, and the two men are vaporized. Discretion being the better part of valor, X allows Banton to flee.

Banton returns to Polarity, asking Davey to help destroy the thing before the government can find him. Ryan seeks to stop him, and Banton reluctantly steps toward her, sucking her into the shadow force. Locked in the chamber, Banton discovers that Davey is part of the conspiracy, saying he's "lightning in a bottle." As Davey calls to alert his bosses that he has Banton a shot rings out, and we see X's face through the portal.

Mulder and Scully arrive to find videotape showing Banton in the particle chamber disappearing, but Mulder knows something is awry. He goes to X, saying that X used him to find Banton and that Mulder wants nothing more to do with him. "You're choosing a dangerous time to go it alone," X counters, stressing that he didn't kill Banton.

At Ryan's funeral, Mulder tells Scully that Davey is missing—and maybe it wasn't Banton they saw in the accelerator at all. Elsewhere, X approaches a man in a lab coat. "We'll be studying this man for a long time," the scientist says, as we see Banton hooked to electrodes, half-crazed, being subjected to a flashing white light over and over again.

Back story: The original concept and teleplay came from Vince Gilligan—whose credits include the feature *Wilder Napalm*—and represents one of the few scripts to come from outside *The X-Files* staff.

Still, substantial revisions were made, particularly as the story pertains to the character of X, who wasn't featured at all in the original draft. Once it was decided that the scientist's fear of a "brain suck" should be more than just paranoia, the writers needed a means of conveying him into the hands of those who wished to study him, and X seemed to be a natural choice. "It had been a long time since X had done anything," says Frank Spotnitz, who was among those who worked on the rewrite, "and the character really needed to grow." The episode showcases X's ruthlessness and dedication to his own agenda, in contrast to the more benevolent presence of Deep Throat.

Bang, bang . . . the guns of *The X-Files.* In the pilot, Mulder carried a Taurus 92 automatic, firing 9mm rounds. Scully carried a Bernadelli 7.65. Mulder later switched to a Glock 19 and Scully changed to a Walther PPK 7.65. In the first few episodes of the second season, they were both carrying Sig Sauer weapons; Mulder carried a Sig Sauer 226 and Scully a 228. They are now carrying the FBI standard weapons, Smith and Wesson 1076. These guns are no longer manufactured.

Our Town

First aired: May 12, 1995

Written by
Frank Spotnitz

Directed by
Rob Bowman

Guest stars:
John Milford (Walter Chaco)
Caroline Kava (Doris Kearns)
Gary Grubbs (Sherriff Tom Arens)
Robin Mossley (Dr. Randolph)
John MacLaren (George Kearns)
Hrothgar Mathews (Mental Patient)
Gabrielle Miller (Paula Gray)
Timothy Webber (Jess Harold)
Robert Moloney (Worker)
Carrie Cain Sparks (Maid)

Log line: Mulder and Scully investigate a murder in a small Southern town and its strange secrets surrounding a chicken processing plant.

Principal setting: Dudley, Arkansas

Synopsis: George Kearns, a middle-aged man, is led into the woods by a young woman, Paula. Suddenly, he's surrounded by lights, turning to see a man in a tribal mask, and screaming as a ceremonial axe comes flashing down.

Kearns was a federal inspector who was about to suggest closing down Chaco Chicken, a local processing plant at the heart of the community, alleging major health violations. Mulder is intrigued by his disappearance, particularly in light of legends about foxfire and a 12-foot burn mark found in a nearby field.

The local sheriff says Kearns was a philanderer who probably chased some woman out of town, and his wife concurs. Later, however, Paula starts to hallucinate on the assembly line, taking the plant manager hostage at knife-point before the sheriff shoots her.

Scully wants to perform an autopsy, so the agents get permission from Paula's grandfather, Mr. Chaco, who founded the plant and built the town. Shockingly, Paula's personnel file shows she was born in 1948, meaning she was actually 47 years old. In addition, she's suffering from the same extremely rare fatal disease, Creutzfeldt-Jacob, that Kearns had.

THE TRUTH
IS OUT
THERE
223

Mulder decides to drag the river, and searchers find remnants of nine headless skeletons, one of them belonging to Kearns. The bones are smoothed at the ends, as if "boiled in a pot," Mulder says, noting that 87 people have disappeared in the area over 59 years and that the polished bones suggest cannibalism, which in some tribes has been practiced with the belief it prolongs life. Kearns's rare disease, therefore, may have been contracted by eating him. "Many religions believe that the reward for eating flesh is eternal life," Mulder observes.

Mulder and Scully find the town's birth notices destroyed. Kearns's wife calls saying she fears Chaco, just as the man in the tribal mask appears behind her. Scully goes to help her, while Mulder visits Chaco's house, finding a display case filled with human heads.

Chaco captures Scully, taking her, bound and gagged, to a bonfire ceremony attended by numerous townsfolk. He argues with the plant manager, but they behead him, preparing to do the same to Scully.

Mulder rushes to the scene, shooting the executioner, who's revealed to be the sheriff. The plant is closed, and though it's unknown how many residents took part in the cannibalism, 27 have become fatally ill with Kearns's disease. The Chaco Chicken slogan—"Good People, Good Food"—takes on an ironic twist.

Chaco, Scully notes in voice-over, spent six months during World War II with the Jale tribe in New Guinea, "whose cannibalistic practices have been long suspected but never proven." He was 93 years old, and his remains "still have not been found." Meanwhile, a workman finds a wisp of gray human hair in the chicken feed, as the birds peck away hungrily.

Back story: Writer Frank Spotnitz began with the premise of cannibalism in a small town, inspired by his fondness for the Spencer Tracy movie *Bad Day at Black Rock*, which also dealt with a town hiding a terrible (if slightly more mundane) secret.

Spotnitz came across an article in UCLA's research library about salamanders getting sick from eating other salamanders, then turned to his brother, a neurologist, who suggested the rare disease that the townspeople contract from eating the chicken plant inspector. "It's very convenient," Spotnitz says of his brother's vocation. "He's been extremely helpful."

Interestingly, some of the material regarding cannibal-

This is only the second episode in which Mulder has killed someone.

Despite rumors to the contrary, the severed heads in the trophy case belonging to Walter Chaco are NOT portraits of various real people. They were made by the makeup department.

istic tribes—and the discovery of rounded human bones
that appeared to have been boiled in pots—relates to
research Spotnitz had done about the Anasazi, the native
people Chris Carter refers to in the subsequent episode.
The name Chaco Chicken, in fact, was derived from
Chaco Canyon, New Mexico, where that tribe was
believed to have lived and such bones were found.

Anasazi

First aired: May 19, 1995

Written by
Chris Carter; story by
David Duchovny and Chris Carter

Directed by
R.W. Goodwin

Guest stars:
Byron Chief Moon (Father)
Bernie Coulson (The Thinker)
Peter Donat (Bill Mulder)
Nicholas Lea (Agent Alex Krycek)
Mitch Pileggi (AD Walter Skinner)
Paul McLean (Agent Kautz)
Floyd "Red Crow" Westerman (Albert Hosteen)
Renae Morriseau (Josephine Doane)
Aurelio Dinunzio (Antonio)
Willam B. Davis (Cigarette-Smoking Man)
Dean Haglund (Langly)
Tom Braidwood (Frohike)
Bruce Harwood (Byers)
Michael David Simms (Senior Agent)
Ken Camroux (2nd Senior Agent)
Mitch Davies (Stealth Man)

Log line: Mulder and Scully's lives are jeopardized when an amateur computer hacker gains access to secret government files providing evidence of UFOs.

Principal settings: Washington, D.C.; New Mexico

Synopsis: A strong earthquake jolts New Mexico, and a young Native American man finds something shiny and metallic in the earth, along with a desiccated corpse that looks not quite human. "It should be returned," his grandfather, a tribal elder, tells him. "They will be coming."

Separately, a hacker named the Thinker breaks into the Defense Department computer system, prompting calls to Japanese, German, and Italian government officials saying the MJ documents have been penetrated. The Cigarette-Smoking Man says upon learning of the security breach, "Gentlemen, that is the phone call I never wanted to get."

Mulder is contacted by the Lone Gunmen, who claim they're being pursued by a multinational black ops unit named Garnet because the Thinker has obtained files containing everything the Defense Department has compiled about UFOs since the '40s. A shot rings out, and Mulder is shocked to discover one of his neighbors has gone crazy, killing her husband of 30 years.

Mulder gets a digital copy of the files from the Thinker, only to discover they're in Navajo, which was used to encrypt messages during World War II. Mulder behaves strangely, mouthing off to Skinner. Meanwhile, Scully is concerned about Mulder's strange behavior. When Skinner asks Mulder about him possibly receiving the missing files, Mulder hauls off and slugs him. Scully meets with superiors at the FBI who warn her that Mulder is in danger of being dismissed, and her with him.

The Cigarette-Smoking Man visits Mulder's father on "pressing business," telling him the documents have been breached. When Mr. Mulder asks if the Cigarette-Smoking Man can protect his son, he simply says, "I've protected him this long, haven't I?"

Mulder tries to summon X, but his father calls saying he must see him right away. Mulder's father begins to tell him about his work at the State Department, but when he steps into the bathroom, he is fatally shot by Krycek, who is hiding in the shower.

Mulder calls Scully, who tells him someone tried to kill her at his apartment but also warns him that with his erratic behavior, he looks responsible for his father's death. He arrives at her place sick and weakened, waking to find both Scully and his gun gone.

Checking the plumbing at Mulder's apartment, Scully discovers that someone had been doping the water, which explains his odd behavior as well as the recent murder. Mulder, meanwhile, encounters Krycek and is about to kill him when Scully shows up, shooting Mulder to prevent him from committing murder.

Mulder awakens in New Mexico, where Scully introduces him to Albert Hosteen, a Navajo code talker during World War II. Scully plans to return to Washington to meet with Skinner and tells Mulder he must learn what's in the MJ files—that her name and Duane Barry's are among the recent entries, having "something to do with a test."

Albert mentions a tribe, the Anasazi, who disappeared 600 years earlier—abducted, he thinks, "by visitors who

X

The Thinker, unlike Mulder and Scully, uses a Macintosh computer.
Throughout most of the series, Mulder and Scully have used IBM clones in their offices. In the field, Scully uses a Mac Powerbook 540C. In fact, she was using one before they were in general release. At one point, the Powerbook in the offices of Ten Thirteen in Canada was the only one in that country.

come here still." His grandson leads Mulder to the alien corpse site, even as the Cigarette-Smoking Man calls, warning Mulder against taking things at face value and saying his father authorized the project.

Mulder finds piles of what appear to be alien bodies in a train refrigeration car. He calls Scully, who's found references in the files to Axis power scientists granted amnesty after the war to perform experiments on humans, called "merchandise." Mulder notices a small-pox vaccination, coming to a sickening realization. "Oh my God, Scully," he mutters. "What have they done?"

The Cigarette-Smoking Man and a contingent of soldiers arrive by helicopter, searching the boxcar but unable to locate Mulder. "Nothing vanishes without a trace," the Cigarette-Smoking Man says, echoing Albert's words, setting the train on fire and flying away as flames dart out of it.

To be continued . . .

Back story: Carter has said that the Southwestern United States is about the only area that can't easily be duplicated in and around Vancouver. To create the Southwestern setting, the producers painted a rock quarry red with 1,600 gallons of red paint, combining that with second-unit composite shots taken to in essence re-create arid New Mexico within an hour's drive of lush Vancouver.

Veteran actor Peter Donat, who plays Mulder's father, is the son of Robert Donat, who starred in such classic films as *Goodbye, Mr. Chips* and *The 39 Steps*.

The Majestic 12 documents are almost as famous among UFO buffs as the Roswell incident. Supposedly documenting the existence of a secret organization dedicated to the concealment of extraterrestrial contacts, they purport to have been compiled for Harry Truman soon after the Roswell crash. Arguments rage about their provenance and authenticity, but perhaps the most telling link to "Anasazi" is the international character of the alleged conspirators.

THE EPISODES

season ③

The Blessing Way

First aired: September 22, 1995

Written by
Chris Carter

Directed by
R. W. Goodwin

Guest stars:
Floyd "Red Crow" Westerman (Albert Hosteen)
Tim Michael (Albert's son)
Dakota House (Eric Hosteen)
Mitch Davies (Camouflage Man)
William B. Davis (Cigarette-Smoking Man)
Michael David Simms (Senior agent)
Mitch Pileggi (AD Skinner)
Don Williams (1st elder)
Stanley Walsh (2nd elder)
John Moore (3rd elder)
John Neville (Well-Manicured Man)
Sheila Larken (Mrs. Scully)
Melinda McGraw (Melissa Scully)
Tom Braidwood (Frohike)
Peter Donat (Bill Mulder)
Jerry Hardin (Deep Throat)
Benita Ha (Tour guide)
Ernie Foort (Security guard)
Forbes Angus (MD)
Alf Humphreys (Dr. Pomerantz)
Rebecca Toolan (Mrs. Mulder)
Nicholas Lea (Agent Krycek)
Lenno Britos (Hispanic man)
Ian Victor (Minister)

Log line: With the Cigarette-Smoking Man pursuing the secret files that prove the existence of alien visitation and experimentation—and Mulder still missing—Scully finds her own life and career in jeopardy.

Principal Settings: New Mexico; Washington, D.C.

Synopsis: In voice-over Albert Hosteen—the tribal elder Scully had brought Mulder to in the previous episode, "Anasazi," to decipher the encrypted MJ Documents—relates an ancient Native American proverb "that something lives only as long as the last person who remembers it," warning that some would seek to change history by eliminating those who know it.

Suddenly, the Cigarette-Smoking Man and soldiers burst into Albert's home. "I want Mulder and I want those files!" he demands, as the soldiers brutally club both Albert and his grandson. Scully arrives once they've left, going to the boxcar where Mulder was last seen and finding only smoldering wreckage. Soon after, her car is stopped by troops, who take her printed copy of the files, which document the government's knowledge of alien visitors.

Back in Washington, Scully is told she is to be suspended for "direct disobedience." Believing Mulder to be dead, she tells Skinner the men who killed him and his father won't be punished. When Skinner says they will, she says icily, "With all due respect, sir, I think you overestimate your position in the chain of command." Scully returns to her desk, only to find the DAT tape containing the secret files gone.

The Cigarette-Smoking Man meets with other shadowy men in a private club, assuring them that the matter of the missing files is being handled and that the media attention will amount to "nothing more than a few scattered obituaries."

Scully visits her mother, breaking into tears. "I've made a terrible mistake," she tells her. "Dad would be so ashamed of me." She's later visited by the Lone Gunmen's Frohike, who shows her a news clipping about the Thinker—the computer hacker who first accessed the files—who has been murdered, execution style.

Back in New Mexico, buzzards lead the Native Americans to Mulder, who's found buried under debris and badly injured, having escaped the boxcar and stayed alive in underground tunnels. "Only the holy people can save the FBI man's life now," Albert says. "He is in their hands." In dreams Mulder is visited by Deep Throat, who urges him to go back and finish his work; and his father, who—echoing Albert's words—says, "You are the memory, Fox. It lives in you. If you were to die now the truth will die, and only the lies survive us." In his dream state Mulder also sees an image of the aliens in the boxcar, being killed by a cyanide canister.

Returning to the FBI office to tell Skinner about the Thinker's death, Scully is scanned by a metal detector, which registers a small implant under the skin at the base of her neck. Removed by a doctor, the device looks like a tiny computer chip.

After three days, Mulder rouses. "Like a rising sun, I sensed in him a rebirth," Albert notes. Scully confides to her sister, Melissa, about the chip, and Melissa encourages her to try and access the memory of her abduction. Scully, however, resists the hypnotherapy, returning to her apartment to see Skinner suspiciously coming out of it and hurriedly speeding off. In her own dreams Scully senses Mulder is still alive. She awakens with a start.

At the funeral service for Mulder's father, Scully encounters a distinguished older gentleman seen earlier with the Cigarette-Smoking Man. The Well-Manicured Man warns her that she's in real danger of being killed, perhaps by someone she knows. The man adds that his colleagues—a "consortium representing global interests"—are "acting impulsively." When she asks what his business is, he merely replies, "We predict the future, and the best way to predict the future is to invent it."

Mulder's mother returns from the funeral to find Fox waiting for her. At home, Scully receives a call from Melissa but, due to the Well-Manicured Man's warning, she is wary when she tries to return the call and doesn't reach her. Deciding to go meet her sister instead of waiting at the apartment, Scully encounters Skinner, who takes her to Mulder's apartment so they can talk. Not trusting him, Scully pulls her weapon as they enter and holds Skinner at gunpoint, while Melissa arrives at Scully's place and—in a case of mistaken identity—is shot by Agent Krycek and another operative working for the Cigarette-Smoking Man.

"I came here to give you something," Skinner tells Scully, who eyes him skeptically. "I've got the digital tape." At that moment footsteps are heard outside the door, and Skinner uses the distraction to draw his own gun. It's a stalemate.

To be continued . . .

Back story: Certain Navajo scholars had alerted the producers to some cultural inaccuracies depicted in "Anasazi," so Chris Carter was invited to attend a Navajo night chant and the Native American Church Peyote Ritual in preparing "Blessing Way," which is named for an actual chant. Carter considers attending the ritual a great honor but does admit jokingly that it was "excruciatingly painful to sit on the ground, Native American–style, for eight hours" during the ceremony.

Continuing *The X-Files* mythology and taking it in bold new directions, "Blessing Way" makes Skinner a much more active character without necessarily changing his fundamental role. Skinner is acting to defend his agents, Carter says, adding, "He's not a member of the X-Files team in any way," but rather merely trying to right what he perceives as an injustice.

The episode contains several interesting nuances relating to the series both on and offscreen—such as having Krycek, played by Nicholas Lea, shoot Melissa Scully, played by his real-life girlfriend Melinda McGraw. Mulder also talks in his sleep about wanting sunflower seeds, having discussed inheriting his father's taste for them in the second-season episode, "Aubrey."

Another startling moment has Mulder, in his near-death ruminations, seeing the alien/human hybrids killed in the boxcar by cyanide gas—echoing the Nazi atrocities committed during World War II. "These are Nazi scientists," Carter notes. "Why wouldn't they behave as they behaved really?"

The producers considered it a coup casting John Neville, whose credits include the title role in *The Adventures of Baron Munchausen,* as the latest in the show's string of uniquely named characters, the Well-Manicured Man.

A tag at the end of the episode reads, "In Memoriam. Larry Wells. 1946–1995." Wells was a costume designer on the series.

Paper Clip

First aired: September 29, 1995

Written by
Chris Carter

Directed by
Rob Bowman

Guest stars:
Mitch Pileggi (AD Skinner)
Sheila Larken (Mrs. Scully)
Robert Lewis (ER Doctor)
Melinda McGraw (Melissa Scully)
Bruce Harwood (Byers)
Tom Braidwood (Frohike)
Dean Haglund (Langly)
William B. Davis (Cigarette-Smoking Man)
John Neville (Well-Manicured Man)
Don Williams (1st elder)
Stanley Walsh (2nd elder)
John Moore (3rd elder)
Walter Gotell (Klemper)
Martin Evans (Factotum)
Peta Brookstone (ICU nurse)
Floyd "Red Crow" Westerman (Albert Hosteen)
Nicolas Lea (Agent Krycek)
Lenno Britos (Hispanic man)
Rebecca Toolan (Mrs. Mulder)

Log line: Mulder and Scully seek evidence of alien experimentation by Nazi war criminals while Skinner tries to bargain with the Cigarette-Smoking Man for their lives.

Principal Settings: Washington, D.C.; West Virginia

Synopsis: Albert Hosteen speaks in voice-over about the birth of a white buffalo—"a powerful omen" in Native American lore, he says, meaning that "great changes were coming."

Scully and Skinner remain squared off at gunpoint. The figure at the door turns out to be Mulder, who enters with his gun drawn. Now it's a three-way standoff, and Skinner reluctantly puts down his weapon. When Skinner says he has the files, Mulder tells him, "Your cigarette smoking friend killed my father for that tape." Skinner insists the tape is "the only leverage we've got to bring these men to justice."

Scully's mother goes to the hospital, finding Melissa in an induced coma. Elsewhere, Mulder and Scully bring a picture he'd found of his father taken in the early 1970s to the Lone Gunmen, who identify a man shown with him as Victor Klemper—one of several Nazi scientists allowed to escape to the United States after World War II in exchange for their research knowledge, under a secret deal dubbed Operation Paper Clip. That program, they add, was supposed to have been scrapped in the '50s. At that point Frohike enters, telling Scully about her sister's condition.

The Well-Manicured Man and his cronies grill the Cigarette-Smoking Man, saying his henchmen have committed "a horrible mistake" in shooting the wrong woman and demanding that he produce the missing tape. They'll have it, he assures them, by the next day.

Mulder and Scully visit Klemper, who cryptically advises them to journey to a mining company in West Virginia. He then calls the Well-Manicured Man to inform him about the visit. "Mulder is alive," the Well-Manicured Man announces. Knowing that the hospital is being watched and that Scully is in danger, Mulder has Albert carry a message to Scully's mother, and he prays over Melissa.

Skinner meets with the Cigarette-Smoking Man, saying he may have located the tape, cagily adding that it could fall into the wrong hands. "Do you want to work a deal? Is that what this is? I don't work deals," the Cigarette-Smoking Man snarls. Skinner merely says he should know of "certain potentialities."

At the mining site, Mulder and Scully find countless cabinets of medical files hidden there, including one for Scully and another for Mulder's missing sister, Samantha, with Mulder noticing that her name has been pasted over his own. Suddenly, the lights go out, and what appears to be diminutive alien figures rush past Scully. Mulder ventures outside, seeing a massive spacecraft hovering over the facility. Scully observes what could be an alien silhouette, but in a flash of light, it's gone.

At that moment several armed men arrive, firing at Mulder as they chase him back into the mine. "We've got a small army outside," he says, before the pair escape through a secret door. Meeting at a cafe, Skinner tells them he wants to trade the tape for their safety and reinstatement to the bureau. Mulder says they need the evidence to expose the truth and learn why his father was killed, why his sister disappeared, and why Scully was abducted. "Is that answer worth your lives?" Skinner asks.

"It's obviously worth killing us for," Mulder replies.

Scully says they've lost control of the situation, maintaining that the truth is no good if they're dead and that she wants to see her sister. Mulder defers to her, and she tells Skinner to make the trade. If they don't honor the deal, Skinner assures them sternly, "I'll go state's evidence and testify, or they'll have to kill me, too."

Skinner stops to see Scully's mother at the hospital,

pursuing a mysterious man into the stairwell, where he's ambushed by Krycek and two other men who beat him and take the tape. When Krycek's accomplices later leave him in the car alone he suddenly realizes they mean to eliminate him, and he springs from the vehicle moments before it explodes.

Mulder and Scully return to see Klemper but are met by the Well-Manicured Man, who tells them that he's dead. After the 1947 Roswell crash, he explains, Nazi scientists were brought to the U.S. to conduct experiments, trying to create an alien/human hybrid. Genetic data was gathered from millions of people through small-pox vaccinations, and Mulder's father—having threatened to expose the project—was kept silent via Samantha's abduction, which was used to ensure his silence. "Why are you telling me this?" Mulder asks, even as Scully cautions him against trusting the man, who says only, "It's what you want to know, isn't it?"

Krycek calls the Cigarette-Smoking Man at the club, telling him he's alive and, since he possesses the tape, warning against any further attempts on his life. The Cigarette-Smoking Man also tells his compatriots there will be no deal with Skinner.

Mulder goes to see his mother, asking if his father had asked her to decide between him and Samantha. "No, I couldn't choose," she admits reluctantly, weeping. "It was your father's choice, and I hated him for it. Even in his grave I hate him still."

The Cigarette-Smoking Man meets with Skinner, telling him the tape is gone and that his own life may be in jeopardy. "This is where you pucker up and kiss my ass," Skinner snaps back, saying Albert has memorized the tape's contents and related it to twenty other men under his tribe's narrative tradition. "So unless you kill every Navajo in four states," Skinner says, "that information is available with a simple phone call."

Melissa Scully dies, and Dana mourns her. Mulder says they've both lost so much, but that he still believes the truth is out there—and can be found through their work on the X-Files. "I've heard the truth," Scully says with grim determination. "Now what I want are the answers."

Back story: The aliens who run past Scully within the mountain storage facility were actually played by eight- and nine-year-old children, dressed up in suits created by makeup maven Toby Lindala. Children were also employed in similar fashion during "Duane Barry," though Carter acknowledges that it isn't always easy keeping such pint-sized performers with the program.

"They are so excited at first," he says with a sigh. "Then you get those costumes on them and about a half-hour later they're saying, 'Can I go home now?'" The same sequence involved a large rigging, in which a massive crane lifted lights over the building to achieve the illusion of the alien mother ship.

Although "Paper Clip" provides greater insight into the circumstances surrounding Samantha Mulder's abduction, Carter quickly points out, "You're still not sure by whom." The story clearly implies military/government complicity with alien abductors, which has become part of the literature in that realm.

Carter likes the notion of using something as low-tech as the Navajo oral tradition as a means to "buy Mulder and Scully some insurance" and undermine the Cigarette-Smoking Man's high-tech government apparatus. He also points to the mythic elements in Mulder being told that he has in a sense become his father—one reason Duchovny has likened the narrative course of these three episodes to another trilogy, *Star Wars,* with a touch of *Sophie's Choice,* perhaps, thrown in for good measure.

Stunt coordinator Tony Morelli—who Carter calls "sort of our all-purpose bad guy"—plays the first man to encounter Skinner in the hallway. Though Skinner ultimately takes a beating in that fight, both Carter and Mitch Pileggi are quick to point out that the odds were three-against-one and that the character "got his punches in" during the tussle. The question of whether Skinner or X won their bout in "End Game" has become a favorite one to ponder at *The X-Files* conventions.

"Paper Clip" also carries a memoriam, this one to Mario Mark Kennedy, 1966–1995, a major fan of the show who had organized on-line sessions on the Internet. Kennedy died in a car accident.

X-philes

Star Trek fans have never particularly warmed to the expression "Trekkie," so it may come as no surprise that enterprising (pardon the expression) fans of *The X-Files* wasted no time in coining their own nickname: "X-Philes," the "phile" derived from the Greek word *philos*, meaning "to love."

While "interactive" is clearly an overused catchphrase in the modern media age, few shows have prompted the sort of emphatic viewer response as *The X-Files* has in such a relatively short time period. Indeed, as with any cultural phenomenon, fan reaction to the series has become as much a part of *The X-Files* story as the show itself, from the conventions that have sprung up around the country to the hours of chat about the series whipping around each week on the Internet.

The X-Files launched its own World Wide Web site on June 12, 1995, but fans were becoming involved in the series well before that. Delphi, the on-line service, estimates that 25,000 people go in and out of sessions pertaining to the show on a monthly basis, more than all other Fox series available via the service combined.

At least four regular on-line ses-

A cap auto-
graphed by
David
Duchovny was
auctioned off
for $180 at
The X-Files
convention in
Pasadena,
California.
A script to
"Duane Barry"
signed by
Duchovny,
Gillian
Anderson, and
Chris Carter
fetched $780.

sions are scheduled, with a Sunday night David Duchovny Fan Club (one group of female fans held a "virtual birthday party" for the actor on his birthday, including gifts; another group call themselves the David Duchovny Estrogen Brigade), a Tuesday discussion of paranormal phenomena, a post-show party each Friday, and another hour discussing the series on Saturday. There's also a less formal but not-to-be-outdone Gillian Anderson Testosterone Brigade, who by all accounts tend to be a bit more restrained than their feminine counterparts.

The Internet has even prompted fans to forge in-person relationships, with some groups who've met over the 'net actually hanging out together — one of the largest being in the Houston area and calling themselves, naturally, "Tex-Philes."

On top of that, *The X-Files* conventions have proliferated since the first San Diego gathering was attended by roughly 2,500 people in June 1995. A total of 20 conventions have been scheduled through the end of calendar-year '95, with conservative estimates that 35,000 to 40,000 people will ultimately participate by the time the year's over.

The one-day events—staged by Creation Entertainment, which has done the same for *Star Trek*, and usually promoted via commercials aired on the local Fox affiliate during episodes of the series—are immediately striking in the wide cross-section of people who turn out. Those who show up are both young and old, from elderly people on walkers to plenty of young parents pushing strollers and carrying toddlers with them. Fans are of every race and color as well, brought together by their common interest in the series.

In addition to personal appearances by some of those associated with the show, the conventions feature a prop museum where one can see the bloody pig's leg, for example, sent to a prisoner in the episode "F. Emasculata," or the replica of an alien corpse showcased in the second-season closer "Anasazi." At the conventions, it's hard not to be taken aback by the passion surrounding the show.

Virtually anything associated with the series has become a collectible, with even the issue of *TV Guide* that featured the show on the cover commanding a premium on the resale market. Fans can buy T-shirts, caps, still photos, posters, and comic books, all topped off by a snazzy and not-for-the-faint-of-heart (or faint-of-wallet) *The X-Files* jacket. Any way you slice it, the series has become big business.

There's also an official *X-Files* Fan Club offering a wide variety of memorabilia.

Still, the series's influence occasionally rears its head in the paranoia department. One woman, asked to fill out information regarding her age and whatnot for the fan club, expresses doubts about being, well, too trusting in divulging such information. "This is *The X-Files*, after all," she tells a friend.

Fans cheer when the stars are discussed, hissing at the mention of villains like the Cigarette-Smoking Man or Krycek.

At one convention over the summer in Las Vegas, Mitch Pileggi, who plays Assistant Director Skinner, patiently signs hundreds of autographs after taking questions from the crowd. Many of the queries are to be expected (How did you get the part? Do you personally believe in aliens?, etc.) but even the seemingly unflappable actor is struck speechless by one. "How much money do you get?" one young man asks bluntly.

"None of your beeswax," answers Pileggi, after a long pause and a hearty laugh.

"I kinda highly admire you," a woman later tells him when she gets her turn at the microphone, the lust practically dripping from her voice.

The follow-up act is Doug Hutchison, who played Eugene Tooms, the ageless liver-eating mutant, in two first-season episodes. Hutchison has proven a fixture on the convention circuit, using his appearances to openly lobby for an encore by Tooms on the series, apparently undaunted by the fact that his character was ground to paste under an escalator. Unrecognizable from the show, Hutchison also displays a humorous side and wit in stark contrast to his dour character, doing the equivalent of a stand-up comedy routine. "I slipped into a slot machine," he tells the Vegas crowd. "The guy put his quarter in, and three livers came up." Hutchison subsequently admits to the audience he's a vegetarian who, in fact, has "never touched a liver in my life."

For *The X-Files* executive producer and creator Chris Carter, all this interaction with the show's fans is something of a dream, and clearly a side effect he never imagined. While there was fan mail in the old days, the modern equivalent has proven noteworthy if only in its immediacy and the manner in which on-line services and conventions allow producers and fans to share the experience. Carter himself acknowledges that he checks out the Internet "almost every day," talking to fans, reading the more thoughtful comments, and sometimes thinking, "Hey, they're right. I'd better watch myself."

"It's like an interactive tool for me," he says, noting that the show was fortunate to be growing in popularity as the computer-literate on-line phenomenon simultaneously bloomed.

Carter also concedes that some of the instant reviews, critical dissection, and obscure meaning read into small nuances in the show "occasionally starts to drive me mad," which may explain a joke in the second-season episode "One Breath," wherein one of the Lone Gunmen invites Mulder over to get on the Internet and "nitpick the scientific inaccuracies of *Earth 2*." Nitpicking is clearly a part of the process, as viewers delight in finding inaccuracies and continuity errors in the series.

For the most part, however, Carter—who grew up catching waves on Southern California beaches—enjoys surfing the 'net, saying the degree of scrutiny by the fans is for the most part fun, forcing him and the other writers to pay closer attention to every detail. Positive viewer response also helped inspire the show to expand Mitch Pileggi's role as Skinner. The actor will appear in more episodes during the third season, having signed a shiny new six-year contract.

In addition, the contact he's had with viewers since the show premiered has altered whatever views Carter harbored regarding people who chase UFOs or claim to be alien abductees—having feared originally when the show went on the air, he allows, that "all the weirdos would crawl out of the woodwork" and turn the switchboard into "crackpot central." "The interesting thing," he says, "is most of these people are not wacky. Most of them are just ordinary folk who really believe this stuff."

Granted, the avidness of the people who show up at conventions and light up the Internet has to be kept in context, since they represent a relatively small percentage so far of the more than 14 million viewers who tune in the series on an average week. It's worth noting, too, that similar on-line followings haven't been able to save low-rated shows with dedicated constituencies like *My So-Called Life*, so the real challenge—as is always the case in network television—is to retain and perhaps expand on the show's broadest audience of millions while still serving the die-hard fans, who've been top of mind with the producers since *The X-Files* really started to take off. As story editor Frank Spotnitz told them at one convention, the goal remains "to meet the high expectations that you set for us."

Carter, too, makes it clear that he feels a special affinity for, and duty to, the show's core audience. "I felt," he says, referring to his early close encounters of the 'net kind, "as if I was working for these people."

"Fallen Angel"

Scene: Mulder's trashed hotel room.

Scully: "What's going on?"

Mulder: "Looks like the house-keepers haven't been here yet.."

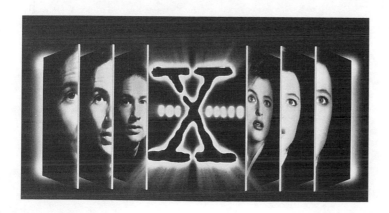

ratings

season ①

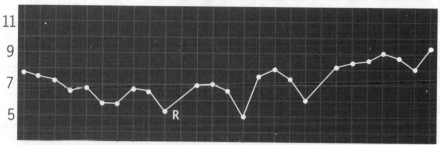

sept.   oct.   nov.   dec.   jan.   feb.   mar.   apr.   may
'93   '94

R=Repeat

season ②

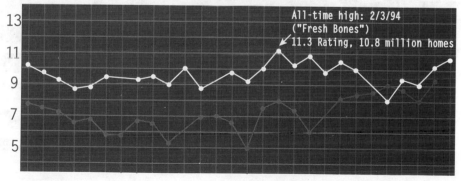

All-time high: 2/3/94
("Fresh Bones")
11.3 Rating, 10.8 million homes

sept.   oct.   nov.   dec.   jan.   feb.   mar.   apr.   may
'94   '95

Airdate	Episode	Homes (in Millions)	Rating/Share
0/93	Pilot	7.4	7.9/15
7/93	Deep Throat	6.9	7.3/1
4/93	Squeeze	6.8	7.2/1
0/1/93	Conduit	5.9	6.3/1
0/8/93	The Jersey Devil	6.2	6.6/1
0/22/93	Shadows	5.6	5.9/1
0/29/93	Ghost in the Machine	5.6	5.9/1
5/93	Ice	6.2	6.6/1
12/93	Space	6.1	6.5/11
19/93	Fallen Angel	5.1	5.4/9
12/10/93	Eve	6.4	6.8/1
12/17/93	Fire	6.4	6.8/1
7/94	Beyond the Sea	6.2	6.6/1
21/94	Genderbender	6.8	7.2/12
/94	Lazarus	7.2	7.6/
1/94	Young at Heart	6.8	7.2/1
/11/94	E.B.E	5.8	6.2/9
/18/94	Miracle Man	7.1	7.5/1
8/94	Shapes	7.2	7.6/14
/94	Darkness Falls	7.5	8.0/14
15/94	Tooms (Squeeze 2)	8.1	8.6/15
/22/94	Born Again	7.7	8.2/ 4
6/94	Roland	7.4	7.9/14
13/94	The Erlenmeyer Flask	8.3	8.8/ 6

Each rating point = 942,000 homes

Airdate	Episode	Homes (in Millions)	Rating/Share
9/16/94	Little Green Men	9.8	10.3/19
9/23/94	The Host	9.3	9.8/17
9/30/94	Blood	8.7	9.1/16
10/7/94	Sleepless	8.2	8.6/15
10/14/94	Duane Barry (Part 1)	8.5	8.9/16
10/21/94	Ascension (Part 2)	9.2	9.6/16
11/4/94	3	9.0	9.4/16
11/11/94	One Breath	9.1	9.5/16
11/18/94	Firewalker	8.6	9.0/16
12/9/94	Red Museum	9.9	10.4/18
12/16/94	Excelsius Dei	8.5	8.9/15
1/6/95	Aubrey	9.7	10.2/16
1/13/95	Irresistible	8.8	9.2/15
1/27/95	Die Hand Die Verletzt	10.2	10.7/18
2/3/95	Fresh Bones	10.8	11.3/19
2/10/95	Colony (Part 1)	9.8	10.3/17
2/17/95	End Game (Part 2)	10.7	11.2/19
2/24/95	Fearful Symmetry	9.6	10.1/17
3/10/95	Dod Kalm	10.2	10.7/18
3/31/95	Humbug	9.8	10.3/18
4/14/95	The Calusari	7.9	8.3/16
4/28/95	F. Emasculata	8.5	8.9/16
5/ /95	Soft Light	8.1	8.5/15
5/12/95	Our Town	9.0	9.4/17
5/19/95	Anasazi	9.6	10.1/18

Each rating point = 954,000 homes   Source: Nielsen Media Research

reviews

Initial critical response to the series was widely favorable, though a number of writers questioned whether the show would survive from a ratings standpoint. Here's a sampling:

September 10, 1993 (premiere)

"One of the more intriguing new dramas of the fall season. . . . a promising drama with a provocative edge."
—Ray Richmond, *Los Angeles Daily News*

"The stories are incredible—that is, truly unbelievable, and that's my problem with *The X-Files*. Otherwise, it's an entertaining crime drama. . . . My score: 8."
—Jeff Jarvis, *TV Guide*

" . the eerie but nonviolent *X-Files* could scare up a cult of curious viewers for Fox each week."
—Lon Grahnke, *Chicago Sun-Times*

"Looks like sci-fi/mystery fans have something they can sharpen their teeth on with this new series . . . If succeeding chapters can keep the pace, this well-produced entry could be this season's UFO highflier."
—Tony Scott, *Daily Variety*

"Duchovny and Anderson are the youngest and most attractive FBI agents in TV history. But didn't you feel safer when FBI agents looked like Efrem Zimbalist Jr.? While it's not bad, I still see *The X-Files* headed for the round file."
—Bob Wisehart, *Sacramento Bee*

reviews

" . . . intelligent writing and sharp plotting lift the series far above the standard for the genre. . . . Friday night is an unlikely time to find that audience at home, but Fox may be betting that the viewers it wants can set their VCRs."
—Gail Pennington, *St. Louis Post-Dispatch*

"Not since Darren McGavin stumbled onto a different monster every week in *Kolchak: The Night Stalker* has there been a primetime series as preposterous as *The X-Files*. Or as much fun."
—Noel Holston, *Minneapolis Star-Tribune*

" . . . this spooky drama . . . could be a hit. It's sure to develop a cult following at the least."
—Walt Belcher, *Tampa Tribune*

" . . . the government coverup is depicted with the right touch of humid paranoia. . . . The problem is . . . *The X-Files* itself seems destined to end up in TV's archive of short-lived phenomena."
—Joyce Millman, *San Francisco Examiner*

October 1, 1993

"If the producers can keep the mood spooky, this show will have its devoted adherents. Deservedly so. Grade: B."
—*People* magazine

reviews

October 8, 1993

"The X-Files is the most paranoid, subversive show on TV right now. . . . **There's marvelous tension** between Anderson—who is dubious about these events—and Duchovny, who has the haunted, imploring look of a true believer. . . . *X-Files* is a hoot about hooey. B+"
—*Entertainment Weekly*

November 5, 1993

"I can safely say this episode of *X-Files* turns out to be one of the **more potent and creepy hours** on network TV in quite a while—with a scene or two virtually guaranteed to make you squirm, and with a story line worthy of honorary passage into *The Twilight Zone*."
—David Bianculli, *New York Daily News* (reviewing "Ice")

"File this under your **'must-see'** heading: *The X-Files* just keeps getting better. And weirder. And scarier."
—Matt Roush, *USA Today*

awards and honors

awards and honors

emmy awards
1995
- Nominee, outstanding drama series
- Nominee, writing in a drama series—Chris Carter ("Duane Barry")
- Nominee, guest actress in a drama series—CCH Pounder as Agent Kazdin ("Duane Barry")
- Nominee, individual achievement in cinematography for a series—John Bartley ("One Breath")
- Nominee, individual achievement in editing for a series, single camera production—James Coblentz ("Duane Barry")
- Nominee, individual achievement in editing for a series, single camera production—Stephen Mark ("Sleepless")
- Nominee, sound editing for a series—Thierry Couturier, Machiek Malish, Chris Reeves, Marty Stein, Jay Levine, Stuart Calderon, Michael Kimball, David Van Slyke, Susan Welsh, Chris Fradkin, Matt West, Jeff Charbonneau, Debby Ruby Winsberg ("Duane Barry")

1994
- Winner, individual achievement in graphic design and title sequences—James Castle, Bruce Bryant, Carol Johnsen
- Nominee, main title theme music—Mark Snow

golden globe award
- Winner, best dramatic series

saturn awards
(presented by the Academy of Science Fiction, Fantasy, and Horror)
- Winner, outstanding television series

television critics association (TCA) awards
- Nominee, best drama series
- Nominee, program of the year

awards and honors

viewers for quality television (VQT) awards
- Nominee, best drama series
- Nominee, best actor in a drama series—David Duchovny
- Nominee, best actress in a drama series—Gillian Anderson

Digital Hollywood Awards
- Winner, best digital writer—James Wong and Glen Morgan ("Beyond the Sea")
- Nominee, best in digital television (series)

mystery writers of america edgar allen poe awards
- Nominee, best episode in a television series—Chris Carter ("The Erlenmeyer Flask")

american society of cinematographers awards
- Nominee, achievement in cinematography—John Bartley ("Duane Barry")

environmental media awards
- Winner, outstanding episodic television (drama)—Chris Carter ("Darkness Falls")

parent's choice honors
- Winner, best series

monitor awards
- Winner, best editing—James Coblentz ("Beyond the Sea")

new york film festival for television programming and promotion
- Finalist, best writing—Chris Carter ("The Erlenmeyer Flask"); James Wong and Glen Morgan ("Beyond the Sea")

CHARACTER X dossiers

Special Agent Fox Mulder

Name: Fox William Mulder
Badge number: JTT047101111
Height: 6 feet
Weight: 170 pounds
Hair: Brown
Eyes: Green
Date of Birth: 13 October 1961
Birthplace: Chilmark, MA

**Current
Address:** (address unknown)
       Apt. 42
       Alexandria, VA
Telephone: (202) 555-9355
**Distinguishing
Marks/Features:** Mole on right
cheek.
Marital Status: Unmarried
Father's Name: William "Bill"
Mulder (see Classified Folder).
Formerly of the State Department.
Assassinated by Alex Krycek.
**Father's
Address:** West Tisbury, Martha's
       Vineyard, Massachusetts
Mother's Name: (unknown)
**Mother's
Address:** 2790 Vine Street,
       Chilmark, Massachusetts
Siblings: One sister, Samantha
Ann Mulder, born 22 January 1964.
Disappeared 27 November 1973.
(X-File X-42053)

Education: Oxford University, A.B.
in Psychology, 1982. Quantico FBI
Training Academy, 1984.
Publications: *On Serial Killers
and the Occult,* Monograph, 1988.
(as M. F. Luder) article in *Omni*
magazine, 1993.
Current rank: Special Agent
Weapon: Smith and Wesson 1056
(9mm rounds)

FBI Career History

1983–1986: Oxford University
1986: Enters Quantico Academy immediately after graduation from
Oxford. Earns nickname "Spooky."
1988: Assigned to the Violent Crimes Unit under the supervision of

ASAC Reggie Purdue. On his first case, Agent Mulder distinguished himself in the pursuit of bank robber John Barnett.

June 16, 1989: Agent Mulder undergoes regression hypnosis with Dr. Heitz Werber, after which Agent Mulder becomes convinced his sister was abducted by extraterrestrial forces.

1991: Agent Mulder persuades his superiors to transfer him to the X-Files section, where he has operated ever since, reporting first to the head of the VCU, Section Chief Blevins, and later to Assistant Director Walter Skinner.

March 6, 1992: Fears that Agent Mulder's work in the X-Files section is getting out of control lead Chief Blevins to assign Agent Dana K. Scully to the X-Files section as Agent Mulder's partner.

1993: Agent Mulder is called in for a hearing with Section Chief Joseph McGrath of the Office of Professional Responsibility after trespassing on a crime scene under military jurisdiction, and after accusations of interfering with a military operation and impeding an investigation were lodged against him. All charges later dropped.

April 1994: Assistant Director Walter S. Skinner investigates charges brought by Eugene Victor Tooms that Agent Mulder was engaging in harassment of Mr. Tooms, who had been released from incarceration. Tooms was later killed in an industrial accident.

May 1994: AD Skinner shuts down the X-Files section and reassigns Agents Mulder and Scully.

October 1994: Agent Alex Krycek is partnered with Agent Mulder.

November 1994: Following Agent Scully's abduction by fugitive Duane Barry (X-File X73317), AD Skinner re-opens the section. Agent Krycek fails to report to work after Agent Scully's abduction, and is currently wanted for questioning in her disappearance.

May 1995: AD Walter Skinner requests a hearing with Agent Mulder, Agent Scully, and members of the Office of Professional Responsibility after an unprovoked physical assault by Agent Mulder. Agent Mulder does not attend the meeting. The following day, Agent Mulder's father is shot to death in his house while Agent Mulder is present.

Personal

Agent Mulder is convinced that his sister was abducted
by aliens while he was paralyzed by some unknown
power, and his memories altered. He believes that
extraterrestrial powers, perhaps aided by rogue government organizations, are continually visiting this
planet. These unusual beliefs have earned him the
nickname "Spooky" among his peers. He is not known to
associate closely with other agents save for his partner, Agent Scully. Although he is well respected pro-
fessionally, personally he is considered a maverick by
other agents. His personality does not fit the profile
of the ideal Bureau agent, although his record of
success in his assigned area puts him among the top
agents now working in the Federal system.

Special Agent Dana Scully

Name: Dana Katherine Scully, M.D.
ID Number: 2317-616
Height: 5 feet 3 inches
Weight: (unknown)
Hair: Red
Eyes: Green
Date of Birth: 23 February 1964
Birthplace: (unknown)

Current 3170 W. 53 Rd. #35
Address: Annapolis, MD
Telephone: (202) 555-6431
E-Mail: D_Scully@FBI.gov
Distinguishing
Marks/Features: None
Marital Status: Unmarried
Father's Name: William Scully, Captain, United States Navy. Served in the Cuban Missile Crisis, 1961. Died December 1993.
Father's
Address: Deceased
Mother's Name: Margaret "Maggie" Scully
Mother's
Address: (unknown) Baltimore, MD
Siblings: Elder brother, William "Bill Jr." Scully Jr. Elder sister, Melissa Scully (deceased). Younger brother, Charles Scully.

Education: B.S. Physics, University of Maryland, 1986. Medical degree, (unknown), residency in forensic pathology.
Publications: Senior thesis: "Einstein's Twin Paradox: A New Interpretation."
Current rank: Special Agent
Weapon: Smith and Wesson 1056 (9mm rounds)

FBI Career History

1990: Joins the FBI directly from medical school. Teaches for 2 years at Quantico Academy.
1992: Assigned by Section Chief Scott Blevins to the X-Files section.
October 1994: Abducted by fugitive Duane Barry (See X-File X73317) under unexplained circumstances. Agent Alex Krycek is wanted for questioning in her disappearance.
November 1994: Discovered in a deep coma in the Intensive Care Unit of North Georgetown University Hospital; no witnesses or records of

her admission can be found. Upon her recovery, Agent
Scully returns to duty, claiming to have no memory of
the events of her disappearance.
April 1995: Agent Scully fails to appear at a hearing
called by Assistant Director Walter S. Skinner into
the activities of Agent Mulder. A bungled attempt on
her life results in the death of her sister Melissa.

<u>Personal</u>

Agent Scully is a well-respected and highly organized
agent, knowledgeable in the areas of forensic medi-
cine and pathology. She does not share Agent Mulder's
beliefs in the paranormal. Dana Scully spent the
first year of her undergraduate school at the
University of California, Berkeley, near the Alameda
Naval Air Station, where her father was stationed. At
Berkeley, Dana had a brush with political activism,
particularly antinuclear protest groups, though her
involvement never went further than reading leaflets
and engaging in occasional spirited "discussions"
with her father. After one year there, Dana transferred to the University of Maryland. Agent Scully's
medical training has been invaluable to the Bureau in
the investigation of several cases assigned to the
X-Files.

Assistant Director Walter S. Skinner

"Tooms"
"Little Green Men"
"The Host"
"Sleepless"
"Ascension"
"One Breath"
"Colony"
"End Game"
"F. Emasculata"
"Anasazi"
"The Blessing Way"
"Paper Clip"

Personal

Assistant Director Walter S. Skinner is Fox Mulder and Dana Scully's supervisor. He is an ex-Marine: stern and demanding. His strict insistence on by-the-book investigative techniques often puts him at odds with Mulder, whose unorthodox methods grate on the senior man. Skinner gets frequent visits from the mysterious Cigarette-Smoking Man, but the exact relationship is ambiguous at best. Although Skinner once shut down the X-Files section on "orders from above," he later reopened them on his own authority, and they have since stayed open.

Skinner's relationship with Mulder is equivocal: while the younger agent's methods and irreverent manner exasperate him, he has found many ways to support Mulder even against the Bureau's hierarchy. In "One Breath," he refused to accept Mulder's resignation, and told him of an out-of-body experience he had during his service days in Vietnam. "I am afraid to look beyond that experience, Agent Mulder. You...you are not. Your resignation is unacceptable."

Cigarette- Smoking Man

Personal

From the moment when Dana Scully was first assigned to the X-Files, the sinister chain-smoking man in the stiff suit has been keeping an eye on Mulder, Scully, and the X-Files. Tall, gaunt, with a tendency to squint, he has contacts in the black ops operations that thwart Mulder in his investigations, but it is unclear whether he is aiding them or parrying their moves.

In "Tooms," the Cigarette-Smoking Man broke his long silence to affirm his belief in Mulder's report. In "Sleepless," he began to intervene more directly than in the pilot episode; he is the superior to whom the perfidious Alex Krycek reports. His chilling dismissal of Scully — "Every problem has a solution" — followed by the stubbing out of a trademark "Morley's" cigarette, implies that he will stop at nothing to shut down the X-Files permanently. Yet in "Ascension," he tells Krycek that it is better not to kill the agents outright, thus risking turning one man's religion into a crusade.

In "One Breath," Mulder confronted the Cigarette-Smoking Man directly, after Walter Skinner reluctantly revealed his whereabouts. Mulder named him "Cancer Man," by which name he is now widely known on the Internet. With Mulder holding a gun to his head, the Cigarette-Smoking Man revealed that he had "no wife, no children, some power," and that he was "in the game because I believe in it."

"Anasazi," the second-season finale, revealed his deepest secret to date: the Cigarette-Smoking Man is very well acquainted with Mulder's father, William Mulder. In a tense conversation, the Cigarette-Smoking

Man claims to be protecting Mulder. Yet when the Cigarette-Smoking Man later speaks to Mulder himself, he blames Bill Mulder for authorizing "the project" that Mulder is about to uncover.

"The Host" (implied)
"Sleepless"
"Ascension"
"One Breath"
"Fresh Bones"
"End Game"
"Soft Light'

Personal

Decidedly more sinister than his predecessor Deep Throat, X loves the
shadows. He rarely emerges clearly enough to be seen, and when he
does he appears tense, edgy, paranoid. From the beginning he has said
that he does not want to end up like Deep Throat, to whom he feels
some loyalty, but not enough to get himself killed. On more than one
occasion, he has refused to help Mulder or Scully.

X has shown himself to be capable of cold-blooded murder in "One
Breath," when he calmly executes an operative sent to steal a vial of
Agent Scully's blood. In "End Game," he meets Dana Scully face to
face when she asks for his help in finding Mulder. He flatly rebuffs
her; Assistant Director Skinner fights him in an elevator to get the
information. In that confrontation he tells Skinner he has killed men
for lesser offenses than hitting him. In "Soft Light," he manipulates
Mulder into revealing the whereabouts of a research scientist whose
research X had been trying to get his hands on. X abducts the scientist, Dr. Banton, and turns him over to the very researchers Dr.
Banton feared most.

Whether he is Mulder's friend or his enemy has yet to be revealed.

The Lone Gunmen

"E.B.E."
"Blood"
"One Breath"
"Fearful Symmetry"
"Anasazi"
"The Blessing Way"
"Paper Clip"

Personal

These three operatives form the editorial staff of a conspiracy-oriented magazine known as *The Lone Gunman*, after the alleged second assassin in the Kennedy assassination. They have contacts and inside knowledge in a diversity of fields, and function as a kind of alternative think tank for Fox Mulder. Byers is neatly bearded, well dressed, and a very precise information systems expert. Langly is tall, rangy, blond, and spectacled. His specialty is communications. Frohike has a decided penchant for Agent Dana Scully. He serves as the photographic and special operations guru of the bunch.

There was a fourth member of the group, known as "The Thinker," a.k.a. Kenneth Suna. However, he appeared only once and is a computer hacking genius, having broken into the Department of Defense Top Secret files and downloaded extremely sensitive information on government involvement with aliens. He was murdered for accessing the MJ files.

While the group is earnest and eccentric to the point of mania, it has provided Mulder and Scully with equal amounts of paranoid theory and objective fact.

Agent
Alex Krycek

"Sleepless"
"Duane Barry"
"Ascension"
"Anasazi"
"The Blessing Way"
"Paper Clip"

Personal

First seen in "Sleepless," where he latches on to an investigation Mulder is conducting, the clean-cut, fresh-faced Agent Krycek at first looked like a younger, less cynical version of Mulder himself. As time went on, however, he was revealed as a double agent, working for the Cigarette-Smoking Man to thwart Mulder's attempts to reopen the X-Files. He materially contributed to Dana Scully's abduction by Duane Barry and attempted to kill Mulder when Mulder went to rescue her.

Afterward he disappeared, only to resurface in "Anasazi," where he killed Mulder's father and framed Mulder for it. Mulder is now clearly aware of Krycek's involvement; indeed, the only way Scully could stop Mulder from killing Krycek was to shoot her own partner. Krycek escaped, only to reappear during a bungled assassination attempt on Agent Scully that resulted in the death of her sister Melissa. That mistake resulted in an attempt on Krycek's life. After a narrow escape, Krycek fled the country possessing a powerful trump card a digital computer tape containing information on the government's involvement with and knowledge of extraterrestrial life.

Deep Throat

"Deep Throat"
"Ghost in the Machine"
"Fallen Angel"
"Eve"
"Young at Heart"
"E.B.E."
"The Erlenmeyer Flask"

Personal

Mulder's most influential secret source was introduced in the second episode of the series, in which he suddenly appears to warn Mulder away from a case. He repeated similar warnings in his other appearances, while at the same time feeding Mulder information to help him with his investigations. Always cryptic, he readily admitted on one occasion to lying to his protege. He stepped in to save Mulder's job in "Fallen Angel," and in "The Erlenmeyer Flask" he saved Mulder's life at the price of his own.

Deep Throat, whose real name and affiliations were never revealed, was a man seemingly caught in the middle. While he claimed to have such a "lofty position" that he can get Mulder box seats in any baseball stadium in the country (a sign of real power), he also confessed that he put his life in jeopardy every time the two met. He claimed to have watched Mulder for a long time, assessing his fitness, before confiding secret information to him. While Mulder believed him implicitly from the beginning, Scully was more doubtful. It was not until she was forced into an alliance with him to save her partner's life that she brought herself to trust him.

There are a few hints about Deep Throat's background. He said he worked for the CIA in Vietnam and belongs to an organization which had been guilty of "heinous acts against man." It appeared to be his goal to bring down this organization, through the actions of Mulder and Scully. He had been able to obtain highly classified Top Secret documents and pass them to Mulder in a very short time. He had access

to some excellent resources for disinformation, as
his faked UFO photo in "E.B.E.," designed to lure
Mulder and Scully away from a "hot" investigation,
was almost good enough to fool an expert like Mulder.

Deep Throat's most remarkable revelation was in
"E.B.E.," wherein he said he was one of three men in
the world to have not only seen but killed an alien.
He detailed for Mulder the setup of an international
conspiracy devoted to the capture and execution of
extraterrestrial visitors. In fact, so shattering was
that experience, that Deep Throat confessed he had
embarked on this mission of bringing information to
Mulder as a form of penance. Yet Mulder found this
hard to believe, as his deep faith in his informant
was shaken by lies and misdirection.

From his hint to Mulder in his first appearance
("*They* have been here for a very, very long time.")
to his dying words ("Trust no one!"), his influence
on Mulder and on the X-Files has been profound.

The Mulders

"Little Green Men"
"Colony"
"End Game"
"Anasazi"
"The Blessing Way"
"Paper Clip"

Personal

The family of Fox Mulder has known considerable tragedy. When she was eight years old and he was twelve, Samantha Mulder disappeared and was never heard from again. Mulder says the experience tore his family apart, and apparently his parents are separated, if not actually divorced.

In hypnotic regression sessions with Dr. Heitz Werber, Mulder was able to recall a bright light, a presence in the room, his own helpless paralysis, and a voice assuring him that all would be well and his sister would be returned. This convinced him that his sister had been abducted by aliens, and he has dedicated his life to the recovery of his sister and the uncovering of government conspiracies concealing their existence.

Yet more suffering is in store for the unhappy Mulder family, when a woman claiming to be Samantha suddenly turns up in the middle of one of Mulder's cases. We meet Bill Mulder, a cold, stern, unsmiling man, formerly of the State Department. We also meet Mulder's mother, warmer, gentler, but not entirely gullible; she, too, questions "Samantha's" bona fides. But in "End Game" when Scully is taken hostage, Mulder is forced to trade Samantha for his partner, and must watch in horror as she is killed in a fall from a bridge. Once again he must face his unforgiving father and tell him that Samantha is lost. Still reeling from this, he is shocked again to discover that his "sister" is in fact one of a number of clones, who claims to know the fate of his actual sister.

In "Anasazi," more of Bill Mulder's past is revealed as we discover he is a former associate of the Cigarette-Smoking Man, with whom he is on a first-name basis. The elder Mulder appears equally concerned that his involvement in a secret government experiment not be revealed, and that his son not be harmed. The Cigarette-Smoking Man reassures him, but the old man calls on his son. After Mulder arrives, his father is on the point of revealing his role in Mulder's case, but is shot by Agent Krycek and Mulder is framed for his own father's murder. On the run, Mulder is contacted by the Cigarette-Smoking Man, who warns Mulder that exposure of the secrets he is pursuing will also mean exposure of his own father's role in it.

The Scullys

"Jersey Devil"
"Beyond the Sea"
"Ascension"
"One Breath"
"The Blessing Way"
"Paper Clip"

Personal

In contrast to her partner, Dana Scully's home life and childhood seem pretty normal. Her father, William Scully, was a captain in the U.S. Navy. He was a participant in the Bay of Pigs in 1960. Scully's mother, Margaret, was called "Maggie" by her father. Maggie once told her daughter that Captain Scully proposed to her immediately after his return from the Bay of Pigs; "their song" was "Beyond the Sea" and was played at their wedding. The marriage seemed happy in every way, and the Scullys had four children: William Jr., known as "Bill Junior," Melissa Scully, Dana Scully, and Charles Scully.

While Captain Scully could be formal and reserved, he called his youngest daughter "Starbuck" after the character in *Moby-Dick* and she called him "Ahab." Although he disagreed with his daughter's choice of profession, Maggie Scully twice assured Dana of Captain Scully's pride in her. His sudden death around Christmas of 1993 was a blow to Dana. When she saw an apparition of him shortly afterward, it shocked Scully so much she began to question her own beliefs. He reappeared in her near-death experience in "One Breath" with a message of love and hope.

Dark-haired Margaret Scully does not appear to have any profession outside of the home, but is clearly the center of the family. Her warm yet commanding presence dominates any family scene. She respects her youngest daughter's independence of mind, even to the point of agreeing to the execution of Scully's living will. This may even have gone against her own conscience, as there are indications Margaret Scully is a devout Catholic. The family is Catholic and Margaret gave

Dana a tiny cross when she was fifteen, which Dana always wears. Margaret may have some psychic ability, as she confides to Mulder on one occasion that she had a premonitory dream about her daughter's abduction by Duane Barry.

Melissa Scully, Dana's older sister, resembles her slightly, with red hair and hazel eyes. She is a believer in miracles and has a tendency to spout New Age jargon. She claims to be able to read auras, announcing that her sister in her coma was deciding whether to live or die, and telling Fox Mulder that he was "in a very dark place," darker than Scully's. She is partial to charms and crystals, and is familiar with pendulum dowsing techniques. By Margaret Scully's account, her oldest daughter was not a tomboy like Dana. In "The Blessing Way" Alex Krycek shoots Melissa, mistaking her for her sister. Mrs. Scully keeps a bedside vigil for her in "Paper Clip" but to no avail. When Melissa dies, a grief-stricken Dana Scully says, "she died for me."

Bill Junior and Charles Scully appear only as boys, in "One Breath," and no mention has been made of their professions or whereabouts.

BRIAN LOWRY is the Los Angeles television editor for *Daily Variety*, the show-business trade newspaper, where he has worked since 1987 reporting on the TV industry in addition to writing reviews and the weekly column "Changing Channels." A native of Los Angeles, he is a graduate of UCLA, who, during and after college, freelanced for various publications, among them *Starlog* magazine.